Dead Line Earth

BY DAVID ALAN FAIRCLOTH

NEW HANOVER COUNTY
PUBLIC LIBRARY
201 CHESTNUT STREET
WILMINGTON, NC 28401

DORRANCE
PUBLISHING CO
EST. 1920
PITTSBURGH, PENNSYLVANIA 15238

The contents of this work, including, but not limited to, the accuracy of events, people, and places depicted; opinions expressed; permission to use previously published materials included; and any advice given or actions advocated are solely the responsibility of the author, who assumes all liability for said work and indemnifies the publisher against any claims stemming from publication of the work.

All Rights Reserved
Copyright © 2019 by David Alan Faircloth

No part of this book may be reproduced or transmitted, downloaded, distributed, reverse engineered, or stored in or introduced into any information storage and retrieval system, in any form or by any means, including photocopying and recording, whether electronic or mechanical, now known or hereinafter invented without permission in writing from the publisher.

Dorrance Publishing Co
585 Alpha Drive
Suite 103
Pittsburgh, PA 15238
Visit our website at *www.dorrancebookstore.com*

ISBN: 978-1-6442-6438-6
eISBN: 978-1-6442-6095-1

THE YEAR IS 2095 and the United States science programs are booming. My name is Marco. I have been in the United States Air Force now for fifteen years. My whole life growing up in Warren, Michigan, my father constantly preached, "Go to college, work hard, make something of yourself." I rebelled under all the pressure my father put on me. My grades in school was shit and so was my attitude towards life. Nothing much my mother could do. Sure, she tried to talk to me but I looked at her like my father did, as weak and not really a voice to be listened to. Don't get me wrong, deep down I wasn't a bad kid or a stupid kid, which could be debated depending on who you ask. I was just misguided and very immature. By my senior year of high school, good old Lakeside, I had already been suspended three times and earning straight-D averages. Hell, at the time I was just happy to get that and get the hell out of there.

My buddy Jack and I were going out one Friday night. It was one week before school ended. He finally got us some good IDs so we could hit the bars and hopefully score some pussy. We arrived at a bar called The Wet Landing Strip, notorious for great liquor and exceptional ass. We got out of our vehicle and headed to the front door.

"Hey, guys, let's see those IDs."

"Sure, here you go."

We both were nervous. He stared at us several times and scanned our cards.

"Alright, guys, enjoy your night, watch out for the cougars, they're hot and heavy tonight."

"Hey, Jack, did you bring some condoms?"

"Um, no. Damnit, Marco, can't you live on the wild side for a change?"

"Not a problem, just don't want my dick to fall off in the next few days."

We got trashed that night, flirted with women. My buddy Jack took a girl into the bathroom and left me at the bar.

"Hey, bartender, need a shot of Jamison Black Label."

I grabbed the shot glass and downed it. I immediately felt a sharp pain to my back and slumped over the bar. Fuck, what the hell! I turned around quickly. There was a huge guy behind me yelling and poking my face.

"What the fuck did you do with my wife, mother fucker!"

"What are you talking about? I don't know you or your wife!"

"Don't lie to me, mother fucker, she told me everything, bitch!"

The next thing I knew was that I had hit the ground. He had hit me so hard, I couldn't remember where I was at for a few seconds. When I came back to my senses, I saw Jack and the same woman he was in the bathroom with come running up. The woman started hitting her husband and yelling. I couldn't understand what they were saying, I was still dazed. I could see Jack was pissed and he and the husband and wife began fighting. The last thing I saw before going unconscious was Jack stabbing the man in the chest with his knife and people rushing around in a panic.

I woke up the next day in a cell, not really understanding what the hell had happened. Two officers walked in.

"Are you ready to talk, Marco?"

"What? I don't understand what's going on."

"Get your ass up, it's time to answer some questions!"

"Okay, I need water, please."

"You have five minutes before we come back for you, if you want water you can drink it from the toilet!"

The door slammed behind them. What the fuck was going on! I crawled to the bathroom and threw up all over the floor, but the cold floor felt great on my skin. I saw the toilet, flipped open the lid, and stuck my face in, sucking up as much water as I could. Minutes later I heard the cell door slam open.

"Alright, Marco, time to talk, let's go."

I was pulled off the floor by two officers and dragged down a long hallway, and then suddenly we stopped moving. I heard a door open and I was picked up off the floor and slammed into a chair. I was still half-drunk, sick, and in shock about what had happened.

A man walked in through the door and sat in a desk that was in front of me. "Well, let me introduce myself there, Marco. I am Lieutenant Bullard with Detroit PD. Well, the way I see things, Marco, you two window lickers are in some serious shit! Let's just take a quick look at a list of charges here. HUM, let's see, we have possession of fake IDs, we have possession of a weapon in a non-authorized zone, drinking under age, destruction of private property, technically adultery, and oh yeah, least to say murder!"

"I didn't kill anyone!"

"Shut your mouth, I haven't asked you to speak yet! We know you didn't kill that man but your ass is still in a lot of trouble. I'm letting you know your court date will be in two days."

"Damn, really, that's fast."

"No shit, it's not the nineties, asshole. Oh, almost forgot, your parents have already gotten you an attorney. You're going to be at the mercy of the judge at this point."

Two days went by very quickly. I slept most of the time and only ate once. Early that morning I was woken up by the guard, who then escorted me into a room with several showers and a haircutting booth. I was ordered to sit in the chair and a young beautiful woman walked through the door.

"Good morning, my name is Julie and I will be cutting your hair today."

"No need, Julie, I don't need a haircut but thanks," and I started to get up.

"Sit your ass down, this isn't an option!"

I sat down. She pulled out the razor and shaved my entire head in less than five minutes flat. I looked in the mirror. What the fuck, I was practically bald!

"Julie, thanks for the cut, you may leave now," the officer instructed. "Alright, Marco, clothes off, shower, and use fucking soap. You have five minutes to finish or I'm coming in after you."

That was the quickest shower of my life at this point. I got out still half wet and he threw me some black jumpsuit clothing. He immediately handcuffed my hands and then shackled my legs.

"Alright, Marco, off to the courtroom we go."

I shuffled my way into court and was escorted to a bench close to where the judge resided. A few minutes later the judge walked in and everyone rose from their seats.

"At ease, everyone, please be seated, thank you."

Judgment

"Marco Rameriez, approach the bench."

I stood up slowly and was escorted by two guards.

"Mr. Rameriez, I have already had talks with your attorney."

"Well, at least you have. I have never seen the guy!"

"One more smart-ass comment out of you, Rameriez, and you will be hating life very soon! I have seen your records from school and your lack of discipline and now the trouble you just got yourself into. I'm feeling very generous today, and do not take that as a sign of weakness; I am not nice most of the time. You have two choices and I am going to let you decide for yourself."

"So what choices do I have, Your Honor?"

"You can serve five to seven years in prison, or you can join the United States Air Force for a minimum four years. If you choose the Air Force and get kicked out in that four-year period you will face me again, and that result will not be fun for you. I hope I am being very clear here! If you make it four years with an honorable discharge, you are free to go and do as you please. So, what say you, Rameriez? Rameriez, I don't have all day, what's your choice?"

"What the fuck, I guess sign me up!"

"Smart choice, Marco. Guards, take him back to his cell."

The Five

My parents did not even say goodbye and I was shipped off to Mississippi for boot camp. Boot camp was a blur, it was over as quickly as it started. I certainly found my path. I got my bachelor's degree in engineering those first four years. I was also in the aviation program. I really wanted to become a pilot more than anything. The aviation program was the toughest thing I had ever done in my life and the most rewarding as well. There was no social life, it was physical training half the day and schoolwork the other half.

    A year into the program, we started doing simulation training and eventually the real deal. The first time I flew with my instructor it was like heaven on Earth. My stomach was up in my throat and the speed was almost orgasmic! The only people I associated with was the twenty members of my training class. To be honest, there really was very little socializing by the end of the day, you were so damn tired all you wanted to do was eat and go to bed. We had two days left before we graduated and at this point ten had already dropped out. The rule for graduation was they only passed the top five in the class. The next two days I worked my ass off, and at the same time there was a lot of shit talking going on from everyone who was left trying to psych each other out. Our last day was done, it was six P.M. and time for dinner. Our instructors told us the wake-up call for PT training was at five A.M. to six A.M. Then shit, shower, and shave in fifteen minutes and ceremony at six-thirty A.M. to find out the top five.

I grabbed my food and took a table in the chow hall like I had done every other day. Can't say I would miss this boring routine, most of the time I was usually about to fall asleep during dinner. This dinner, however, was different.

I began to eat when a pretty young lady from my class with curly brown hair and a mocha complexion asked, "Do you mind if I join you?"

"Not at all, feel free, it's just dinner."

"Well, that was a warm welcome."

"Well, what did you expect? It's been this way for the entirety of our training."

"Whatever, anyway, I am Samarra, in case you were wondering."

"Well, Samarra, I am Marco, by the way. I guess we are pleased to meet each other."

"Well, Marco, I was trying but you seem to be a self-centered dick. I guess I will leave then!"

"Hey, hey, hey, wait, I am sorry, just a lot of stress. I am sorry, please sit down. I would love to talk."

"You sure? I don't want to put you out or anything with you being so popular and all."

"Okay, SSamarra, you're a dick too, please sit down and enjoy dinner. So, Samarra, where are you from?"

"Your mom's anus, that's why she would want me to marry you someday."

I busted out laughing. "I admit you are a woman of my heart, funny and a pain in the ass."

Samarra laughed. "I am from Idaho, born and raised, and if you make fun of that watch how far I can shove that baked potato up your ass. I was a pro at it back home."

"Wow, this is an awkward first date."

"It's not a date, dick, just a get-to-know-you, don't flatter yourself."

"So how do you feel you are doing so far, Samarra?"

"Don't know don't care, but I'm sure I did much better than you."

"Once again, I'm blown away. Can you bear my children, you so classy and all?"

"Well, Marco, this was lame; however I guess I'll see you in the A.M. to watch you cry."

"Same to you, it's been the best entertainment I've had in a while."

"Doesn't surprise me a bit."

Top Five

I left chow laughing and wondering what the hell that was all about. Very cute, tough girl, but what a bitch. I lay down in my cot and I could hear a lot of people talking, but I was too tired to give a shit and instantly fell asleep. Holy shit, what the hell. I heard loud banging in the dorm. Shit, not now, damnit! I snapped to attention, did my bed quickly, and was as presentable as I could be.

One of the instructors jumped in my face. "What kind of dick sucker are you, Chubby Lips!?"

"One that sucks hard, sir!"

"How hard can you suck, Chubby Lips!"

"So hard I could snap the cartridge in your dick, sir!"

"Love that answer, Chubby Lips, from now on you will be called Cum Dumpster. Cum Dumpster, give me five miles full gear in less than ten or I will shove my baton up your asshole so far you will think an elephant's dick is small!"

"Sir, yes, sir!"

Five miles of hell, I threw up twice while they yelled "Pussy!" at me, calling me a pussy the whole way. Why did I do this, I really could not tell you. It went from five miles until the torture finally ended around four A.M. I returned to my cot extremely tired and afraid if I went to sleep I would miss the ceremony.

Grad day came very quickly. I was exhausted and still in pain from my overnight activities. I hit the shower, got myself in tiptop shape, and put on my best uniform. Graduation day was at hand. I saw everyone in my class and even saw

Samarra. I slightly waved to her and in all her classiness she flipped me the bird. At this point I didn't really give a shit, when today was done I would know where I stood. It was a beautiful ceremony orchestrated by the Air Force. Many family members were in attendance, but not mine. I guess they had given up on me. I had not heard a word from them since I had been arrested. They would be extremely proud of me, but I guess they have moved on.

It was finally time to announce the top five of the class and I was literally shaking, this was it. I either made it or my dreams were shot! Did I screw something up? Was that why I had extra PT that night or what? I really didn't know.

They called my name. "Marco, number two in the class."

I almost passed out. I don't even remember the other names called. As soon as it was over we were dismissed to visit family. I went straight back to my cot, I was done. Several hours later I woke up very disoriented with glued-on nipple pasties all over my face. I looked over and saw Samarra there laughing.

"Marco, you did better than I thought, but just to remind you, Slap Dick, I am number one."

I heard her, saw her, and was out again.

New Life

Five years later I was in charge of a top-secret group that tested new aircraft and trained pilots to fly them. It was a great job, paid me very well, kept me busy, but just like the academy no time for socializing or finding the woman of my dreams, and yes, there was that everyday PT training I loved so much.

"Captain Marco, sir!"

"At ease, Sergeant, what can I do for you this morning?"

"There's a call for you, sir, on the secured private line!"

"Are you pulling my dick, Sergeant? I'm too busy for bullshit this morning!"

"No sir, Captain, I'm very serious!"

"Thank you, Sergeant, I will get it."

I walked down the hallway, used my security pass to open the private elevator, and took it all the way down to the bottom floor, which was ten miles underground. I walked up. I tell you what, if you were not a computer with a voice like that I would marry you today!

I took a deep breath and picked up the phone. "Good morning, Mr. President, it's Captain Marco here, what can I do for you, sir?"

"Captain Marco, I am so glad to be able to talk to you for the first time."

"Thank you, sir, it is a honor for me to be able to talk to you!"

"Captain, I will cut to the chase, if you don't mind."

"Not at all, sir, what can I do for you!"

"I have been following your career and I am extremely impressed with what you have achieved thus far."

"Thank you, sir, that means more than you know!"

"Listen, Captain, I have a top-secret and important mission I need someone like you to be a part of. Are you interested?"

"With you asking, how could I say no, Mr. President?"

"Great answer, Captain, take the rest of the day off, that's an order. We will pick you up at nine A.M. tomorrow and send you to a new location for the meeting."

"Yes, sir, thank you, sir, see you then."

What the hell did I just get myself into? Now my mind was racing. I took the elevator back upstairs and called for my sergeant.

"Yes, sir, Captain?"

"At ease. I am off for the rest of the day and at nine A.M. I will be gone, don't know for how long, but until then you are in charge."

"Yes, sir, thank you, sir!"

"Don't let me down, Sergeant."

"I won't, sir, good luck."

"Thanks, I will see you when I get back. You know while I am gone, if you do well this could be great for you."

"I do, sir, let me prove myself."

"I know you will, Sergeant, cannot wait to see you when I get back."

"Thank you for trusting me, sir. I will see you when you return, be safe."

I had a lot of whiskey that night trying to relax. I remember watching the news and falling asleep around eight o'clock or so. I woke up with the alarm clock kicking and screaming at six A.M. I jumped up, made my bed, and began the shit, shower, and shave routine in under five. Old habits never die. By seven I was ready to meet the president but I was two hours early.

A limo showed up at nine A.M. on the dot and I got a call from the sergeant.

"Sir, your ride is here."

"Did you clear them, Sergeant?"

"Yes, sir, they are waiting on you."

"Thanks, I will be out."

I walked out to the main hangar and saw the limo. Two very large men exited both sides of the vehicle. They definitely were Secret Service.

"Captain Marco, I am Mark and this is Chad. Please get into the vehicle."

The trip was long, at least ten hours, not much talking, kind of silent and weird, if you ask me.

"Okay, this is it, Captain, go to the second floor and knock at door 505 and say, 'I have a nice ass but you can't have it.'"

"Are you fucking bullshitting me!"

"Welcome to the top brass, Captain."

The Briefing

I walked up to door 505, knocked, and said that ridiculous passcode sentence. The door opened and to my surprise I was greeted by the president himself, along with two Secret Service agents.

"Come on in, Captain Marco, let's go to this back office, sit down, and discuss some business."

"Sounds good, sir."

"Captain, can I get you a drink?"

"Sure, do you have whiskey?"

"A man of my own taste. Sure thing, whiskey it will be."

One of the Secret Service came in and poured us both a shot, and we sat at the table.

"So Captain, I'm sure you are wanting to know why I have asked you to come?"

"Yes, sir, I have been wondering ever since I received the phone call."

"I am sure you have. As you know, Captain, the Air Force has made many changes over the last fifty years and especially in the area of flight technology."

"I do, sir, I work with it every day."

"That is why I have called you here today."

"I am not following you, sir?"

"You know, Captain, about ten years ago we were the first to break through the ability to travel one light year into space in a reasonable amount of time without putting the crew at risk."

"Yes, sir, I know, it was amazing to accomplish that goal and I actually helped work with that particular aircraft."

"I know you did, son, and you and your crew did a wonderful job at that. To get to my point, Captain, what if I told you now we have the ability to go two light years out with travel time only being one week to get there and one week to get back?"

"What, are you serious, how?"

"I am not a scientist, Captain, but they have made great improvements on the last aircraft to go that far and now we know ways of speeding up the trip using wormholes for travel while conserving aircraft energy."

"My God, are you serious!"

"I am and that is not all. Here comes the fascinating part. We have discovered a planet two light years away that has the same distance between the sun as Earth does. In other words, Captain, there could be life like ours. It could be a second home for our planet, we just don't know."

"So are you asking me to work on the aircraft that's going?"

"Sort of, but I have more in mind of you actually leading an expedition to the new planet for research purposes."

I was speechless and did not know what to say or even think at that moment, he caught me off guard.

"So what do you say, Captain, are you up for serving your country?"

"Can I have some time to think about it?"

"Well, it is a three-man crew and two others have been chosen. There's little time, we are ready to launch soon."

"What is in it for me if I go and return safely?"

"All of you would be allowed twenty million a year to spend tax free as you wish, never to pay taxes again, and full retirement pensions. On top of that, your fame and whatever you decide to do with that would be tax free as well. And never forget, you would go down in history as a pioneer of this age."

"You should have been a car salesman, Mr. President. Maybe when I get back I may finally have time to find a wife."

"I am sure you could, Captain, probably any woman you wanted. So are you in?"

"Yes, sir, let's get started!"

"I knew I could count on you, Captain. We are flying you home tonight, take tomorrow off, pack your things, get arrangements made, and we will send you the information you need to fly to our new training facility."

"Yes, sir, I will, and thank you, sir, my parents did not believe in me."

"That is a shame, Captain, we will see you soon."

I arrived back at my base around 7:30 that night and was greeted by the sergeant at the gate.

"Sir, is everything okay?"

"Yes, it is, Sergeant, but look, I am probably going to be gone for a while, and as you know I need you in charge and on top of your game."

"I understand, sir, what is going on?"

"I can't talk about it, Sergeant, it's very classified and I hardly can believe it myself, but hopefully one day we can talk about it. I have to pack my things tomorrow and leave the next day, so from now on you are the man, you got it?"

"Yes, sir!"

"So excuse me, Sergeant, I need to get some sleep, busy day of packing tomorrow."

"Goodnight, sir!"

The Move

Woke up early that morning, took my time, made breakfast, watched the news. Wow, this was great. I had not done this since I was in high school. I started packing my things and boxing up other things I was not bringing with me to put into storage. Sargant had called me, told me I had mail from the president, so I had him meet me for lunch and bring the mail. We sat and had chow together. I opened up the letter and there was a plane ticket to Seattle, Washington, and instructions that someone would pick me up using the passcode "Into the darkness you will see the light." Okay, better than the last code, I will give you that.

Sargent was nervous, questioning me on his job, and it was hard for me to follow him when I had a lot on my mind as it was.

"Sargent, just relax, you know what you're doing. You will be fine, and by the way if I don't come back, I have loved working with you. It has been a real honor."

"Do not say things like that, Captain."

"You never know. I have to get going and finish up early."

"Yes, sir, Captain, I will see you off in the morning!"

"Thank you, just call me Marco."

"Yes, sir, I will try."

Seattle

That morning came early and sure enough Sergeant was there to escort me off. The limo was waiting to take me to the airport.

"Hey, Captain, please be safe."

"I will, and hope to see you soon, and make sure you hold down the fort for me."

"I will do my best, Captain," and he snuck in a quick hug that took me by surprise.

We headed off to the airport. I was nervous and excited at the same time. Once we arrived at the airport, we went through security protocol checks and then finally boarded the plane. Estimated flight time was three and a half hours to Seattle.

My fellow passenger sat down beside me. She looked to me around high school age or a little older, hard for me to tell these days.

"So stranger, where you going?"

"Seattle, and you, miss?"

"Do not call me 'miss,' dickhead. I am not your fucking daughter!"

I could relate to her attitude. She reminded me of where I had come from. "Sorry, going to Seattle on business."

"Me too, just got a gig in a band, going to hit it big and rock ass the rest of my life, you know! And you?"

"Well, let's put it this way. I hope to change the world."

"That's cool, old man. I am going to drink to the both of us on this flight! By the way, I'm Trina."

"I am Marco, and time for my earplugs and a nap."

I was woken up by a flight attendant.

"Sir, we are here."

Looked over and Trina was gone.

"Okay, thank you, sorry I overslept."

"That's okay, sir, you can exit now."

I slowly dragged myself off the plane and headed outside to where my escort was supposed to be. There were three limos outside waiting, and I was having trouble remembering the secret passcode. I just yelled out into the darkness, "You will see the light, or whatever it was!"

I saw the second limo flicker its lights. As I approached the limo, the passenger-side window rolled down.

"Get in, Captain, we have been waiting on you."

"Sorry, guys, I fell asleep on the plane."

About a half-hour later, we arrived at a location I had never been to before.

"Hey, guys, where are we?"

"No need to know the name, you're just going to be here for one day for briefing on your mission and to meet your fellow brothers. Then they're flying you guys to Florida, where eventually you will start your mission there. Alright, Captain, we are going to escort you to your room so you can get settled for the night. Someone will come get you at eight-forty-five A.M. and the meeting starts at nine sharp. Try not to oversleep this time."

"Sure thing, thanks."

Eight-forty-five came quickly and there was a knock at the door.

"Morning, Captain, are you ready?"

"I am coming."

We walked down the hall and took the elevator up two floors.

"Second room on the right, Captain."

"Thanks."

I opened up the door and the first face I saw was Samarra's. *Oh, shit, abort mission* screamed through my head.

"Holy shit, if it's not number two. This has to be a bad Air Force joke," came muffling out of her mouth.

"Come in and take a seat, Captain Marco. Just to let you know I am Peter from NASA. I see you and Samarra already know each other?"

"Oh, yes, you could say that."

"Captain Marco, this is Daniel, who will be on the mission as well."

"Good to meet you, Daniel."

"Likewise, Marco."

"Alright, everyone, sit down so we can get started. I am going to make this as simple as I can. You already know we now have the capability to go two light years away from our own solar system. Marco, this is why we chose you. You and your crew worked on the last aircraft that went one light year out. It is the same design but it has been obviously modified, we will brief you on that later. We have found a planet with roughly the same temperature and seasons as Earth, also that planet's sun is equal distance to that of our own. It is almost like they are twins except in a whole new system. We do know this planet contains oxygen, we think enough to support life; however with the great distance, we cannot be completely sure until you get there and take samples. Once you get there is where Daniel comes in. He has a lot of critical scientific knowledge and will be in charge of collecting samples and testing them."

"Excuse me, Peter, what am I here for?"

"Samarra, you are one of the best pilots the Air Force has. We need your skills on that ship and also to help and assist anyone you can. I have been told that Captain Marco will be the commanding officer on this mission, so everyone is to report to him."

"Commander-in-Chief, that is complete shit. I am surprised he can wipe his own ass!"

"Enough, Samarra, you two can work out your issues later. This is serious business!"

"So, Peter, just how are we getting to this new planet?"

"Well, Captain, our top scientists at NASA have mathematically calculated a way to travel through three wormholes that should shoot you to the planet's location quickly in a short timeframe."

"Should or will?"

"You're right, Captain, it is all mathematical and theory. That is why this is serious business. My responsibility is to inform you on the risks of this mission and not to candy coat things. You have two hours to officially decide if you want to take on this mission. You are dismissed. I will see you back here in two hours."

I started down the hallway and headed back to my room when I heard that irritating voice.

"Hey, number two, you better check those boxers. I smell a poop stain, or shall I say bacon strip from back here."

I arrived at my room and sat down, pulled out a beer from the mini fridge, and began to think, *Hell, why not? Nothing to lose but my life, right? No wife, no kids, it's just me. Hell, who knows, if we make it I can retire and focus on getting a family and settling down. Okay, it's settled, I guess.*

Eleven o'clock came quickly and everyone was already in the room when I got there.

"Well, we are all here, let's begin, time is short. So, Daniel, in or out?"

"Count me in."

"Samarra?"

"You know I would not miss out on this."

"Captain Marco?"

Samarra was staring me down like a hungry lion. Our eyes connected.

"Hell yeah, I'm in!"

"Great, everyone, come up front and center and sign the paperwork."

Florida

Early the next morning we woke up like clockwork and headed straight to the airport. This time we were not flying by civilian plane. There was a military transport aircraft waiting on us. We all got loaded up in the aircraft and were ready for takeoff. As usual Samarra had not shut her mouth since we left the briefing. We arrived in Florida around two o'clock P.M. and were taken quickly to our new living arrangements while we were there. Admiral Jacobs came around and greeted everyone face to face and to let us know to meet him for dinner at six P.M. Dinner could not come quick enough, and I was starving. I was sure the food would be excellent while we were here.

"As all of you already know, I am Admiral Jacobs. I personally want to welcome each of you and thank you for taking on the historical journey. I do not sugar coat anything. This mission is dangerous and there is a high probability none of you will survive this mission. In saying that, many people before you have accepted the challenge and made history and died doing so. Either way, sacrifice is what has made mankind very special and unique. The next three weeks you will be trained on your own individual duties away from each other so you will know your roles front and back. I will say this only once! Captain Marco is chief commander of this mission. If anyone has issue with that, they need to leave now. Now training starts at six A.M., a thirty-minute lunch at noon, and training ends at six P.M. Chow will be between six and seven P.M. and then you go straight to your rooms. There will be no playtime outside this facility. Is everything understood!"

"Yes, sir."

"Louder, soldiers!"

"Yes, sir!"

"Better. When you're done with chow, report to your rooms."

Training was intense as to be expected, and of course that damn physical training I loved so damn much. If I survived this and got out of the force, I'd never exercise again as long as I lived. I was taught inside and out about the new aircraft, every nook and cranny of it, over and over. Flight simulation over and over, every possible situation they could think of. This was going to be the longest three weeks of my life.

"Samarra, what the hell was that shit?"

"That was damn good piloting, sir!"

"No bullshit, you would have had the aircraft split in half!"

"No, sir, I do not crack aircrafts, sir, just people's balls."

"You better take this shit serious or your ass will be the one cracked, understood, Samarra?"

"Yes, sir!"

My God, once I was done with this three weeks of bullshit training I would be ready to move to another fucking planet. Day in and day out I worked my ass off and I was the fucking best pilot in the force, but because I was a woman I still got treated like shit. Fuck them!

"Hey, Daniel, wake up. Is you brain too tired or is it the fact you're not up to date on your physical training?"

"Sorry, sir, no sir, just got tired after lunch."

"Well, get your ass up, flat worm dick. We have shit to review!"

"Yes, sir, sorry, I am on my way."

My entire life I had always been at the top of my class. How I wound up here, I did not know, but the force had become part of my life. This mission could be a scientific breakthrough and something I would be destined for, but how much more could I take? Who knows, but I was here for the long haul!

Today was the last day of training and Admiral Jacobs walked into the chow hall. All of us stood up and saluted.

"At ease, soldiers, enjoy your chow tonight and get some good sleep. All of you have worked very hard and come a long way since training has begun. I am more than proud of all of you. The three of you represent what is so great about our country and the force. Sleep in as late as you want tomorrow. There are no restrictions tomorrow on chow, and liftoff will be at six P.M. I trust all of you will live up to expectations and succeed. God bless. History starts tomorrow!"

The Launch

The only good part of the training was I had three weeks of not hearing Samarra's mouth, but I was sure that would change soon. I woke up at around 10:30 that morning. It was great to have slept in, but reality was starting to set in and I was getting nervous. I decided to have my last big meal on Earth around two because I had to be at the launch site by four. To my surprise I ran into Daniel at chow and we sat together for dinner.

"Well, Daniel, we haven't really had much time to talk, but how was your training?"

"Intense but good. I am really excited and nervous, how about you?"

"You could not have said it any better. I am with you on the nervous part. Have you seen Samarra today?"

"Marco, I have not seen her since we left Seattle."

"Well, hell, hopefully she has quit. Oh shit, too late, there she is."

"Hey there, boys, are you up for the challenge?"

"Which challenge are you referring to, the one going to space or the one having to deal with your mouth?"

"Well, Captain, that actually was pretty funny, did not know you could be. So boys, I know that I am the only woman on this mission, so do yourselves a favor and relieve yourselves before takeoff. Try and remember, don't let the little head screw up what the big head needs to do."

"It is going to be a long trip, Daniel."

"I agree, sir."

It was game time. All three of us suited up and began walking down the transport corridor to our new home for the next few weeks. We climbed the long ladder that led us to the main door of the ship. We all ducked our heads and stepped into the cockpit and took our respective seats.

"Okay, guys, here we go, uploading system checks."

I was loving it, so many gadgets to play with. I was in heaven.

"Samarra, will you do the honor and fire up the engines?"

"Hell yeah, in three, two, one, firing it up!"

The power of the newest most technologically advanced rocket engines just blew me away.

"Daniel, how is your systems check doing?"

"So far so good, Captain. It is almost complete, sir."

"Hey, guys, just call me Marco, please, no need to be so damn formal on this mission."

"Can I just call you 'Dick' for short?"

"Love you too, Samarra. Samarra, upload the maps to full screen. We sure as hell do not want to make a wrong turn."

"Uploading now!"

"Hey, guys, we are being hailed. Daniel, connect call to full screen."

"Connecting, sir."

"At ease, soldiers. I just wanted to say a few words before you embark on such a historical trip. The three of you have done a wonderful job in your careers and in your training. I have full confidence in each of you and know if you three work together there is nothing you can't accomplish. Make the force proud, I know you will, and God bless. See you when you get home."

"Thank you, Admiral, we will see you soon, Captain Marco and crew out."

"Okay, guys, get prepared, we have five minutes until launch time. Can anyone think of a nickname we should call the ship?"

"How about 'Redemption'?"

"Interesting, Daniel, what do you think, Samarra?"

"Sounds good, Daniel, very catchy, I like it. Then the Redemption it is. Get ready, we have one minute and thirty seconds until launch."

"All is clear, Marco."

"Thanks, Samarra, on my mark, hit launch sequence. Three, two, one, you're on, Samarra."

"Launch sequence activated, everyone hold on to your asses so it does not end up in your throat."

BOOM!!!!!

Flyer Miles

We shot up so fast, I could not even talk or think and we quickly slowed down as soon as we broke Earth's atmosphere and began to slowly orbit the Earth. Slowly I began to get my senses back and yelled out, "Is everyone okay!"

Not much response, just some grumbles. At least I knew they were alive.

The first words I heard were, "What the fuck just happened?"

"Good, you're okay, Samarra, how is Daniel?"

"I am good, Marco, just give me a minute."

"Samarra, let's see the map. We have to exit Earth's orbit at a certain time to connect with the wormholes for travel."

"I know that, dick, uploading now!"

"We have ten minutes, Marco, before we have to hit light speed to reach our first wormhole."

"Thanks, everyone, get prepared, no time to waste. This trip is going to be a bitch!"

"Okay, Marco, time to launch!"

"Lead the way, Samarra, it is your call now."

BOOM!!! Off we went, same thing. We came almost to a halt, and all of us lost consciousness. All of us started to slowly come around.

"Where are we, Samarra?"

"Hold on, dick, I am working on it."

"Daniel, you okay?"

"I think, but my pants need to be changed."

"Yeah, mine too!"

"Marco, we are one mile away from the first wormhole, we can launch anytime."

"Thanks, Samarra, let us get our senses together and then we will proceed. Look, guys, this is the first encounter into the unknown, this travel as you already know is based on theory and math. When you guys are ready, let me know."

Silence was the new language of the Redemption.

"Fuck it, I am in charge. Samarra, hit launch sequence now!"

"You got it, Captain, launch is on!"

BOOM!!! A huge burst and we entered the hole!

Dark Travels

Almost immediately I fell into a state of unknown. I could not move or see. Was I asleep, was I dreaming? I could not tell. Thoughts of my past filled my mind and came crashing down like a powerful waterfall crushing every part of my body. Emotions and senses began to override my soul. Loud booms and bangs filled my ears, and then the visuals began. Odd-shaped colors of distortion came and went, and then they began to clear out. Odd visions of my favorite dog as a kid appeared along with visions of my grandmother's funeral as well. Things I hadn't much thought about in years flooded my mind and emotions were at an all-time high. The vivid odd-shaped colors appeared again as quickly as they had left. I sat there drained of emotion but fascinated by the complexity of it all. They began to spin counterclockwise from slow to eventually fast. The center began to pull itself inward and took the shape of a funnel and me staring right into the middle of it. I could barely see something moving in the center of the funnel, slowly crawling its way up to my direction. What was it? My heart was racing, adrenalin pumping, and emotions drained, I could not take much more. Then I could not see it anymore, just the spinning funnel and silence. Silence quickly broken with screams from a million people flooded my ears and a predominant voice talking to me, saying, "You are already dead, you just don't know it!" My body shot up from my chair and my restraints quickly threw me back into my seat. My body was pouring sweat and tears had flooded my eyes. Every ounce of my body hurt. I felt like I had been to hell and back. I could hardly get my words out.

"Samarra, Daniel, speak to me!"

Samarra mumbled, "I am good, Marco."

"Okay, check out Samarra for me."

"Yes, sir."

"Samarra, are you okay enough to check our status?"

"Yep, just give me a sec. Marco, we are in slow cruise control at 1500 mph. At this rate we will be there in forty-five minutes to the second hole."

"Great, everyone, get your shit together. We have two more to go!"

"Marco, we are approaching the second hole."

"Thanks, Samarra, it is your countdown, lead us in when you're ready."

"Yes, sir! On my mark, three, two, one, engage."

BOOM!!! As quickly as we entered, the state of illusion began once again. This time I could hear voices talking, but they were muffled and distorted. Was this just another wormhole illusion, or was I going crazy from the stress on my body? Slowly I was starting to be able to understand bits and pieces of the conversation. The voices were not familiar to me. I could hear a woman and two men talking, which turned into arguing. The woman lashed out, screaming about millions of people that were dead, and no one did anything to prevent it. One of the men told her not to worry, we were safe now under new leadership.

She began to yell again, "It's all lies, you have been deceived."

The men began to laugh, and the conversation quickly faded away into the darkness as did my mind. I was awake and in as bad of a condition as I was the first time. Now I understood why PT was so damn important.

"Samarra, coordinates, please."

"Marco, we are twenty-five minutes away from the last hole. If we make it we will arrive at our destination."

"Hey, guys, we can do this, just one more and we can make history. Who is up for it?"

Screams and "hell yeahs" filled the Redemption.

"Sir?"

"Yes, Daniel, when we arrive permission to change underwear, sir?"

All of us began to laugh, and you could tell the trust for one another was starting to grow.

"Permission granted, Daniel."

"Marco?"

"Yes, Samarra?"

"I am setting coordinates so when we pass through the hole the ship will come to a slow stop so we can observe the planet first and get ourselves together."

"Sounds good, Samarra, great thinking. Lead us in when you're ready."

"Aye-aye, Captain!"

"Who are you, SpongeBob SquarePants, are you flying a pineapple under the sea?"

"Sorry, could not help myself, in three, two, one."

BOOM!!!

Again, reality or not, I am not so sure, but the conversations continued to increase. I heard lack of food, overwhelming disease, mutation, wars. Your fault, their fault, it cannot be fixed, we are all going to die. I was awake and the ship was still. I sat in my chair and my eyelids flung open and the phrase "Your death or mine" rolled off my brain.

"Hey, we made it, we fucking made it!"

Screams filled the cockpit of the Redemption. All of us knew we just made history and so far we were still alive.

"Just to let everyone know, all of us did a great fucking job. I am proud and honored to be a part of this with you!"

Screams and yells ensued.

"Hey, sweet cheeks, let me know our position when you're ready."

"Captain, are you flirting with me?"

"Maybe, but do not ruin the moment."

Observation

"We are twenty-five hundred miles away from the planet's atmosphere, sir."

"Okay, Daniel, let's start taking readings and check for any kind of radar detection systems."

"Yes, sir, Captain. I am ready to interpret the results as soon as they come in."

"Thanks, Daniel, we need it as soon as possible, do not want our dicks in the wind if we can be detected."

"Captain, data is being transferred to Daniel now."

"Thanks, Samarra. Daniel, when you're ready."

"Looking now, Captain. Captain, there are no radar systems that I can find unless they have technology that we are not familiar with."

"Good, thanks, Daniel."

"Hold on, Captain, I am interputing some new data just coming in. The planet's oxygen levels are ten-percent less than Earth's but we should be able to manage that. However, unfortunately I see other environmental factors such as radiation that is much higher than our levels on Earth."

"Okay, Daniel, are we able to go to the planet or what?"

"Yes, we just need to wear some proper protecting clothing and we should be fine, as long as we don't overstay our welcome."

"Okay, anything else, Daniel, I need to know?"

"Yes, sir, just a sec, getting more feedback. Sir, there is movement on the planet so there is life down there. Population wise, though, it is not even a quarter of Earth's current population. Interesting, though, I am not picking up any kind of major power sources from the planet."

"So what you're saying is the life detected is probably a primitive species?"

"That would be my guess, sir."

"Well, everything is dark down there, so let's all get some rest, we need it, and will proceed in the morning, when the planet's sun is up."

"Captain, it is amazing, this planet is almost a brother to our own but different."

"Hell yeah, boys, this bitch is tired and needs her rest. It's tough being this hot and talented. See you simple dicks in the morning."

"On that note, goodnight, guys, see you in the morning."

Morning came quickly.

"Everyone up, we have work to do, eat breakfast. We do and will have a long day ahead of us. Are you up, Daniel?"

"Trying, sir."

"Samarra?"

"Yes, dick, I am up!"

"Morning to you, my little ray of sunshine. Never a bride, just a bridesmaid, I can see why. You have thirty minutes for breakfast and let's get started. The quicker we get the mission done, the faster we get home and live on Easy Street. Samarra, fly us in closer so we can get a better visual read out of the land."

"Yes, sir! Marco, I am getting some strange readings."

"What is that, Samarra?"

"The structures that are on the ground show similar properties to the dwellings on Earth but not the same at all. There is a lot of radiation in the materials that is making it too difficult to get a clear analysis. Captain, this is strange!"

"What do you think, Daniel?"

"No, I agree, something is odd here. I would proceed with caution."

"I agree, everyone get prepared and ready for anything."

The Unknown

"Samarra, take us in slowly and take us and land us four miles outside of the dwellings."

"You got it, Captain."

Off we went. The landing was slow and smooth.

"Captain, we have arrived."

"Great job, Samarra. Okay, guys, hydrate, get your supplies together, lock and load your weapons, time to take a tour of the unknown."

We all were nervous and a little on edge as the door to the Redemption opened slowly. Wow, very similar to Earth, a little harder to breathe but it felt like we were home. Where we had landed was very sandy and next to no vegetation or life to be seen. Instantly Daniel began taking soil samples and the data came back.

"Nothing can grow here, sir, no minerals, no nutrients, but a lot of radiation, sir, similar to a radiation fallout on Earth if it would have happened. If we would have had a nuclear war this would be the result!"

"So what the hell is this?"

"I don't know, sir."

"Everyone proceed with caution! Let's head toward the dwellings."

The land was sandy and hot as hell, making it even harder to breathe. We walked until we arrived at the edge of the dwellings.

"Okay, guys, keep alert, let's check out the structures and get some better readings from the inside."

We got about ten steps in when suddenly the ground gave way. We were in some kind of trap, and quickly the sand filled the ends around us, only exposing our necks. We were all terrified. None of us could move. The sand had cemented in our bodies with nowhere to go. I felt a sharp pain in my neck and began to feel dizzy, and then everything went black.

I woke up to a woman yelling at me, "Do not try to fuck us, you already have done that."

I yelled out half dazed, "Who are you?"

"I am Eve, the beginning to a new start!"

Your Mine

The confusion was slowly clearing out of my head, and I could feel my body being dragged across the floor and propped up against a wall. I could feel my hands and feet were restrained with some very coarse rope. I looked over to my left and could see Daniel and Samarra were tied up as well.

"Are you two okay?"

Silence.

"You only answer my questions for now!"

"Who are you?"

"I have already told you, I am Eve. So the question remains, who are you?"

"Rank Captain 010587."

"Your name, I asked you!"

"010587."

"You idiot, forget your military bullshit, I want your name! Oh, no answer? You want to play the strong, silent type? Before I start cutting up each one of your friends here, you should know the military does not exist anymore! You have questions, solider, and so do I. So your name first or people are going to start getting cut." Eve held the knife firmly on Samarra's throat and a trickle of blood ran down her neck.

"Stop, I am Captain Marco with the United States Air Force!"

Eve began to laugh uncontrollably. "Most of the time I would laugh at you and say the radiation finally got to your head, but I have seen your ship and we have taken your weapons."

DEAD LINE EARTH | 39

"Where are we?"

"Where do you think, Captain? Think about it, Captain, to be as high rank in the wonderful United States Air Force you should be able to figure it out! I speak your language, hell, I can even speak Spanish. Doesn't those two forms of language sound familiar to you? The size of the planet, the similar closeness of the sun? Think you may be able to take an educated guess now! Speechless, Captain, I figured you would be. Welcome home, Captain, you are on Earth!"

"No, you're wrong, this is not Earth, we just left Earth a week ago!"

"What year, Captain, did you leave?"

"2095."

"Well, Captain, this Earth is more than a hundred years after that. This is what the world has created, are you proud?"

"Daniel, can this be true!"

"Captain, I cannot be sure but from my readings I got I cannot disprove what she is saying."

"Why try to fight the truth, Captain, you are here and it's the new existence that your people have created."

"We have not created any of this, we are a strong and smart society."

"Silence, you're wrong, your culture created all of this, do you understand me!"

History Lesson

"Do the three of you want to hear the truth, do you!"

"Sure, whatever you want."

"Do not be an asshole, Marco, I have no problem with cutting off your head!"

"Sorry, please explain."

"The year was 2095, in early October, I think, on the second or third day."

"Wait, stop, Eve. Daniel, when did we leave Earth?"

"2095, on August tenth, sir."

"The dates make no sense or the time difference."

"Do not ever question me, Marco!"

"Captain Marco!"

"Yes, Daniel."

"We do not know how the time travel has affected everything. Eve, we can fix all of this once we get back."

"None of you are getting back! You do not deserve it, and you should pay for everything that you have done! The new law around here is technology is outlawed."

"We can save the world, why don't you want us to help!"

"Let me explain about your technology! Everything started with the world's weapons system completely controlled by computers. There was some sort of glitch or virus in the system. The United States fired nukes at North Korea and which in return China attacked the US. In which the UK fired on China. Then Japan, Iran, and Israel all got involved, including Russia. Within twenty-four hours the whole world went to shit! There was no winners, everyone lost and humanity was destroyed! Governments collapsed, nations collapsed, there was famine, disease, and mutations all around us. Most of the survivors would rather have been dead! Have you ever seen, Captain, another human eating another human alive and including innocent babies, have you! Of course you have not, you're pathetic!" Eve in her anger punched me in the face.

"Eve, look, we can fix all of this. It does not have to be this way. Surely you do not want the world to stay this way?"

"Why not, Marco? Even if you went back and fixed it, it would just be a matter of time before you fucked things up again anyway! It will never change, you're too ignorant to understand what has already happened." Eve began to choke up. "The children, I do not even want to talk about it, from the fallout and even today! Any of you have children?"

"No, we do not."

"Of course you don't, and you will never understand. My group of people, and when I say my people it is exactly that. They are mine and I love them and they love me. My people as a collective body are none as realists and our motto is very easy. We do not believe in advancing technology any more than what it is now. We want to live simple, grow our food, raise our livestock, simple as God had originally intended. Do any of you know who God is?"

"I do!" Samarra shouted.

"Tell me, then, who is God? A manmade legend from centuries ago!" Eve began to smirk. "Once again you're wrong, just like you were about technology and led to the downfall of mankind. I am really not as mean as I sound, so I am willing to make you a deal."

"And what kind of deal are you offering, Eve?"

"You want to save the world, here is the new realistic way you are going to do it. A couple of miles from here, outside of our society, is a mountain called the Devil's Dumping Ground. To get to the top of the mountain it is a twenty-five-mile walk, and also going down as well. The dumping ground is roughly 85 miles wide and full of things you have never seen or wish to. If you make it up the mountain and back down here to the surface, you are free to go try and save your technological world. However, I will tell you you're not going to live, but in the meantime you will see and learn what technology has done to our planet."

"And Eve, if we do not agree to your deal?"

"It will be simple, all of you will be executed by first light!"

"I guess we do not have much of a choice, we accept your deal."

"You're a sick bitch, you are lucky my hands are tied!"

"Guard, free Samarra, please."

"Yes, ma'am, I certainly will."

"Okay, Samarra, you're free, show me what you would do since you're such a bad-ass military solider."

"Samarra, no, back down, that's an order!"

Samarra grabbed Eve and they began to struggle with each other. Eventually Eve flung Samarra on her back and hammered her foot into her chest, knocking the wind and the fight out of her.

"Guard, take her away! See, Marco, life has not been easy for us. We have been well trained in combat as well thanks to our new lives. Oh, before I forget, I will not let you take this journey unarmed. I am not that cruel. However, you cannot have your guns back, that would be stupid on my part. So each of you will be given a choice of a weapon to choose from. Your choices are a bow spear or knife. Each of you must choose now. Marco, you're first, what will it be?"

"A spear."

"How long do you want it?"

"Six feet."

"Daniel, and you?"

"A knife."

"And since Samarra is not here, I will ask her myself a little later. See, there, I am not really hard to deal with. Your journey will start at daybreak, and tonight I will feed you and give you a good place to sleep. Guards, take them away, let them eat and drink, and remember the rules!"

We were escorted to another holding area, where we were personally fed and then escorted to a room for sleeping. They separated us for bed and guards were posted at each door. I was hoping Samarra was okay; we were going to need her for tomorrow.

New Day

Daybreak came very quickly. I slept very little and was nervous about what we were all up against. A sharp knock on my door.

"Yes?"

"It is time to go, are you ready?"

"I am."

The guard led me to a door. He opened it and I walked outside. The sun was hot and very bright. It took my eyes a little bit to adjust. It must have been the effects from traveling through space for the last week. Daniel and Samarra were already standing outside, looked like they were waiting on me to get there.

"You okay, Samarra?"

"Pissy but peachy!"

"You, Daniel?"

"Never better, sir."

"Enough talking!" Eve shouted. "The people that you see behind me are our lawmakers within the realist movement. I have told them about your quest and if you were to succeed you will be freed. I keep my word and so will they."

My hands were freed and we were given our weapons of choice.

"Any words for us before you leave?"

"I want my ship in perfect shape when we get back. We will toast to your departure and good luck, you will need it."

"Okay, guys, are we ready?"

"Hell yeah!" Samarra shouted.

"Daniel?"

"I got your backs."

Country Living

We headed into the dumping ground and found a trail that was an easy passage in. As we walked in the vegetation was starting to increase and more and more signs of life. We started to see some birds, which was the first time I had seen one since we got here.

Unfortunately I also saw a lot of rats that didn't care we were even there. The further we went, the air began to get more humid and stale smelling. The fog started to slowly creep in, making it more difficult for us to see very far ahead. It began to sprinkle rain and our skin began to burn.

"Sir?"

"Yes, Daniel?"

"We need to try and find some shelter, this is acid rain. We do not want to be exposed to it for long periods of time."

"I agree, everyone keep your eyes open for any kind of shelter."

At this point we had been at least walking for three miles or so.

"Marco, look up ahead, looks like a cabin on the edge of the clearing."

"Sharp eyes, Samarra, good job. Alright, let's approach very slowly and quietly, who knows what we may run into. Samarra, scope out the back perimeter and meet Daniel and me around the front and be careful!"

"Will do."

The cabin appeared very small and looked very old and tattered. Also I noticed in the back was a barn-looking structure that was fairly large.

"Samarra, did you see anything?"

"No, seems quiet. Do you think anyone lives here?"

"Not sure, but we are getting ready to find out. Samarra, you and Daniel get on each side of the door and I will knock. Be ready for anything."

"Don't worry, Captain, we have your back."

I knocked on the door three loud times and paused to listen. No response. I could not hear anything inside. I knocked again and this time the door just popped open slightly on its own. There was no movement inside that I could see.

"On the count of three, let's move in. One, two, three."

I kicked the door fully open and we rushed in with weapons ready. The cabin looked like it had been abandoned. There was an old couch with a huge hole in the center of it and a makeshift-looking bed made with old torn-up sheets that smelled like an animal had died on it.

"Okay, let's make a quick sweep of the cabin to make sure we are not alone."

There was only two other small rooms, and Samarra and Daniel swept those.

"Hey, guys, are we clear?"

"I think so, Captain."

"No, we're not!"

"What is wrong, Samarra?"

"Come quick, we have visitors."

Daniel and I rushed into the room.

"Look outside."

Shit, there were two people walking from the barn to the cabin.

"Let's go meet our new friends and be ready!"

We stormed out from the house and quickly surrounded them with our weapons ready. It was an old man and woman, their clothes were torn dirty and had quite the smell coming from them. Neither one of them appeared to be in very good health.

"What are your names!"

The old man replied in a deep, scratchy voice, "I am Alton, and this here is my wife, Lynn. Who are you?"

"I am Marco, this is Daniel and Samarra. You two have any weapons on you?"

"No weapons, just our knives for harvesting our food."

"Daniel, search them."

"Yes, sir, Captain."

As I did my search I could feel both of them shaking with fear.

"Sir, they are clean."

"Good, you can lower your weapons. Alton, is this you and your wife's home?"

"It is. We farm and live our lives. We don't get many visitors here. It has been a few years since we have seen anyone around here."

"We are not here to hurt you, we were just looking for shelter to get out of the rain."

"You're welcome to stay and have dinner with us if you like."

"That is very nice of you two, we may take you up on the dinner. Do you have any water to spare?"

"We do, let's get back to the house so I can rest. I am not getting any younger and my bones are cramping up."

"We are following you, Alton."

"Lynn, can you get our guests some water?"

"Yes, dear."

"Alton, how long have you and Lynn been married?"

"Hell, who knows now, it's been a while. I hardly remember the day before."

"Here you go, there is more water if you need it."

"Thank you, Lynn, very nice of you. What is wrong, Samarra?"

"This water is awful, where did you get it?"

"It is okay, we get it from a well I dug when I was a younger man. The ground helps filter out the bad stuff, never gotten sick from it."

"Daniel, what do you think?"

"Well, he is right, the ground will filter out the bad stuff and as you know we do not have many options now."

"Marco, the misses is going to be making delicious grazier fingers today."

"What is that?"

"Let me show you my livestock in the barn."

"Alright, I am going with, Alton. You stay here with Lynn and we will be back soon."

We walked to the barn at a very slow pace. It appeared he had really bad arthritis and his tough life had beaten him down.

"Alton, you seem really proud of your livestock."

"I am, Marco, just wait and see. I am the best farmer around the parts, I assure you dat."

I helped him pull back the big latch to the barn door and it swung wide open. I gazed into the barn and everything began to go in slow motion. My brain and my mouth temporarily forgot how to work together. There was five rows of ten humans buried up to their necks like vegetables in a garden. Behind the rows was a makeshift smokehouse with different human parts being smoked like jerky.

"Alton, what the hell are you doing? These are human beings! You need to let them go, now!"

"Marco, have you lost your mind? These are graziers, everyone knows that. They're more animal than human, they don't talk, they forage the land eating like animals and breeding like them as well. It is tough keeping their populations in control, hell, they will try and eat anything you try to grow. The human side of them left many, many years ago. In my younger days I used to hunt them down, but now I set traps to catch them. I tend to my livestock very well. I bury them up to their heads in the ground, give them water every day, and feed them mostly protein and fat from parts of their own kind. You know, the leftover stuff. Once they gain weight, the ground starts to crack and then I know they are good for harvesting."

"My God, I cannot believe mankind has fallen this bad!"

"Marco, are you some kind of grazier lover? What is wrong with you?"

"UMMM, no, Alton. Alton, I noticed you have a lot of knives. Is there any way you can spare a few?"

"Sure, I have made many over the years. How much you need?"

"Three if you can spare them?"

"Sure, here you go."

"Thanks, Alton, and I am sorry."

"For what?"

"Never mind."

We headed back to the house slowly, and Lynn, Daniel, and Samarra were on the porch talking.

"Okay, let's move out."

"Is everything okay, Marco?"

"Yes, Daniel, we just need to get moving."

"Do you need more water to take with you?"

"That would be great, Alton, thank you once again. Okay, fill your canteens and let's move out. Alton, Lynn, thank you both, be safe!"

Swamp Death

We continued our track farther north.

"Spill the beans, Marco, what did you see? I saw the look on your face."

"The downfall of our society, Samarra. I am sure we will see a lot more."

All of us were starting to get hungry.

"Keep your eyes out for anything we can get our hands on to eat."

"No shit, this bitch is hungry!"

"Never lost for words, are you, Samarra?"

We walked for several more miles and decided to stop and rest and have a water break.

"Holy shit, Captain, look what I found."

"Damn, Daniel, excellent find, looks like we are having turtle for dinner. Let's get a fire started, cook the turtle, and try and find shelter before nightfall gets here."

The turtle, well, it was a turtle and it filled our stomachs and gave us the protein we needed to continue with our mission. The further we went, the wetter and nastier the ground got.

"Marco, we need to find shelter soon. It is getting darker and I think we have about thirty more minutes of sunlight left."

"I know, Daniel, you guys keep your eyes peeled. We need to find something soon."

"Um, guys, what's that moving in the mud ahead?"

"Hopefully more dinner of some sort."

"No, Marco, I see hands now. It is coming out of the mud!"

"Daniel, behind you!"

"Shit, Marco, we are surrounded, there must be twenty of these things!"

"Okay, get prepared, they don't look friendly, engage them now! I will spear the ones coming out of the ground, Samarra and Daniel, attack the walking ones! No mercy on them!"

I went from one to another, spearing them in the head as they continued to crawl out from the mud. Daniel and I were fighting hard but they outnumbered us. As quick as I stabbed one, another was on top of me again. I fell to the ground with one of them on top of me, snapping its dirty, slimy teeth, trying to bite me. I heard in the distance Daniel yelling out in great pain. He had been bitten. I was trying to fight the ones off around Daniel. I could not hold on much longer. I was getting tired and this thing was not letting up. I held my hands around its throat, trying to keep its mouth away from my face, when out of nowhere a giant club came down and smashed its head in. Blood and brains splattered my face and into my mouth. Just as quickly both my arms were grabbed and I was being dragged through the woods at a quick pace, screaming and yelling.

"Samarra, Samarra!"

Out of the woods three men showed up, beating off the creatures, and they began to leave.

"Follow us, it is almost dark and the mud people will return in greater numbers."

"I can't, they have Samarra!"

"You have no choice; your friend is very sick and needs treatment. There is nothing you can do for her now. Let's go now, time is short, the dark is way too dangerous! Help me get your friend and let's go!"

We grabbed Daniel. He had already passed out, and they led me through the woods to the small village about a half a mile away. The village was amazing. Their makeshift huts were all built into the trees with ladders that could be pulled up, I assumed for safety reasons.

A lady came running out. "What's wrong, and who are these people?"

"This one has been bitten by a mud person. Can you start making the antidote to help him?"

"Yes, get him up into my tree and I will start right away."

"Thanks, Jane. We did not have time to introduce ourselves. I am Josh, and you are?"

"Marco, and thank you for your help out there."

"Your friend will be fine, Marco, once he gets the antidote. A bite will not kill you but you would wish it did. A bite will instantly paralyze and give you extreme pain, makes it easier for the mud people to overcome you and eat you alive."

"Who and what the hell are these mud people?"

"You mean to tell me you don't know where the hell have you been? After the fallout the radiation mutated a lot of the human DNA, forced them to live in the water and moist areas or they will dry up like termites in the sun. They're not really human anymore, more of a hybrid species of the fallout."

"What about Samarra, Josh, who the hell has her?"

"That is a different story. Those were mountain people."

"And who the hell are they!"

"Where are you from, Marco, really you don't know?"

"No, just tell me!"

"Mountain people by name primary live in caves and underground enclaves. They scavenge for food. After the fallout most of them cannot speak very well. They have lost all sense of reality. They are what we would consider your modern-day caveman."

"My God, I have to go after her!"

"Just wait a minute, Marco, you don't know what you're saying."

"No, I have to go!"

"You go tonight and the both of you are dead. They're not going to kill her. If they would have grabbed you or your other friend, you probably would be dinner. They keep women, especially the ones they find, for breeding purposes and to help raise the young."

"How is Daniel?"

"He will be fine, trust me. You and I need to talk, Marco, let's go back to my tree. I have questions for you."

We went back to his tree. It amazed me how large and homey his hut was.

"Take a seat, Marco, we're going to talk. Do you know what alcohol is, Marco?"

"Oh, yes, I do!"

"Well, that is a first." He began to laugh. "Take a sip, Marco."

"No, you first and try yours and mine together."

"What's wrong, you think I am going to poison you?" He downed both shots. "Are you finally satisfied, Marco? Go ahead, please have a shot."

I did and it got my attention.

"What's wrong, Marco, never had liquor before?"

"Not like that!"

"Cut the shit, Marco, you have never seen mud people or mountain people and by that sip of that shot you have never had liquor before? I am not stupid, Marco, who are you and where are you from?"

Three shots later I began to talk. I was in a buzzed stupor. "I am Captain Marco, United States Air Force, on a secret mission on the discovery of a new planet, and come to find out it was Earth of the future and I am here and fucked! What say you, Josh!"

"I would say you are an honest drunk and I do appreciate your honesty. What are you doing in the dumping grounds?"

"We were going to be executed, but Eve told us if we survived we could go back and try and save the world."

"Eve did you say? Eve!"

"Yes, you know her?"

"I know that crazy bitch very well. She does not want technology to advance. She thinks it is the root of all evil. She only wants it that way so she can remain in charge and control everyone! That is why we are here, Marco. We had an establishment on the outside lands, and when she found out we were teaching our children and trying to better ourselves she got a small army behind her and drove us out. We are a peaceful people, Marco, as you can see, and we are not crazy. We want mankind to return back to a civilized society."

"A-men to that, Josh. I need another shot!"

"Tomorrow, Marco. I need you to talk to an elder in our group. He has vital information to give you for your trip home. He is very sick, so you need to see him first thing tomorrow."

"What about Samarra?"

"We will work on that, first thing is you need to talk to him and let your friend get better or staying here will be no good. Get some sleep, Marco. I promise you I will help you. All of us need you to succeed."

I woke up the next day confused, hungover, and Josh staring at me face to face.

"Breakfast is ready. Eat and let's go talk to Evan. He has a lot of information that is important to tell you."

"Okay."

It was wild bird eggs and berries. It was good enough to do the trick.

"Let's just see what Evan has to say. Did you sleep well, Marco?"

"I guess, pretty hungover, though, would love to have your special recipe for when I get back."

"Here we are. Remember, Evan is very ill. He has been informed of who you are and has something he wants to share with you, so please be patient with him."

We opened the door and a frail old man lay in the bed, propped up with the help from his caretakers.

"So you are Marco?"

"Yes, sir, I am pleased to meet you, Evan."

"I know who you are and why you're here. If you want to save the Earth from what has happened…."

Then the coughing spell began. The caretakers raised him up more and began pounding on his back. He caught his breath and spit up some blood and mucus into a wooden bowl.

"The one who sent the virus to the computers came from Iran but was raised in the UK."

"Do you know his name?"

He began coughing again and up came more blood. "His name is Abbas Tahan. Kill him and none of this world will have ever existed!"

"Thank you, sir!"

"Just fix it."

The coughing began again and we were asked to leave.

"What do you think, Marco?"

"It is a start, Josh, but now I need to get Samarra back."

"I understand. I see you're very loyal to your friends. However, Daniel is not ready for this. We will back you up but time is getting short."

Samarra: New Surroundings

I was dragged through the woods and down a hole in the dirt. My body ached and it was very cold where I was. They kept dragging me through the dirt. We must have been in some kind of underground tunnel or cave. The air was dense and smelled very sour, almost like bad body odor but worse. Quickly we stopped changed directions and I was being dragged again. Shit, were we ever going to stop? I was yelling at the top of my lungs to let me go but with no reply. Finally we stopped in a room with a fire that was just below the surface of the ground. I could see a small makeshift chimney and could see the stars outside. I could barely see my captors' faces. Their hair was really long, nails even longer, and dirt covered their faces. I just froze, not knowing what to expect. Both men were saying something to each other but I could not understand them, but they looked angry at each other.

I yelled out to them, "What do you want with me!"

They yelled back in my face with gibberish.

A few minutes later another man walked in with a woman along his side. He stood beside me and put his hand through my hair, feeling and playing with it. The next thing I knew he was playing with my boobs. I smacked his hand away and he grabbed my hair and slung me backwards. I yelled out in pain. He had strained my back and then he flipped me upright.

"You here, you ours!"

Wow, half-broken English but at least I could understand, even though I did not just like what he had just said.

"No, I am not yours, and I need to leave." I started to walk away and he stopped me very quickly.

"No, you here, you ours!"

I tried to make a run for it but he grabbed me and slung me to the floor, and the other two men began tying me up with vines that had very sharp thorns on them. I could feel them cutting into my skin. The more I moved, the worse it got. The two men picked me up, carried me down another tunnel to a smaller room, and tossed me in and sealed the hole with a very large boulder. Shit, I was going to die!

At some point that night, I do not know when time stood still, and I must have fallen asleep. I awoke to the sound of the big boulder being moved away and I was guessing a six- to eight-year-old girl came into the room with wooden bowls in her hand.

"Hey there, little one, how are you?"

She hissed at me like a wildcat and put the bowls on the ground and quickly moved away.

"Can you speak? I am Samarra."

She looked pissed and approached me and sat down in front of my face. She grabbed one of the bowls, scooped some stuff out of it, and tried to put it in my mouth. The smell was horrible. She forced it in my mouth.

I spit it out and told her, "No! Get that shit away from me!"

She started to cry and hit me in the face and ran out, and the boulder slammed behind her. I sat there still confined to vines and thorns, pissing and shitting myself now.

"You fuckers better let me go, assholes!!!"

Daniel

"Hey, man, it's Marco, how you feeling today?"

"Better, thanks, just really fucking tired. What the hell happened?"

"Sorry, long story, no time to explain but Samarra is gone and we need to get her back. Daniel, are you up for the challenge?"

"I think so. I need food and water first."

"Look, Daniel, Josh has had his men doing night patrols. We think we have a really good idea of where she may be and they are willing to help us."

"Marco, I just need one more day to get strength back and I will be ready."

"Suck it up, Daniel, we do not have another day!"

Samarra

I lay in shit and piss and then the broken-tongued mother fucker came in the door.

"You mate, make baby, you take care, we feed."

What the fuck was he talking about?

"You mate!"

"Eat shit, dick!"

I was almost out cold. He knocked me to the ground and I could hardly remember my name. I felt him fucking me, then I passed out!

Daniel

I woke up in a cold sweat. The last words I remember was Marco telling me basically to man up. I got up, threw my clothes on, and grabbed my knife. "I am coming after you, Samarra, I am going to save you!" I was pissed and for the first time in my life I was angry and had a purpose.

It was early morning. The sun barely shined. I crept through the woods in stealth mode like I was instructed in training. I stopped behind a tree and waited, one swift move. I turned around and stuck a knife in the back of his head! I could see the possible entry holes in the ground. My mind was racing at this point. Should I smoke them out, or should I just go in and kill everyone I saw!

Samarra

I woke up sometime later and the little girl was in the room with me. She was very attentive and I think she knew what I had gone through. She lay with me, cuddled me like she was my own child I never had. It was strange but she gave me comfort. She stroked my hair and I kept her close, felt like something that I was missing in my life. I told her I was going to name her Tanya. I repeated the name over and over, I did not think she really understood, and then I passed out. I awoke to a lot of noise from people yelling in a strange tone, and

Tanya was gone. Somehow I was free from the vines and thorns. Was it freedom or a deception?

After sticking my blade through his skull, I decided to go into stealth mode. I took off his clothes. Shit, he stunk! It should give me an advantage when I made my move. I crawled down into the first hole and was instantly met with someone on top of me. I quickly drew my knife and a quick stab to the head ended that! I crawled down the tunnel and met another. Before he knew who I was, he was already dead!

"Josh, where is Daniel?"

"I don't know where he is. Fuck, he is probably looking for Samarra. I have to go!"

"Damn you, Marco, you cannot go alone. All of you will die!"

"Then get who you can to help or I am leaving now!"

"I have people, Marco, just give me enough time to assemble them."

The killing spree continued one after another. I dropped them like flies. They had no clue what was coming at them.

"Where are you, Samarra?"

I could start to hear yells and panic. They must have discovered the bodies. I was in the zone, killing was coming easy to me now. I did not like it but I knew I had to do it to save my friend.

"Okay, Marco, let's go. I have four men and myself, let's go get her! Samarra comes back today, no exceptions, even if I have to kill them all! Today, Marco, there could be a heavy price to pay!"

"Maybe, Josh, but I leave no one behind."

"Marco, remember your mission!"

"I am and she is part of it."

Josh became silent.

Tunnel War

There were six of us. I wished we had better numbers but that was all the volunteers we could get. Josh led the way through the woods. We were running at full speed towards the caves. The closer we got, I began to hear yells and screams in the distance. We slowed our pace and started to creep slowly toward the caves. I could see people running around in a panic and knew the Daniel must already be inside.

I continued searching from room to room. Some of the cave dwellers went right past me. Maybe it was the smell of my clothes or the dim lighting, either way it was working to my advantage. I entered a new room and sitting there on the floor were two women tied up, backs facing each other. I cut them free and told them to leave, but I did not think they understood me too well and they were terrified. I began to have a bad feeling and turned around. When I did there was a cave dweller standing there facing me from the other side of the room. Shit, my cover was blown! He looked to be around six foot four and well over two hundred pounds. Long-ass black burly beard, mud all over him, and a very sharp stick shaved into a knife.

I crawled to the entrance of my room and peeped out to see what was going on. There was a lot of chaos going on and people were running in all directions. I was wanting to escape but knew I could not leave without Tanya anymore. She had to come with me.

"Okay, Marco, let's enter that hole over there. It does not seem to have so much activity going on."

"Okay, everyone, ready, let's go in!"

We slowly crept to the hole, not to make it so obvious. However, that did not last long. We were spotted and five of them started running at us full speed. Nowhere to hide or run, we had to fight them before we could enter the cave. I had the advantage. The first asshole ran at me and with my six-foot spear took the blade straight to his heart. The fight ensued, a lot of yelling, cussing, and screams filled the air. The smell of death filled the air, organs and blood exposed to the elements gives off a distinct odor. I had just speared my last one when everything became silent. I turned around and observed our fight. We had lost three men, blood was everywhere, but no time to feel or think, we had a mission to do!

I was scared and pissed. I yelled out to him, "Bring it on, mother fucker!"

He screamed at the top of his lungs and began to charge me. When he got close enough I fell to the ground and stuck my leg out to trip him and he fell, hitting his head against the dirt wall. He quickly got up and charged again. I ducked as he approached, and with his full force he tripped and fell to the floor. Now he was really pissed off. He got up screaming, veins throbbing from his head. He charged again, this time I tried to outmaneuver him but his wooden knife snagged my shoulder and clothes and threw me to the ground. Both of us had lost our weapons and he picked me up, took three steps, and threw me against the wall. I bounced off it like a rubber ball hit the ground, and all I could hear was him yelling like a wild animal. He picked me up again and for the second time slammed me several times against the wall. The fight that was in me was quickly fading.

The three of us entered the tunnel. I led the way. I had the longest weapon. The tunnels were dark damp and smelled like shit! The three of us crept the cave. I just started randomly spearing people as they came by. It was so dark and they were confused. They did not know we were even there. I yelled out, "Daniel, Samarra, where are you!" No responses.

I left the room. I had to find Tanya and get her out of all this madness. I crawled the floors and went down the hallway until I heard yelling from the room to my left. What the fuck was going on? I peeped through the hole in the wall and saw that fucking asshole who knocked me out and raped me. He had someone against the wall choking them and then I saw a wooden knife on the floor. I slowly crawled in the entranceway, grabbed the knife, slowly stood up, and was right behind him. I touched his left shoulder and he turned around and I shoved that wooden knife through his fucking head! He dropped to the floor on his knees and then I slit his throat for insurance. I quickly dropped to the ground to see how the other person was doing.

"Daniel! Daniel, it's me, Samarra!"

We continued through the caves. Josh shouted out, "Shut up!"

"What, Josh?"

"Shhh! Listen, I hear normal speech! Samarra, Daniel, where are you?"

"It is me, Samarra, where are you guys?"

"Do not come out, Samarra, keep talking, we will find you!"

We followed the voice and were amazed that both of them were together.

"Thank God, let us get the fuck out of here!"

"No, Marco, not yet!"

"What are you saying, Samarra?"

"We cannot leave without Tanya!"

"Who the fuck is Tanya, Samarra? We need to leave now!"

"No, not without her, you go, I will find her!"

"No fucking way, Samarra, who is she?"

"My new daughter!"

"What?"

"We need to find her. I will explain later, Marco!"

We continued to search the cave and nothing. Samarra was yelling her name the whole time.

"She is gone, Samarra, we have to leave now!"

"No, I am staying!"

"No, you are not, Samarra, that is a fucking order, damn you!"

As we left the cave and exited a hole Samarra stopped and picked up a child.

"I guess this is Tanya?"

"It is, Marco, and I love her!"

I kissed her cheek and welcomed her to the movement. "Okay, everyone, time to head back to the trees for safety and get some rest!"

I walked over to where Samarra was staying. "Samarra, how are you doing?"

"Okay, Marco, I am good. I am thankful for everyone coming after me. You could have just left me."

"You know better than that, Samarra, we do not leave our people behind, and you know I would have missed your smart-ass mouth anyway."

She kind of grinned with a crooked smile.

"Samarra, what happened to you?"

"Look, Marco, thank you. I do appreciate the rescue but make that the last time you ask me what happened to me. I do not want to talk about it, okay!"

"Understood, but if you do you know I am here."

"I do, thanks."

"So where is our new edition, Tanya?"

"They took her to clean her up and feed her. Marco?"

"Yes, Samarra?"

"We need to get the fuck out of this place soon. We cannot allow the world to end this way."

"I understand, and we're not going to let it, trust me. Get some rest. I will see you in the morning and we will move on. I am going to see Daniel next and let him know we are heading out soon."

"Daniel, how are you doing?"

"I am good, Captain, very bruised throat but I am alive."

"That is good, but however I am going to tell you that was the most fucking stupid piece-of-shit trick I have ever seen! You ever do that again I will personally kill you myself! Stupid, irresponsible, and not your fucking orders!"

"I am sorry, sir!"

"No, you're not, Daniel! We need you, Daniel, but for what it is worth I am very fucking proud! I will let everyone know when we get back how much of a warrior you are!"

"Thank you, Captain!"

"Get some rest, Daniel, we move out early tomorrow."

"Yes, sir."

"Hey, Marco, meet me at my tree for dinner and drinks so we can talk."

"Sounds good, Josh, I will be there in a few minutes. Thank you, Josh, for inviting me for dinner and drinks. I need a good, stiff drink after today."

"Me too, Marco. I just got done telling the family members about the deaths."

"I am sorry to hear that. I know that is very hard. We are leaving tomorrow morning, Josh, we need to get back as quickly as we can to prevent all of this."

"I agree, Marco. I will provide you some smoked deer meat and fill your water containers in the morning for your trip. Just remember one thing, Marco, keep your eyes open, do not trust anyone. People are starving and will do anything to stay alive. I pray for you guys, please stay safe. You are our only hope! Eve knew when she sent you out here you would probably die. Prove her wrong, make her understand that humanity is worth saving, that it was not really technology that destroyed everything but one evil man's heart that did."

"Oh, I almost forgot to tell you, Evan died while we were gone."

"I am truly sorry to hear that."

"Yes, me too, he was a great man. He will even be greater for giving us the knowledge of who did this. It will not go unrecognized, I promise!"

"Well, they call you Captain?"

"Indeed they do."

"Well, Captain, this drink is on me."

"Yes sir, Josh, let the fire water flow."

It was a great night but time for bed.

Forward On

Morning came early. I woke up, the sun was just peeking its head above the horizon. The three of us assembled outside and had breakfast with many others from the community. As he promised, Josh gave us deer jerky and water for our mission.

I turned to Daniel and Samarra. "Before we leave I need to say a few words to the people. Attention, everyone."

The crowd became silent.

"Thank all of you for everything you have done. Our mission is to make sure this world you live in now never will exist. There is hope. I knew it the first time I met your leader, Josh. Love each other, help one another, and always be kind, that is the true meaning of humanity. Thank you again, but we must leave."

The crowd exploded with chatter and clapping and began to disperse into their everyday activities.

"Marco, where is Tanya?"

"Samarra, she is staying with Josh, where she will be safe."

"No, damnit, she is coming with us!"

"No, she is only six or seven, she belongs here. She will be safe here, Samarra!"

"No, she is my child, she belongs with me!"

"What the hell is wrong with you? She is not your child."

"She is, Marco, and I am not leaving here without her!"

"It is too dangerous, Samarra, for her. You saw what happened last time. Come to your senses. If you love her let her be safe here. They will treat her very well, Josh has already promised me that."

"You mother fucker, you set this up without even talking to me first!"

"Mind yourself, Samarra, this is an order. It is too dangerous for her, so get your shit together. Do we have an understanding!"

"What the fuck ever!"

I was pissed at Marco and heartbroken all at the same time. We started to walk away from the village when I felt a huge bump into my legs. When I looked down it was Tanya. She had a death grip on me and would not let me go. I bent down and hugged her. She had tears flowing down from her big brown eyes and it crushed my heart. I tried to explain to her that she could not go with us, but I knew she did not understand. I carried her back to Josh, gave her a big kiss, and hugged and tried to explain she would be okay with him. At this point I could not hold back the tears, and she knew I was upset as well. I kissed her again and did not look back and regrouped with Marco and Daniel.

"Samarra, I am sorry."

"Shut up, Marco, do not talk to me right now!"

Liar

"You wanted to see us, Eve?"

"Yes, Raz and Brinn, have a seat. I have something I want to talk to the two of you about. I need the two of you to carry out an important mission for me."

"Anything you need, Eve, what can we do?"

"The three soldiers from the past is what!"

"What do you want us to do?"

"Track them down in the dumping ground and make sure they do not survive and get back here."

"What, I thought you said if they make it they were free?"

"I have changed my mind. They are too dangerous to live."

"Have you consulted the council, Eve?"

"I am the council, I make the final decisions and this is an order!"

"But?"

"No buts, it is too dangerous if they live!"

"Why, Eve?"

"History cannot be changed, it can be altered, and if they go back we may not exist as we are now, so it is imperative that you make sure they do not survive, do you understand? I am going to give you their weapons and ammo. You will be safe. Get your rest, you two will be leaving at daybreak."

"Yes, Eve, thank you."

We walked and walked through the woods and trails. By the look of the sun it was around midday.

"Okay, guys, let's take a break, have some water and a little food."

As we sat I spotted several graziers and when they saw us they took off like any other kind of wild animal.

"Don't worry, we don't eat our own kind."

"Samarra, Daniel, how you holding up?"

"We are good, Marco, but it won't be that long before we need to be looking for shelter for the night."

We continued to walk and eventually came to a clearing just ahead of us. It was a long dirt road of sorts, which appeared to have wheat grass growing on either side of the road. The wheat grass was around five feet tall and reminded me some much of the Midwest. We walked the trail but we were still on high alert. Who knew who might be using this road? We marched on and I began to notice the grass to the right of us was moving and heading our way, but we could not see anything. All of us stopped, weapons ready, adrenalin pumping. The wheat grass parted and out shot a Huma, or at least I thought it was?

"You got food for me?"

"Sorry, friend, no food here."

"You have food, you big people, take a lot of food to be big."

"Sorry, who are you?"

"Me Jappel, you be who?"

"I am Marco, this is Samarra and Daniel."

"Good meet, me Jappel, me hungry, no stories, me smell food on you."

"You got me, Jappel, I have a stick of jerky, would you like a piece?"

"Jappel need food."

"We have food, Jappel, do you have a place for us to sleep tonight?"

"Jappel do but first Jappel need meat stick."

"Okay, Jappel, here you go."

I reached in my pocket and handed it to him. He seemed scared but took it. I thought he was harmless. Jappel chowed down on the jerky stick. He was a very small person, barely over three feet tall, and no telling what his weight was. One side of his face was sunken down and appeared to have a lot of scars there as well. He did not have much movement in his left arm, and he hobbled as he moved.

"Jappel, where do you live?"

No response, he just ate. When he was done he asked for more food.

"Yes, but we need a place to stay tonight, Jappel, more food for you when we get there."

"You follow me now, let's go, dark coming soon, will die in dark. Let's eat and hide."

"Sounds good, Jappel, lead us away."

"Is it safe, Marco?"

"I cannot be completely certain, sir, Samarra, but he seems pretty harmless and we do not have much of a choice."

We followed Jappel. Even though he had his disabilities it was a struggle keeping up with him. We arrived at his home. He pulled up a huge square-shape cut-up board off the ground that was covered by leaves and tree branches. We climbed down inside and Jappel said to stay there, he would be back. He crawled through another hole, went outside, and covered the board back up with leaves and branches. He retreated back inside and covered the other hole with a boulder.

"Here you go, Jappel, more food."

The four of us ate together and he seemed very satisfied.

"So Jappel, do you have any friends or family around?"

"Jappel has no one. Jappel's parents disappeared, not know where they are."

"We are sorry to hear that, Jappel, and thank you for letting us stay with you tonight."

"Jappel want to know where you going."

"We are trying to get to the top of the mountain and down the other side to where the realist movement lives. Their leader is Eve."

"No, no, no, bad, no, don't you, Eve mean, likes nobody!"

"You know who she is, Jappel?"

"Jappel do, she tried to catch Jappel, me too fast for her! She gets mad comes into dumping ground and hurts others. She is bad, Jappel no like her!"

"Why does she try to hurt people, Jappel?"

"Jappel thinks she thinks she is in charge, the boss, but not Jappel's boss."

"You're a pretty smart guy, Jappel."

"Jappel know he smart, thank you."

We all got a big laugh out of Jappel. He was amazing and very smart.

"Jappel, what else is out here in the dumping grounds I need to know about?"

He got very serious when asked that question. You could see the anguish on his face and could tell he had seen a lot of bad things.

"Jappel tell you not trust many people, death is everywhere. Jappel very tired, must rest. Jappel has a lot of work to do in morning."

"Jappel, goodnight and thanks once again."

We all lay close together for body heat. It was much colder under the ground. I awoke with the sun hitting my face through a hole in the cave. I guessed Jappel was up and gone, attending to his work. I woke up the other two.

"Hey, guys, it is time to go. Samarra, leave Jappel a jerky stick, please."

"Sure thing, hey, that little fucker took one of mine."

I started to laugh. "Well, at least he did not clean you out. I will give you one of mine."

We crawled out of the cave. I did not see Jappel anywhere. I was hoping to at least say goodbye, but we had to be on our way, no time to spare.

"Are you two ready to save what is sacred to all of our lives now?"

"Yes, Eve!"

"Here are your weapons and water and food supplies. Do not let me down. We have fed your horses and watered them, worst-case scenario you can use them as food if need be. Remember, Raz and Brinn, we are all counting on you."

"We understand, we will not let you down!"

"Great, then go, may you return very quickly!"

Brinn and I left at full speed ahead into the dumping grounds. We had one thing on our minds: kill the soldiers and get back home.

"Okay, chicken tenders, let's move out, lol."

"Look, dick, if you talk about chicken tenders again, Daniel, I will carve you up for dinner tonight!"

"Love you too, Samarra."

We got back to what we thought was the wheat fields and got back on the road to move us forward. We marched on very cautiously with unknown dangers all around us. It was a long day but we got started early and were making the most of it. I was guessing it was late afternoon, we started to see workers ahead in some fields. They stopped what they were doing and just stared at us. Oh, shit, not a good feeling.

"Who do you think these people are, Marco?"

"Who knows, but keep your eyes peeled and keep moving. It is starting to get late."

We kept walking and the workers began to disappear from sight.

Bloody Highway

We kept on the path when a man and two women walked out on the road and blocked the path. The man was carrying a metal baseball bat that had spikes welded to it. One of the women was carrying a sword with two sharp blades separated at the end. The other woman had brass knuckles with three sharp knives extended from them.

"Look here, ladies, looks like we have three strangers with very odd clothes on."

"None of you are allowed to talk! If you can't speak, you better fucking learn because I have questions. Let's start the conversation. I am Z, easy to say, easy to spell, just one fucking letter and easy to carve into your ass if you don't talk. So now that I have introduced myself, who are you?"

"I am Marco, this is Daniel, and she is Samarra."

"That was a great fucking start. I love it! So what are the three of you doing out here on our lands?"

"We are just traveling through the dumping grounds to get to the other side is all, we do not want any trouble."

"Well, trouble has found you and you're in deep shit, my friends! Have you been the ones stealing our crops?"

"No, we just got here today, never have been here before."

"Damn, ladies, did you hear that?" and the women began to laugh.

"As I said, we have never been here before until today."

"Stop it, Marco, you're giving me a chubby just hearing you lie so badly."

"Look, we're just passing through, you can see what we have."

"Oh, I will, believe me, and this is typically the place where I make you choose."

"Choose what, Z?"

"Which one of you gets to die today for trespassing!"

"You know what, Z?"

"What, Marco?"

"Go fuck yourself, not today!"

One of the women hit the ground very quickly and was dragged through the woods. She had a snare attached to her leg and was screaming! Z and the other woman took off after her, and I ordered Samarra and Daniel to run! As I was running by I could see four or five people. They barely looked human to me, dragging her with the rope. They dropped the rope and began ripping her apart with their hands and teeth. Her screams were awful. I could not believe my own eyes and ears, it was like time was standing still. The last thing I saw was Z and the other woman trying to fight them off, but I could tell it was already too late for her. We ran and ran until it almost got dark.

"We need to stop, Marco!"

"I know, Samarra, let's rest and spend the night under those trees. Daniel, you keep first watch, Samarra, you second. I'll take the grave shift."

"Yes, sir!"

"We will take off again at first light."

"If it isn't Raz and Brinn. What do I have the honors of both of you showing up at my peaceful village?"

"Cut the shit, Josh, feed and water our horses!"

"Maybe if you act a little nicer. Remember, boys, I am not under Eve's law. This place is mine. Diane, please feed and water our guests' horses. This should, I hope, be a quick visit."

"You never change, do you, Josh? Still in the old mindset, are you?"

"Yep, and as usual, Raz, you talk and Brinn still does not understand much English. I guess you can't teach an old dog new tricks."

"Shut your mouth, Josh, we are here on business. We have questions from Eve, and you better be honest or it could be your downfall!"

"What the hell do you want? I am already tired of seeing your faces already."

"There are three people from the past who have come back to save the world. Have you seen them?"

"Are the two of you seriously asking me this? I would expect Brinn to but not you, Raz."

"Let me show you, Josh, how serious I am!" Raz pulled out a gun and stuck it to Josh's head. "How stupid is this, Josh? Now do you want to talk?"

"I do not know what you have, Raz, but I have no clue about what you are talking about."

"Well, Josh, if I find out that you do I surely will come back and kill all of your people and make you watch!"

"Such a nice guy, Raz, are we done?"

"No, I want some of your famous homemade liquor for tomorrow and Brinn will drink it first. If he dies so will all of you! We are staying here tonight and leaving in the morning, we expect to be fed as well before we leave."

"Whatever you need, Raz, maybe one day you will grow up and understand the truth!"

"Get out, Josh, we are staying in your place tonight. Do not forget to see us off in the morning!"

"Sure thing, see you in the morning."

"You have our food, water, and liquor, Josh?"

"I do, here you go, I cannot say I have enjoyed your company. Tell Eve I said hello and not to dump her trash here anymore!"

"One day, Josh, I will kill you no matter what anyone says."

"Sure thing, Raz and Brinn, have a nice day. Oh, shit, sorry, Brinn, forgot you still can't understand very well."

We woke up early. The sun had just risen and all of us were a little sore from sleeping on the ground.

"Alright, grab your gear and let's head out."

We headed through the fields and got back onto the road and kept heading north. About an hour later we saw a sign on the path that said "Turn back now."

"What do we do, Marco?"

"We have to keep going, Samarra, there's no way of getting around it."

"What do you think, Daniel?"

"I agree with Marco, we do not have a choice."

We kept pressing on only to stop for some water and a little bit of food we had left. We heard in the distance the sounds of engines coming our way.

"Everyone, hide in the trees and get down!"

We saw what looked like three four-wheelers riding through the fields. They all met on the road and began talking.

"Daniel, what do you see? My vision is not that good from this distance."

"Looks like three four-wheelers. Oh, shit, looks like one of them has an old-school shotgun. Weapons, engines, gas, very old school but they must be smart, we may be in luck."

"Do not go down there, dumbass, you do not know who they are!"

"I am not, Samarra, just watching, relax!"

The three vehicles took off and we came out of hiding.

"So what the fuck are we doing, Marco?"

"We need to find out more about these people, Samarra, they may be able to help us."

"Yeah, right, Marco, like the cave-dwelling people! You heard Jappel, you cannot trust anyone!"

"Relax, we are not going to be stupid but we have to get back soon to Earth. Let's move out, guys, daylight is wasting!"

We strolled back down the path. Mistake number one, we had been discovered and surrounded, how the fuck did that happen?

Lockdown

At least twenty people came out from the woods and we were totally surrounded. There was nowhere to run or hide.

"What do we do, Marco!"

"Not really sure, Daniel, but everyone stay cool, maybe we can get ourselves out of this."

"Samarra, please keep your mouth shut!"

They began walking and closing in on us when a man on a four-wheeler slowly crept through the crowd.

"Well, well, can it be? Holy shit, it's Marco and friends, does not look like you got very far."

"Shit, it's Z!"

"You're really lucky, Marco, I'll tell ya why."

"Why is that, Z?"

"At this point I would normally just blow your fucking head off in front of your friends for being an asshole. However, I was informed by the Giver to be nice and treat you well until he decides what to do with the three of you."

"The Giver, what is that?"

"Not a what, Marco, but a who, and you will find out soon enough. First things first, drop all your weapons and back away and lay on the ground! I mean it, Marco. He said to be nice, but don't piss me off!"

We lay on the ground, our weapons were taken and our hands were tied behind our backs. A small vehicle drove up with a cage in the back. We were picked up and tossed into the cage.

Z slapped the driver's door and yelled out, "Let's go. I got to report back to the Giver!"

The truck slowly began to take off.

"Who do you think this Giver person is?"

"I am assuming, Samarra, it must be a leader of some sort. What the hell did you think, Samarra?"

"Shut up, Daniel!"

"Whoever the Giver is, they seem to have a lot of control."

"I agree, Daniel."

We rode at a slow pace for a good fifteen minutes or so when we arrived at a large wooden gate. There were two guards on the outside of the gate, both appeared to be at least seven feet tall. They appeared to be human shape except for the legs were bent like a grasshopper's. I could not see any facial features at all, their bodies were covered in some kind of biomechanical suit that conformed to their bodies. It only took them one step to reach the back of the truck. No chance in hell of outrunning them for sure. They opened up the gate, pulled us out, and dropped us to our knees. I could not believe the strength they had. A red light shot from their foreheads, nearly blinding us. There was no pain but they were scanning us for something. The two guards turned to the gates, and a sequence of noises emerged and the gates began to open up.

"Hey, guys, umm, what planet are we on again? I have never seen anything like that before."

"I agree, Daniel."

All of us were in a state of shock.

"Marco?"

"Yes, Samarra?"

"What the hell, fearless leader, are we going to do?"

"Nothing yet, let's just try and figure out what is going on. I am little loss for words myself."

We were marched inside and greeted once again by Z.

"You idiots ready to go? No answer, that's fine. I told you good treatment by the Giver. Guards, escort them to their room."

They grabbed our arms and dragged us off. They were incredibly strong. There was no way we could escape them. We were taken to a room. It had cool air, places to sleep, and fresh water and food laid out on a table. The guards locked us in.

"What the hell is going on?"

"I don't know, Samarra, but do not touch anything, it could be poisoned."

"Screw you, I am eating it. If I die at least I will die with a full stomach."

Samarra stuffed her face. Daniel and I waited for an hour and eventually gave in.

"Well, boys, I am starting to like these people already."

"Not so fast, Samarra, something is up, you can feel it."

"All I am feeling is good and full."

"No, something is off, Samarra, the two guards, that's not normal."

"Daniel, you got too much brain shit going on, if you would get laid from time to time you would not be so damn paranoid."

"Sorry, Samarra, I agree with Daniel, something is not right."

"Marco, you were the first one who said they could help us and now you're backtracking."

"Samarra, relax, take a nap, but this is reality, do not let your guard down."

There was a knock at the door.

"Yes, who is it?"

"I am Ada, I am here for your comfort."

"Okay, come in, you have the key."

"I am here to offer you a naptime drink. It makes sleep a lot easier and more fulfilling."

"Sorry, Ada, I do not trust it."

"The Giver said you would not trust it, so I will shake it up and have a drink myself. Normally he does not allow that, but under the circumstances he said I could."

"Ada, who is this Giver?"

"I cannot talk about that, and I do not really know much except how well he treats everyone."

"You know, Ada, we could take you as our prisoner!"

"I know and so does the Giver, he just wants peace and thinks you want the same."

"He has put you in jeopardy, Ada!"

"Not really, I trust the Giver and you should as well. If it weren't for him we all would be dead now. You could kill me if you wanted to, but it is not in your nature to do, just like the Giver."

"Come on, Ada, who is the Giver, please?"

"You will see tomorrow, after you get your rest. You will have breakfast and then he will explain everything to you when he is ready."

"Shake up your juice, Ada, and drink then."

"I will. I cannot wait to taste it. I have heard so many wonderful things about it."

She shook up the drink and took a big gulp of it. The first words out of her mouth were "Oh, wow," and then she began to start laughing. The last words out of her mouth were "Smile, Marco, life is not so bad. I will see all of you later."

The door opened and Ada was escorted out by the guards.

"Well, boys, let's party, pass it my way!"

"No, Samarra, we're not touching that!"

"You two boys are idiots, I swear. I do not see how you two made it through the academy! I am having some shots and then going to bed. You two can fiddle dick each other all night, just keep them to yourselves."

"No problem, Samarra, knock yourself out, that way we do not have to hear that mouth run all night!"

Samarra took a shot and went to bed.

"Thank God, Daniel, she is asleep!"

Daniel and I never did drink the juice, but morning came quickly anyway.

New Awakening

"I bet you two do not feel as well as I do. That shit was awesome. That was the best rest I have ever had. I could run twenty damn miles today."

Ada walked in the door. "Good morning, everyone. I hope you all slept as well as I did?"

"Yeah, we're fine."

"Okay, well, follow me. I will take you to breakfast."

"Hell yeah, Ada, I am starving!"

"When aren't you, Samarra?"

"Kiss my ass, Marco."

"Alright now, no need for tempers this early in the day. Here is the kitchen, tell the cooks what you want and find a seat and enjoy."

We approached the buffet bar. There were at least ten different items on the bar from meat to eggs, vegetables, and even cakes, and best yet more clean water with actual ice!

"This is odd, Marco, why do they have all of this and no one else does?"

"Great question, Daniel. I am sure we will find out soon."

Ada approached us and escorted us to a table, and we all sat down together.

"I hope everyone is pleased with their meals?"

"Yes, thank you, Ada."

"Don't thank me, thank the Giver when you see him. You three must be real special. He usually does not meet with new people. I myself have only seen him once and that was from a distance. I am usually informed of what he wants me to do from others under him, so I must admit I am a little jealous."

"Ada, look at me. You seem like a very nice, caring person, but what is really going on here?"

"Nothing, Marco, just eat your food and relax. He will explain everything to you in due time."

She had a great smile and voice that appeared to me she had been brainwashed.

"Are you three ready to meet the Giver?" She was way too excited, like a kid thinking they were really going to the North Pole.

"Oh, you bet we are!"

"I will escort you there and someone else will bring you to him. I am not allowed at the meeting."

Ada escorted us to the meeting room and shit, Z was standing at the door!

"Well, good morning, Marco. Hey there, Samarra, I never forget a pretty face. And Daniel, right? Before we go in, let's try and start over again. Who knows, we may become allies."

"Don't count on that, Z!"

"Never say never, Marco, you may just change your mind." Z pulled out a handheld device similar to an old-school walkie-talkie. "We are here, is the Giver ready for us?"

"Copy that, it is a go, proceed."

The doors opened and we stepped into the room.

"Brinn, we need to ride hard, we do not want them to get too far ahead of us."

"Me know, me know, they can't be too far away, we catch up fast, they be in trouble."

"I like your style of thinking, Brinn, keep your eyes peeled."

We rode as fast and as hard as we could until up ahead we could see people blocking our path.

"Slow it down, Brinn, possible trouble up ahead."

We came to a halt, our guns were hidden and we kept a good five feet of distance away from the group.

"Do you mind getting out of our way? We have things to do!"

A man stepped forward. "You are not going anywhere, my friend!"

"I am not your friend, and you are going to let us pass! We want your food and your horses, and if you're lucky we might let you pass!"

"The answer is no, so what are you going to do about it!"

He took about two steps toward us when I pulled out my gun and blew the back side of his head off. Brinn pulled out his gun and we pointed at each one of them.

"Back off or we will kill all of you!"

A woman began to cry, "Please let us go!"

"Do you have any food?"

"No, we were hoping you did."

"So nothing to offer my friend and I?"

"Nothing, we're sorry, we are starving and move around all the time in search of food."

"Well, I am feeling awfully generous under the circumstances of your group trying to rob us and even kill us. So here goes, you have ten seconds to run before we start killing all of you! One, two…."

They all started running as quick as they could through the fields, heading towards the woods.

"Brinn, shoot the bitch!"

Brinn raised his gun and shot while she was on the run, and the bitch dropped like a rock!

"Damn, Brinn, you may not talk well or very smart, but you're one hell of a shot!"

"Tank you, me good at something."

"Yes, you are, let's head out."

We rode hard and during our ride Brinn asked me a question.

"Why do people tink me not so smart?"

I did not want to hurt his feelings. "Brinn, you are very smart, it's just you do not speak very well so they assume you are stupid. Eve and I know you're smart, she would not have sent you otherwise."

"Can you help me talk more good?"

"I will, Brinn, let us finish what we got to do, get back, and that is the first thing we will work on, I promise."

"Dat good, make Brinn happy."

"Raz?"

"Yes. I killed dat woman, was dat good or bad?"

"It is okay, Brinn, you had to, sometimes we do not have a choice. In times like these it's kill or be killed, and they were going to kill us, so don't worry, you are okay."

I lied to him. He did not know better. Part of me felt bad, also I just tried to ignore my feelings and shut them down, no time for being weak.

We rode up to a field full of people working.

"Who and what the fuck is this? Keep your weapons hidden."

"Brinn, we have some people approaching on some kind of riding machines. Three men approached us. I do not understand what they are riding on, but they're a lot faster than our horses."

"What are the two of you doing on our land?"

"Looking for three people who are in trouble. Have you seen them?"

"No! But the two of you are in trouble, get off your horses!"

"I'm sorry, we cannot do that!"

"Get off your horses or you will die!"

Brinn pulled out his gun and shot the man, and he fell down and began to slowly get back up. One of the other men shot Brinn in the head. He slumped over on his horse and fell sideways to the ground. He was dead and I was fucked!

"Any weapons you may have are not going to help you get off your horse and bow down to us!"

I got off my horse and saw Brinn's body lying there in a pool of blood, it made my stomach sick. I dropped to my knees and submitted without regard.

"What is your name?"

"Raz."

"Lucky for me, Raz, I was given protection to wear from the Giver! It still hurts like hell and now so will you!"

I was struck in the head and everything went black.

We entered the room, it was very large, reminded me of where political meetings would be held for passing laws. There were roughly ten people sitting in seats at the end of the room, I was assuming the Giver must be one of them.

One of the men began to rise from his seat, turned around, and faced us. "I am Trent, you have nothing to fear, you are safe here. I will return. I am going to get the Giver so we can proceed."

The three of us stood there looking at one another, not knowing what to expect. One thing was for sure, I was not getting good vibes from this place. The back doors opened and I could not believe what I was seeing. None of us could, we just stared in disbelief. Out walked a creature around seven feet tall. I could not guess its weight, it was very slender in size. The body was all black and its skin reminded me of the texture and look of a lava rock. It had two broken back legs, the same as the other two guards I had seen earlier. The face was small, shaped like an egg, and had no neck. The front of the face had designs on it, but I could not really see any features of a mouth, nose, ears, or eyes on it. The creature moved with grace and a long stride. It began speaking to Trent, and then the mouth appeared, it was small and round. When it stopped talking the mouth disappeared and the face became solid again.

Samarra turned to me. "Marco, what the fuck is it!"

"I do not know, but for the love of God, please do not run your mouth!"

"Believe me, Marco, I am silenced."

"Daniel, what's up, you're quiet."

"Not much, I think I just shit my pants once again."

The Giver took a seat in a huge chair that looked like something a king would sit in. He raised his long skinny figure to Z and motioned for him to come over. Z went over and kneeled down beside the Giver and they whispered back and forth with each other. Z stood up beside the Giver and told us to approach. We were ordered to stop about three feet from the Giver. He began to speak.

"I am the Giver. You are welcomed here and you are in a safe place where no harm will come to you unless you make poor choices."

I tried to speak.

"Do not talk, I am not done. First I have questions and then you will have time to talk. I know your names, but where are you from? Marco, you are the leader, answer my question."

"From Earth, just like the rest of us except you, I think."

He began to laugh, not an angry laugh but out of amusement. "Marco, I have seen your uniforms. I haven't seen those in a while, especially as good of condition as they are in. So be honest, this is how we develop a trust."

"I am Captain Marco of the United States Air Force. I was sent here to investigate the prospect of a new planet."

He began to laugh in an innocent voice. "Thank you, Marco, I actually believe you. It all makes sense now. Where are all your weapons?"

"Taken from us by Eve!"

"Oh, yes, I know who she is, but she knows nothing of me but in time she will."

"My turn, Giver, who or what are you?"

"Not yet, Marco, I am not done but I will answer all your questions in time. Now you say, Marco, you have come from the past?"

"Yes."

"What year in Earth time?"

"2095."

"And your mission is to do what?"

"Now it is to save the world so it does not end up like this!"

"Marco, I love your devotion but it will get you nowhere."

"Why not, Giver, don't you want peace and happiness for everyone?"

"I do and I have with this place, as you can see."

"What exactly do you do, Giver, to help all of humanity survive and to prosper?"

"Look around, Marco, can you not see it? You are surrounded by it. Humans have jobs, they need to keep themselves living and having a purpose. In return they help me. I give them food, security, and a need to live, what else do they need?"

"Freedom!"

Loud laughs ensued. "Freedom? Your species gave that up a long time ago. Let me explain, Marco, your people gave up everything on their own stupidity and self-gratification. I have stepped in and shaped things into a more peaceful existence."

"And how is that, Giver?"

"When I arrived here several years after the blast, I already knew humans could not live in this type of environment. My kind, we are very different and

I know we could thrive here. We feed off of radiation as a support substance, just as you need vitamins we need radiation. Humans were dying, starving, and killing one another over food and greed. My planet around the same time was struck with some sort of virus that was killing my people off by the thousands. Over half of my kind were dead or almost there and our planet's resources were quickly running out. Once we found out what was going on with the Earth we could feed off the radiation and yet help humans sustain life because we need them in many ways."

"What ways are those, Giver?"

"Marco, you need to understand this. I am what humans a long time ago referred to as a butcher. I herd graziers and the sick and the old and the sufferin; harvest their bodies and ship them off to my planet for consumption, the meat is good and the radiation is even better. It keeps those on my planet alive and healthy. We also need human DNA at some point soon, we are going to mix the two species together and create a superior race that nothing can destroy."

"It sounds sick to me, Giver, I do not like it. I have a chance to save humanity and all you talk about is making things worse!"

"You are wrong, Marco, you cannot change the past, it is too late for that, but however, I am rebuilding the future for both our kinds."

"I know, Giver, how to fix it all, and you do not even want to talk about it."

"Interesting to me, it already sounds like you're pretty clear about what you want. You're just not seeing it clearly, Marco, but you will in time, but before we leave, who is the pretty one again?"

"I am Samarra, sir."

"See, Marco, she is so polite, what a beautiful human she is. Samarra, I smell your baby growing inside of you, so far it is healthy. Z, make sure she receives medical treatment. I do so love human babies. As for the rest of you. You are free to explore the town but you cannot go outside of the gates and the guards will be watching you. Now excuse me, I am going to sleep for a little while. I am more of a nocturnal species. Remember, Marco, it is a new world out there. I want you three to be a part of the change."

I woke up with my head pounding, visions of Brinn dead, lying in his own blood lingering through my head. My vision was off. I was having a hard time focusing but could see legs moving in front of me. I was pulled up by my shoulders and shoved into the corner of a wall.

"Who are you?" someone yelled. Then cold water was flung into my face. "Again, who are you!"

"I am Raz," I slowly blurted out.

"What were the two of you doing on our land?"

"Looking for some people," and then I noticed my hands and legs were tied up.

"Where did you get your weapons from?"

"The ones I am trying to find, the bad people."

"Why do you think these people are bad?"

"They are trying to change the world for the worst. Where are you from, Raz?"

"Not from the dumping grounds, just on the outside realm. I am with the realist movement and Eve is our leader."

"Yes, we know who Eve is. We have quite the predicament here, don't you think, Raz?"

"Why is that?"

"Well, first, murder is not tolerated here. If you kill you will be killed, just like your friend. As for you, I am not sure what we are going to do with you, it is not up to me to make that decision. I have to go back to my leader on your situation and in the end he makes the final decision. In the meantime you will stay here, you are for now a prisoner and a criminal. Do not be stupid and try to escape or you will surely die. Tell your leader not to take all day, I have a job to do!"

"Watch your mouth, Raz, or you will just suddenly disappear."

Z escorted Samarra to the medical facility. We could not believe she was pregnant. We began to stare at one another with suspicion.

Ada came back to escort us back to our room. "So what do you two think about the Giver?"

"We are not sure what we are thinking at this point, Ada, it is a lot to take in."

"I know, it is just amazing, the kindness and thoughtfulness that he gives us. We are so lucky to have such a loving, kind leader to help our people. Okay, people, we are back, stay in your rooms, a guard will watch you for now. You will be escorted but you will be allowed to walk the grounds and see what you think. Later this evening before dinner, we will let you know what your jobs will be and you can start at eight A.M. tomorrow. You two are lucky, tomorrow is the fifth day of the week, so you only work tomorrow and then you will have two days off to rest. Enjoy your day, and I will see you at dinner."

"Z."

"Yes, sir, Giver, what do you need?"

"I want you to bring me the new prisoner your men captured earlier."

"Yes, Giver, I will be right back. Time to pay a visit, Raz, our leader wants to see you now!"

"Well, that was fast, I like that. Maybe I can be on my way soon."

"Do not count on that, Raz. Let's go, time is wasting. I do not like making the Giver wait too long."

I was dragged into a room and in front of me was something I had never seen before. Over and over in my mind I kept thinking, what the fuck is that?

"Your name is Raz is what I was told?"

"Yes, I am, and you?"

"You do not need to know. I have been informed you are with Eve and her people, is this true?"

"Yes, why?"

"Your friend tried to kill one of my security team members, is it true or is it not? He was defending himself."

"Bad, bad answer, he tried to kill one of my men!"

"See, you do not understand, I am in control of everything and soon enough the rest of the planet will be ruled by me and my people."

"Eve will never allow that."

"Eve will bow to me before it's all over with."

"Once I tell her she will stop you!"

"You are a funny human, how will you be able to tell her anything considering you will be dead soon? I am putting an order in for you for your execution in two days. We execute criminals once a week and you showed up just in time. We will take you to the swamp behind our walls, tie you up, and feed you to the water people."

My heart dropped into my stomach.

"Z, take the prisoner away!"

"Wait, wait!"

"Silence, we are done talking!"

"Guard, my friend and I would like to start looking around the grounds now, if it is okay with you?"

"Of course, let's go."

"Guard, what is your name?"

"I am Tinzo."

"I am Marco and this here is Daniel."

"Yes, I know. Feel free to roam around, but remember I am watching every move the two of you make, so don't get stupid."

"We won't, no worries there. Daniel, what do you think about what we heard at the meeting?"

"Marco, I have the feeling he has bigger plans for Earth besides helping people and just biding his time."

"Agree, he gives them safety, food, protection, things they are not used to having. These people don't really know any better, their lives have been a day-to-day struggle for survival. He shows up and it's like he is a Godsend from heaven, or space I should say."

"Agree, Marco, let's take a look around."

City Life

As we walked around, it appeared like everyday living, as well as it could be under the circumstances. Inside the walls were blacksmiths in their shops hard at work. There were small gardens inside, as well were some women planting, watering, and picking crops. We continued to walk a little farther down, where we ran into many different chicken coops and children laughing and giggling inside, collecting eggs. A little further down there was a shop with a couple of men inside. The two men were making different types of furniture out of wood, their skills were amazing, such craftsmanship. All of this reminded me of the medieval times that I had learned about in school as a kid, but it was a huge step forward from the rest of the planet.

"No wonder, Daniel, these people put all of their trust into him."

"I agree, Marco, he is giving them the tools they need to better themselves but in a primitive way, in my opinion to keep them under control. Tinzo, what is that building over there?"

"It is a school for children, do you want to see it?"

"Sure, I would love to."

We walked through the door and the students and teacher stopped what they were doing and just stared at us.

"It is okay, this is Daniel and Marco. I am just giving them a tour of the compound, you may carry on. Marco and Daniel, this is our teacher, Miss Ellis. She has been with us now for five years. She teaches speech, math, and survival skills, and does a great job. I must say, her students really excel and the Giver loves her work."

"Nice to meet you, Miss Ellis."

She looked at both of us and began teaching again.

"Don't mind her, guys, she is very serious about her job and we interrupted her lessons, she really is nice, so let us move on. So as you two can see, we are very productive here and ahead of the game, especially over the ones outside of this compound. And the Giver has been very generous with his knowledge and it has definitely been great for all of us. Tinzo, how do you feel about the Giver packing up humans and feeding his own people with them?"

"It is a way of life now, his people are starving, they need the food and the radiation to survive. We have a lot of very sick and crazy people that can no longer function as humans. It is a give-and-take deal, in return the humans that can function survive off of new technology and ideas, it has made us better people."

"Tinzo, don't you think that maybe when the Giver's people can rally around aren't you afraid when they get here they will take full control and use all of you as slaves and food?"

"Lower your voice, Marco, if someone hears you say such things and you get reported you won't live very long."

"I am going to pretend I did not hear you say that."

"Marco, settle down, let's just keep looking around!"

"Sorry, Daniel. Tinzo, can we see the farmlands outside?"

"Sure thing, follow me."

We walked up to the main gate and the guards let us through. We walked through the gate and Tinzo stopped us.

"This is as far for today that I am going to take you, but I will explain what you are seeing right now. In front of you is about two thousand square acres of crop land. We grow corn, beans, and wheat. The other crops are things that the Giver brought to us to grow crops from his planet we had never seen before. When the big blast hit, almost all crops were lost but he supplied more. During the day we have very well-trained guards hiding in the woods, protecting the workers and watching out for intruders like yourselves or graziers trying to steal our crops."

"What about at night?"

"Great question, Marco, you are ahead of the game. You would be good at working security. No wonder the Giver likes you, he can see your potential. At night we release the Ag-Wazs."

"What the hell is that?"

"Well, the Giver explained it to us like this, they came from his planet. He said they were kind of like a tiger or lion from Earth but much faster, bigger, and stronger and meaner. They are not domesticated animals, they do not feel love and affection. They run in packs, have no fear, and their only purpose in life is to hunt and kill anything, sometimes including each other. The Giver in the beginning helped us out with them, we began to feed them, there is a small bond there, we give them shelter and they protect the fields but that is all the bond there is. They are very hard to kill and very relentless creatures who feel no pain and will not stop until they get what they want. They are primarily nocturnal creatures who hunt when the sun goes down."

"I want to see one of them."

"You can when we go back inside."

We headed back to the gates and the guards let us back inside. We continued to walk when we saw another guard with a prisoner in front of him with his hands and legs tied up.

Daniel poked me with his elbow. "Marco, who is that? I have seen him before. Hey, that is one of the guys that was with Eve!"

The man saw us and began flipping out and tried to grab us when the guard knocked him to the ground.

"Keep moving, you two, the guard will handle him, just move on."

"Who was that, Tinzo?"

"Not sure, just someone they picked up in the field is all I know, looks like a crazy to me. He was from Eve, Marco."

"I know it, okay, Daniel, shhh, we will talk about it later."

"So you ready to see the Ag-Wazs' housing area?"

"More than ready to see this."

I could tell Daniel was just fascinated by all of this. He looked like a kid that was going to pee himself because he could no longer hold out. We approached a large building inside the compound, and Tinzo looked into the lock and the doors automatically opened. It was very dark inside. We could hardly see where we were going, and it definitely smelled like some kind of animal lived here.

"Just a little farther, you guys, and you can see them from the observation tower. Here we are, let me flip on the light."

The Giver gave us a type of light that would not disturb them so we could evaluate them periodically. He hit the light, it was an odd shade of blue, and what came next was unbelievable! I had never seen anything like it in my life before, they were curled up together in large packs. They averaged about four to five feet in height. No fat, all muscle, and four-legged like a dog. The claws on their feet were as long as a raptor's and the heads were the size of two basketballs put together. The teeth were sharp and so big, they stuck out of their mouths as they slept. No doubt a killing machine by far.

Daniel was amazed and his scientific mind began to flow. "Tinzo, what kind of environment do you have them in?"

"Well, Daniel, it is very secure, they cannot get out, the materials are from the Giver's planet that keep them in. We have structured the inside of their manmade cave with rocks from the Giver's planet and designed their den just like it was on their planet. When we let them out at night, they do their thing and come back at dawn. This den is their home on a strange planet to them."

"What do they eat, Tinzo?"

"Anything and everything, they're not picky."

"How much food do they require to survive?"

"Cannot really say, Daniel, they kill even when they're not hungry. I take it, Daniel, you love science?"

"I do!"

"Well, in time maybe you can help us with many projects."

"Maybe, you never know."

"Marco, you have been very quiet, what do you think?"

"I am just overwhelmed about what is going on here. It is hard for me to wrap my mind around it."

"I understand that, but life is now becoming beautiful again. It just takes time to adjust."

"Indeed it does, Tinzo. Oh, shit, getting close to dinner time. I have to take you guys back to Ada for dinner and your new assignments. I have enjoyed this tour with you, guys. I hope soon you can be a part of all this. We need smart, hardworking people like you to complete our mission."

"What did you say?"

"I enjoyed the tour."

"No, the second part."

"Be a part of our mission. Why, what's wrong, Marco?"

"Oh, nothing."

Tinzo walked ahead of us. I turned to Daniel and said, "I am not worried about their mission but humanity's mission means everything!"

"Hey, you two, did you enjoy your tour of the compound?"

"We did, Ada, not nearly enough time, though."

"That is okay, you will get to see more in due time. Let's go eat and I will tell you about your new assignments, okay?"

"Lead the way, Ada, Marco and I are starving."

Ada giggled with amusement. "Here we are, grab your food and I will meet you at the table so we can talk."

Daniel and I stood in the line, picking out what we wanted to eat.

"Look, Daniel, let's ask questions and go with the flow. I feel like with Tinzo if we act real interested and content on staying here, we may be able to find out more information we need."

"I agree, Marco, let's play the game and get the hell out of here. Marco, what about Samarra?"

"I am sure we will see her soon, she's probably being pampered. We won't leave without her, I promise."

"Marco, I do not mean to be rude, but is Samarra pregnant with your baby?"

"Are you kidding me? Hell no! She must have gotten pregnant shortly before we left, I am assuming. It creeped me out when he said he could smell it. Anyway, let's stick to the plan, we need to leave soon."

"Aye-aye, Captain."

"You're a dumbass, let's get back to the table."

"How do you guys like your food choices?"

"Could not be any better, Ada, you have your protein and vegetables, I love it, thanks."

"For now, Marco and Daniel, we need you working in the fields, this is a crucial time for harvesting and we need all the hands we can get. I was told future work is for Marco to be in security detail and for Daniel to be in the scientific department when the time is right. What do you think about that?"

"Well, Daniel I think it suits both of us very well, do you agree?"

"After I saw the Ag-Wazs today I am all in for that!" Ada giggled some more. "I am glad you two are so excited. The Giver will be so happy to hear you want to be a part of history in the making."

"So Ada, when will we get to see Samarra again?"

"Soon. The Giver is letting her get the rest she needs and the nutrition as well. You will start work at sunrise and be done an hour before sunset. Then you will have dinner and be free to roam the compound as you please. You are new here, there are guards out on the compound, so behave just like everyone else, understood?"

"Yes, we got it."

"Oh, yeah, just one more thing."

"What is it, Ada?"

"I should not be telling you this."

"It's okay, Ada, you have been kind to us, what is it?"

"Yesterday very early the guards had a run-in with two men and their mission was to kill the three of you. I do not know who they were, but they had very strange weapons, the guard said. One of them was killed by one of our security agents and another was taken prisoner. I have heard the Giver is going to execute him the last day before our work week starts again. That is when we do executions if we need to so everyone can see the enemy die face to face."

Daniel smacked my back very hard.

"Do you know who was trying to kill you?"

"No, I really don't, Ada, but thank you for the information."

"Well, you boys get some rest, it will be a tough, long first day. I will see you in the morning."

"Goodnight, Ada, and thank you."

"Fuck, Marco, I knew I recognized him, he is one of Eve's fucking people! She broke her own word, she is trying to kill us as well!"

"I get it, Daniel, let's go to bed, it will be a long day tomorrow and we have work to do."

Garden Talk

My body's clockwork was at the top of its game. The sun was coming up soon and I yelled out to Daniel, "Get up, we need to eat breakfast before we go to work."

Daniel was dragging ass but we quickly threw on our new work clothes and headed to the breakfast hall. Breakfast was great and we quickly met the guards outside so we could go through the gates and off to the fields. We were given two sacks a piece to store our crops, and when we were full we had to raise our hands and a guard would pick up the full sack and deliver us a fresh empty one.

"Fuck this, Marco, I feel like a damn slave!"

"No shit, Daniel, we just need to bide our time until we can figure a way out of here."

I had an older lady working with me on the opposite side of Daniel. Her hair was ragged and skin very leathery from the sun, and she was very slow.

"Hey there, I am Marco, who are you?"

She slowly looked up at me and said, "Why do you care?"

"I was just asking, nothing wrong with talking while you work. It makes the day go by so much faster."

"Maybe for you, you're still young. I am old and tired. Soon I will just be a slab of meat for the freaks."

"Do not let anyone hear you say that."

"Why would I care? Now it is almost that time for me, at your age it did not bother me but now it does."

"What is your name, please?"

"Why, so you can report me and it go quicker!"

"No, I agree with you!"

"Marco, shut up!"

"No, Daniel! Please, your name?"

"I am Lena and go report me, I don't care, death is coming soon."

"Lena, I will not tell, I understand!"

"Marco!"

"Daniel, stop it!"

Apparently Daniel was trying to warn me about a guard who had been watching.

"What is going on here?"

"Nothing, sir, my friend stepped on something that hurt his foot."

"Fix it and get back to work."

"We will, thanks."

"Lena, how long have you been working the fields?"

"At least twelve harvests, I guess, maybe more."

"Where is your family?"

"They are all dead and I cannot wait to meet them again, and you will wish the same when it is your time."

"Not my time, Lena, we are going to get the hell out of here."

She began to laugh so hard, she got the attention of the guards once again.

"What is wrong with you?"

"Oh, nothing, these boys think they can out-pick me."

"Okay, but it is work time, get back to it."

"You cannot escape here, you fool, you are working food!"

"Lena, please quiet down, please."

"Look over there, you see all those workers in that faraway field?"

"Yes, I see them."

"That is where those weird people are going to live!"

"What weird people, Lena, who?"

"The Giver's people is who, those are new homes for them when they come and when they do we will all be dead!"

"Lena, quiet down, please!"

A guard approached. "Okay, this is the third time I have had to talk to you, what is your problem?"

"All of you are trying to kill us, use us as food, you're murderers, leave us alone, just leave us alone!"

The guard slammed her to the ground and called for a vehicle to pick her up. She was flung into the back of the vehicle and taken back to the main gate.

"Jesus, Daniel, you heard that, right?"

"I did, Marco, basically we are in an alien meat processing plant."

"Okay, Daniel, let's not bring any more attention to ourselves today and just play it cool."

"I agree."

It was quitting time for the day, and we had two days off of rest with the exception of the execution the day before work started again. We arrived back at our new home and Daniel immediately hit the bed.

"Daniel, get up, we need to go eat."

"No way, I am tired, I need rest first, they killed me today, I will eat later."

"Okay, well, I am going to chow, I will see you a little later."

I headed out to dinner, there were a lot of people there and I really did not know any of them. I got my food and sat down at a table and began to eat.

I heard a pleasant voice ask, "Do you mind if I sit here with you?"

I looked up at her, she was attractive and appeared to be very soft-spoken. "You can if you like, but I am not a real big talker."

"That is fine but it is nice to at least eat with someone."

"Hey, I think I may recognize you."

"Who do you think I am?"

"Not sure, I am horrible with names, aren't you the teacher?"

"Yes, that would be Miss Ellis to you."

"I am Marco, nice to meet you, sorry we interrupted your lessons earlier."

"It is okay, Marco, I know you guys are new, so what do you think about our compound so far?"

"I must say it is very well organized and much more advanced than the rest of society."

"I have to say, Marco, you appear to have been educated very well, your English is good and with a perfectly clear dialect. You are not like the average person from here."

"Well, neither are you, Miss Ellis, I can tell you love children and teaching, you take your profession very seriously."

"See, there you go, you used the word 'profession,' most do not know what that means. Look at me, Marco, I can tell you are hiding something, where are you from?"

"Whatever do you mean, Miss Ellis?"

"Come on now, Marco, tell me the truth?"

"Why, so you can have me locked away like a criminal? Besides, the Giver already knows who we are."

"There is more than just you? Please tell me, Marco, you have to trust me."

A long pause. "Do not make me regret this, the world is at stake!"

"I promise, go on."

"Yeah, I have seen many promises broken in the past. Okay, Ellis, I am from Earth of 2095, we thought we had discovered a new planet two light years away. We finally had the technology to arrive at this planet. When we did we found this Earth in shambles and chaos. Now we have figured out a way to stop all of this, but we have to get out of here to go back and fix the wrongs in history."

"I knew it, I knew you were different!"

"Calm down, Ellis, we do not want to draw attention!"

"I knew there was something special about you, Marco, when I first laid eyes on you and I will tell you the Giver is not good either."

"Yes, I am quickly learning that. Ellis, he is using what's left of mankind to feed his own agenda and that is to bring his kind here and feed on humans and take this planet over without anyone ever noticing it."

"I have been observing, Marco, for years now, I believe you. I have always felt the same but no one to talk to or no one I could really trust. People here are so fooled by the lie because they were so desperate when he arrived, they would do anything to stay in his good graces to survive. How do you plan to escape?"

"I do not know, Ellis, but if I did I would not tell you, we have to build trust first, all of humanity is riding on us getting back and stopping this."

"Fair enough, Marco, I understand, if you need me here is where I live on the compound, visit me anytime during our free hours. I will do whatever you need me to help out. I must go now."

"Thanks, Ellis, I hope this was a productive talk?"

Ellis began to laugh. "Productive, I love it, do not hear that very often, I love it. Goodnight, Marco, and sweet dreams."

She began to walk away and headed out the chow hall door when I heard the words, "How is it going, dick face?" Instantly I knew who it was and jumped up and squeezed her tight. "Hey, hey, back off, dick, you're going to squeeze this baby out of me early."

"How are you, Samarra, are you feeling okay?"

"I am, Marco, but we need to talk, there are things I need to tell you but not in public."

"That is fine, get something to eat, Samarra, and we will go back to our room and talk. Where is Daniel?"

"Sissy boy had to work out in the heat all day today, so he skipped dinner but I am sure he will get up when he knows you are here."

"Great, I will put extra on my plate for him."

We arrived back at the room and Samarra jumped on Daniel, scaring the shit out of him. We all laughed our asses off at his surprise.

"Thank God you're back."

"Wow, Daniel, did not know you cared so much."

"Sometimes I do but you're still a bitch," he laughed.

"Look, guys, there is something seriously wrong with this place. When I was in medical there were several women I heard talking, and they have had several births. After they had given birth they never saw their babies again."

"Where did they go, Samarra?"

"I am not really sure, but there are rumors where they think the Giver sends them back to his planet. The mothers all claim they never see them again after birth."

"My God, Daniel, we may be right. Is he attempting to breed the two species, is it for food also?"

"I do not know, Marco, but either way it is not good."

"I met the schoolteacher that we saw today in the chow hall, we talked and she knew I was different, I hope she is not lying but she claims not to trust the Giver as well."

"Dammit, Marco, you are all going to get us killed!"

"Relax, Daniel, it is all on me, but I have a gut feeling she was telling the truth. Tomorrow morning I will get up, eat breakfast, and meet her at her house. In the meantime, everyone, keep your eyes and ears peeled. Samarra, where do they have you staying?"

"Just across from you two, I can show you later."

"Let's meet around midday tomorrow and go from there."

Samarra left and Daniel and I hit the sack, both of us were tired and I had an early day coming.

Big Head

I woke up early that morning, the sun had not fully risen yet but it was peeking its rays out above the horizon. There was not a whole lot of people in the chow hall yet, I guess it was a little too early for most people. I needed to fill up on protein, you never knew when we'd have a chance to escape. I took my time eating, waiting for the sun to fully come up. We were not allowed to walk outside until the sun had fully risen due to the Ag-Wazs still being loose. It was about a three-block walk to where Miss Ellis lived. I was shocked she did not have a dorm or room but in fact a cute little house to herself. I knocked on the door and no answer. I knocked again and then I heard a very quiet voice say, "Who is it?"

"It is me, Marco, sorry I am here so early."

"That is okay, just give me a minute, I will be right there." The door slowly opened and she invited me in. "Believe it or not, Marco, I have coffee, would you like some?"

"I would love some, please."

"What brings you out so early, Marco?"

"I want to pick your brain about some things."

"Okay, well, let's get some coffee first and go sit out on the porch, it is nice at this time of the day."

We walked outside and sat in the chairs.

"I have to say, Ellis, I am very impressed with your home."

"Thank you, I do enjoy it."

"How did you get such a nice setup?"

"I knew you would ask me that." She began to laugh. "Well, the Giver knows that I am smart and gives me a teaching job that looks great to the community and makes him look wonderful as well. Also, I do not question him, I play along like I know nothing that is going on and he keeps me happy and honestly he thinks it is working. I do know, Marco, the birthrate is getting higher yet enrolled students are dropping. Makes no sense, does it, Marco?"

"Actually now it is making a whole lot of sense, Ellis. We both know, Ellis, what is really going on."

"So what do you want to do, Marco?"

"I am going out on a limb here, but the first thing I want to do is make love to you."

"So what's stopping you?"

I slipped her shirt off and started sucking her nipples, they were very hard, and she moaned heavily. I went down on her, sucking and gracefully biting every inch of her body. My dick was so hard, I put it in her and slowly made love to her, and she orgasmed several times. I finally could not hold back any longer and came all inside her.

"Oh my God, Marco, that felt so good," she licked and kissed me everywhere.

"I am sorry, Ellis, this is not what I was sent to do."

"I know, it is okay, I enjoyed every minute of it!"

We lay in bed for a while. It had been a long time for me as well but a heavy weight had been lifted and now I could think clearer.

"Ellis, I need to find a way out of here."

"I know you do but how?"

"I am not sure but now I know nighttime is definitely not an option. My only option would be during free time, when everyone is out."

"Even then, Marco, it will be tough with the guards and you have to get over the compound wall. The wall, Marco, is at least twelve feet."

"I know, but I am working on some ideas I hope may work. Ellis, do you know where they keep their transport vehicles?"

"Usually with them but at night they leave them outside the wall with Ag-Wazs. Marco?"

"Yes."

"Stop talking, I want some more!"

"I thought you would never ask. Nothing like getting schooled by a teacher first thing in the morning."

It was a great morning but now it was time to head back.

"I hope, Ellis, I will see you again soon."

"Anytime, Marco, you know where to find me."

She kissed me intensely. I did not want to go, but there was a lot I needed to figure out. I left her house with a smile and the thoughts of a new world and happiness overwhelmed me. I started to head back to my side of the compound, the streets still did not have much activity going on. I was enjoying the quietness and peacefulness of the morning when I heard a voice call out, "Hey, asshole, come here!"

I looked around and did not see anyone.

"Down here, asshole, are you fucking stupid!"

I looked down to my right, there was a man laid down on his stomach, his body was buried in the Earth and his head was the only thing I could see. There was a board around his neck and it was nailed into the ground.

"Who are you?"

"Who do you think!"

"You're one of the ones trying to kill us. Looks like you're a lot worse off than me there, buddy."

"Your friends will not be able to protect you for long, Marco!"

"They are not my friends, and you are very misinformed, buddy! Eve will avenge us!"

"Sorry to tell you, my friend, no, she won't avenge you, she knows nothing of this place and if she did she would have a different attitude."

"What the fuck do you mean!"

"Are you ready to listen?"

"Well, does not look like you have much of a choice. What is your name?"

"Raz!"

"Well, Raz, this compound is a human death trap, the one who rules this place is not from this planet. It has one agenda, feed its people and take over the planet to rule and slaughter. You know why, Raz? No answer, I will tell you our technology is so weak now and they're swooping down under our noses and slowly taking over while lying to everyone that they are here to help!"

"Bullshit, you are a liar!"

"No lies, Raz, you're going to die soon, not me, we need to tell Eve before it is too late for everyone!"

"Marco, what the hell are you doing! Get away from that prisoner, he is off limits for the public!"

"Sorry, Tinzo, I was curious, did not realize who he was, I am still learning the rules."

"Did he say anything to you?"

"Not really, just wanted some water and called me an asshole."

"Hey, piece of shit in the ground, remember the rules, no talking to anyone, the next time I catch you I will smash your fucking head in, do you got it?"

Raz had no response.

"Oh, really, you piece of shit, you won't talk!"

My thoughts raced. "Raz, you better say something."

"Okay, mother fucker, I just had a great breakfast, now you're going to see just how damn good it was!"

Tinzo pulled down his pants and took a shit all over the back of Raz' head. "Wow, that even stinks for me, at least I feel better now! No water for this piece of shit, Marco, let's go!"

"Yes, sir, Tinzo." I looked back at Raz as we walked away and was thinking I hope he got it now.

"Do not worry about people like him, Marco, he is a crazy killer who just wants to cause harm."

"No, I get it, Tinzo, but how does it make you feel doing what you just did to him?"

"Well, Marco, my ass sure feels a lot better, why?"

"Just wondering, do you ever think about maybe trying to talk to find out what the differences are?"

"Why would I do that, Marco, I already know what is right."

"Just a question and look, sorry, once again I did not really know what he was, I was just exploring and learning."

"I bet you were, I followed you to Miss Ellis' house, how was that?"

"It was great, we talked, she was very nice, I thought."

"Great, the Giver would love to hear that, he really likes Miss Ellis, I think she is his favorite."

"Why do you think he likes her so much?"

"She is very smart, helps out a lot with teaching people, and she is no trouble at all. The two of you are a good match, I hope it works out for you guys. The Giver really wants you on the security when you're ready, he feels your skills are wasted being out in the fields."

"Me too, Tinzo, just waiting for my opportunity."

"Okay, Marco, I will let you go, enjoy your free time. I will be around if you need me."

"Sounds good, Tinzo, you be safe, okay, and be smart."

"Always, I will see you later."

I headed back to the dorm to see Daniel and Samarra. The door was locked and no one answered my knocks. I went around the building, opened a window, and crawled inside. I walked into the bedroom and to my surprise, or shock I should say, Daniel and Samarra were having a little playtime of their own. I quickly shut the door.

Midday

"I hope you two got it out of your system. I guess you do not have to worry about getting pregnant, do you, Samarra?"

"You are just jealous you're not getting laid."

"Not really, I got laid twice this morning, thank you."

"You must not be lying, you are not usually this nice and smiling."

"Well, Samarra, it is a new day and the world can be full of surprises."

"Where were you this morning, Marco?"

"Daniel, if you must know I paid Miss Ellis a home visit, you remember the teacher, it was a productive visit. She is concerned as well about the motives here as well and has kept her thoughts to herself. She actually confirmed, Samarra, about the missing children, which goes along with what you heard as well. Also to catch you up, Samarra, there were two assassins sent by Eve to kill all of us, one is dead, the other's name is Raz and he is supposed to be executed soon."

"What, are you serious!"

"Very much so, I just saw Raz on my way here. I tried to put a voice in his head that he should leave with us."

"Marco, that's crazy!"

"No, Daniel, it is not, he may be the only one to convince Eve of the truth if she sees us all together."

"Sounds risky to me, Marco."

"I know, Samarra, but it may be our only chance of getting out of here alive."

"Any ideas of how we are going to escape?"

"Not sure yet but I am working on it. One thing is right, it will have to be done during the day. Daniel and I have both seen what protects this place at night, and there is no way we would survive."

Out of nowhere things began to get real exciting. We saw many guards including Tinzo with weapons in hand, running for the compound door at the main entrance.

I yelled out to Tinzo, "What the hell is going on?"

Tinzo yelled back, "Stay there, we have it under control!"

The compound doors opened and immediately they were overtaken by mud people. The guards fought hard but started to quickly lose their ground, there were too many of them and they were starting to drag into the compound streets. Some of them already began feeding on the dead guards. It felt like I was in a horror movie. The three of us ran into the combat zone and picked up weapons from fallen guards. The water people were slow but dangerous in high numbers. We forced ourselves on them and began hand-to-hand combat one after the other, we cracked their skulls with knives and swords. The guards frantically began to close the main compound gates.

I yelled out to them, "Stop, some of your men are still out there!"

"We can't, we have to shut it!"

"Open it enough for me to get out!"

"No, we can't!"

"Do it now or the Giver will hear about this! You two stay here, I will be back!"

"No, Marco, no!"

The door shut behind me. I was on my own now. Quickly I saw Tinzo, he had two of them on him and he was fighting to stop them from biting him. I ran over to him and with two quick strokes decapitated both of them.

"Come on, Tinzo, let's go!"

I pulled him up, both of us exhausted and realized we were surrounded by at least twenty of them.

"Marco, what the hell are we going to do now?"

"Looks like we are going to have to fight, my friend!"

We heard yelling and screaming all around us. The grass was moving but we could not see anything or what it was. Then it flashed out of the thick grass. It was Jappel, he was yelling and making movement. The water people saw and heard him and they began to get distracted. Most of them were now focused on Jappel and not so much as us as Jappel was loud and crazy. I yelled out to Jappel, "Thank you," as he led some of them off. Now we could manage the rest.

Tinzo and I slashed our way through the rest. we were killing machines and ran back to the compound gates.

Tinzo screamed out to the guards, "Open the gates!"

The doors opened and we hit the ground exhausted! Daniel, Samarra, Ellis, and more guards, along with people from the community, surrounded us to see if we were okay. Many people in the compound looked on in disbelief, wondering what the hell just happened.

Tinzo reached his hand over to me. "Thank you, Marco, you have earned my trust and respect, you went out of your way to save my life when you did not have to, I will always be in your debt."

"Don't worry about it, Tinzo, there are bigger things to worry about."

"Huh, I am not following you, Marco?"

"Don't worry but you will; however, thank you for the kind words."

A woman came rushing up to Tinzo, threw herself to the ground, crying and hugging and kissing him.

"Hey, Marco, I want you to meet my wife, her name is Lenetta. Lenetta, this is Marco, the man who just saved my life."

"Thank you, I can't thank you enough, anything you need or any help please let us know, we owe you!"

"I will, Lenetta, thank you, it was nice meeting you, unfortunately under these circumstances, though."

I stood up and looking at me with the biggest most beautiful smile was Ellis. She ran to me, we kissed and she hugged me so tight I could hardly breathe.

"Easy, girl, I am a little sore," I laughed.

"I'm sorry."

"Don't worry." I kissed her cheek. "Ellis, I would like for you to meet the other two. This is Daniel and Samarra."

"Nice to meet the two of you. I cannot wait until we have a chance to talk."

"I can't wait either, at least if we are all there Marco won't be able to put his creepy mind tricks on you."

"Shut it, Samarra! Excuse her, Samarra can be an ass at times."

"No, she's not, I kind of like her sense of humor. We need some of that around her."

"Oh, God, my worst nightmare come true, someone actually loves your mouth."

Tinzo and his wife were leaving. He yelled to me, "Hey, Marco!"

"Yes, sir!"

"I will see you in the morning, we need to talk."

"Sounds good, and Tinzo, get some rest. Look, guys, I need to get some rest, that took a lot out of me."

"Hey, can the three of you come to my house for dinner tonight?"

"Sounds good, Miss Ellis."

"Just call me Ellis, Samarra, and the same for you, Daniel."

"Yes, ma'am."

"Be there two hours before dark or earlier is fine."

"Will do, we will tend to lover boy over here and make sure he is all good."

"Okay, thanks, guys, and I will see the three of you a little later."

"Okay, just a little water and let me sleep an hour and then let's get over there so we have enough time before we have to get back before they shut down the compound."

"You did good today, Marco, don't let it go to your head."

"Thanks, Samarra," and I was out cold.

"Wakey wakey, dick face, you have a date and time is a-wasting."

I got up, body was still sore as hell, but we got ready and were on our way to Ellis' house. We got there, dinner was still cooking but almost ready. She greeted me with a huge hug and a big kiss. I was not used to this but I loved every second of it.

"I know your story from what Marco has told me thus far. After today, Marco, if you play your cards right escape may be easier than you think."

"Explain, Ellis, I am all ears."

"It's like me, for example. I am smart, the Giver knows that, but I am trustworthy at least until this point and I never give him any reason for concern. You proved yourself today, all of you did. You defended the compound, you did not have to, and you saved one of his commanders from death who was left for dead by the other guards. What I am trying to tell you is maybe you will be able to obtain more knowledge and access to things to make escape a lot easier."

"I agree with her, Marco, she makes a lot of sense."

"I second that, sir!"

"Okay, guys, I agree too, but time is precious, we do not have much of it.

We had a great dinner and even better talks it was a great time all around. We talked about the past and present and time went way too quickly. Daniel and Samarra walked out onto the front porch, I told them I would be right there.

Ellis grabbed my face and kissed me very gently. "Be safe, Marco!"

"I will." I kissed her and had my right hand on the small of her back. It felt like we were always meant to be together. I told her I would see her soon and get some rest. We kissed again and off we went.

It was a very quick trip back to our living quarters. It was kind of odd seeing Daniel and Samarra kiss but they looked very happy. Samarra left for her dorm and Daniel and I hunkered down for the night.

"What a day, don't you think, Marco?"

"Yes, it was, I don't know what disturbs me more, mud people or you and Samarra in bed." I began to laugh. "Goodnight, Daniel, let's get some rest."

"You won't get an argument out of me, Captain."

Status Change

Daniel and I awoke just a little after daybreak.

"Are you ready for breakfast, Marco?"

"Hell yes, I am starving and still a little stiff."

"I guess sex and fighting mud people will do that to you."

"You're probably right, Daniel. I am guessing the sex, it has been way too long."

We headed down the hallway and could instantly smell the food.

"Damn, Marco, the smell is just like soaking up in every pore I have."

"Yeah, well, Daniel, I am first," and we both took off running.

"Hey, slow down, you two."

We stopped and turned around. It was Tinzo and his wife, Lenetta.

"Just kidding with you guys. Hey, Marco, come find me on the compound when you are done."

"Will do, I will see you later."

We walked into the chow hall and lo and behold Samarra was already stuffing her face.

"Geez, Samarra, can't even wait for your boyfriend or me?"

"Shut up, dick, you know I am eating for two."

"I was guessing more like five."

She looked at me and opened her mouth, exposing her chewed-up food, and rolled her eyes. "Oh, Daniel, such class, you should be proud."

Daniel and I got our food and sat down at the table with her.

"What's the deal today, Marco?"

"I am meeting with Tinzo after breakfast, he wants to talk to me, not sure what about."

"What do you want Daniel and me to do while you're gone?"

"Please refrain from sex, it took a lot out of me yesterday. Just joking, you two, but go out, walk the compound, look for weakness, and eye out any kind of supplies we may need. I will get with you later."

"We're on it."

I walked the compound, there was a lot of activity today. The weather was warm but not as hot as usual and a cool light breeze with it. I could smell the breakfast food in the air mixed with the odors of the great outdoors, it was actually very relaxing. I saw the prisoner Raz and he saw me but I did not talk to him I was trying to not bring any more attention to myself. I heard a voice behind me.

"You think you're so damn great and smart, don't you?"

I turned around and it was Z.

"Z, I have not seen you since we met the Giver. Where have you been hiding?"

"I have been busy. I have a lot of things to do, you know."

"I'm sure you do."

"Look at me, Marco. I do not trust you. I should have killed you when I found you!"

"Where is all this anger coming from? You were nice in front of the Giver."

"It was just for show. You are lucky he demanded to see you or you would be already dead!"

"You know, Z, I pulled my weight around here yesterday, what else do you want?"

"Maybe you should just give me a reason to kill you now!"

"You have a knife, I have nothing. If you have any fucking balls, Z, here is your chance!"

His face cringed and he slowly pulled out his knife.

"Hey, what the fuck is going on here, Z?"

"Mind you own business, Tinzo, this is personal!"

"Not anymore it's not, what's your fucking problem, Z!"

"This piece of shit here he cannot be trusted, he should be executed along with the other piece of shit that was trying to kill him!"

"You need to mind yourself, Z, or should I just take this matter up with the Giver!"

"Fuck you, Tinzo, do not threaten me!"

"You watch yourself, Marco, I am watching every move you make!"

"What the fuck is his problem, Tinzo?"

"Marco, let me explain some things to you that you may not know about, Z."

"Please do."

"We found Z about five years ago starving, he could barely walk, we were trying to help him out but he was in full survival mode and fought us every inch of the way. We finally had to knock him out and we kept him in isolation, fed him, and basically nursed him back to health. Once he started to come around we slowly integrated him into our society and he slowly began to trust us. We knew he had great survival skills and would be a good match for our security team. We also know he can be what you call a loose cannon at times. I have seen him myself lose control and convert back to his old ways. It is a cruel world, Marco, all of us have to do what we need to survive, you know."

"I do, but he seems to have a lot of issues."

"He does and not only that, I must tell you something else you don't know. You and Miss Ellis getting closer and let me remind you, I do not care, but Z and her had a relationship early on but it fell apart very quickly due to his aggressive nature. That could be part of why he hates you so much. Just be aware of him, do not turn your back on him, okay?"

"No, not at all, I won't, thanks, Tinzo, for the warning."

"Oh, yeah, by the way, Marco, the execution of the prisoner has been postponed until the next date, which would be seven days from tomorrow. The Giver is worried about more attacks on the compound, it has been one of the worst in a long time, they usually do not do that unless they are starving and it has been a very dry season this year."

"I hope you know, Tinzo, I have your back?"

"I know you do, Marco, but listen, the wife wants to know when you and Ellis can come over for dinner"

"Anytime tomorrow, it is the last day before work starts over, how about three hours before sunset?"

"Sounds good to me, Marco, I will let her know."

"Thanks, tell Lenetta we are honored to come."

"Will do, see you tomorrow."

Tinzo left and I headed straight to Ellis' house. She must have seen me coming, the door flung open and out she came with a big hug and a kiss.

"Hey, can you come to dinner with me at Tinzo and Lenetta's house tomorrow?"

"I can if you want me to."

"You know I do, and I also know about you and Z."

"I am sorry, it was nothing, he was very abusive. I probably should have told you about him."

"No, I understand, I would not really want to talk about him myself if I was in your shoes."

"So are you sure you want to go with me?"

"You don't have to even ask, Marco, I am here for you, I love you!"

That phrase scared me, but I really felt the same. "I love you too and thank you." I gave her a hug and a kiss. I had to leave to catch up with Samarra and Daniel.

"So far, Daniel, I have not seen any real weakness with the compound walls, have you?"

"Not really, and there is a lot of guard presence as well. We just have to keep looking, there is always a weak spot somewhere."

"Maybe, Daniel, I do not really know. Is everything okay with you, Samarra?"

"Why do you ask?"

"I don't know, you seem a little out of it like your mind is somewhere else."

"I am fine."

"No, you're really not, please tell me what is going on. I do not judge and you know I really care for you."

"That is odd for me, Daniel, do you really care?"

"I would not have said it if I didn't mean it."

"I have been thinking a lot about Tanya."

"You mean the little girl from the caves?"

"Yes, her. I miss her so much, she was so sweet and innocent, I felt like she was my child I never had and I can't stop thinking about her. She was the only thing that kept me sane while I was held captive there until my big hero came looking for me." Samarra began to smile.

"You know, though, Samarra, the good thing is now she is safe, she does not have to be afraid anymore, she is with good people who are not going to hurt her, only love her. Her life will be better, thanks to you for getting her out of there, I promise she will never forget that."

"Daniel, there is something I want to talk to you about, okay?"

"Anything you want to talk about, I am always here to listen, I hope you know that?"

"I do, but you know me, sometimes it is hard for me to open up." I started to laugh. "I think everyone knows that."

She began to smile and gave me a kiss. "I know that you and Marco are probably wondering who the father of this baby is, and I have not said much about it."

"Yes, but I figured that eventually you would come around and say something, especially that we are together now. It would be something I think I should know about."

"I am sorry, Daniel, I know you deserve to know."

"Marco and I just thought a boyfriend or something before we left to go on our mission."

"No, not exactly, I wish that was the case but it is not."

"Okay, Samarra, I am now confused, who is it?"

"I was raped in the caves, Daniel." Samarra began to cry.

I heard a lot of commotion around the main gate of the compound. Four guards walked in through the doors and Z was leading them. Two of the guards were carrying something I could not see because the crowd was so thick.

Z was speaking to the crowd. "Do not worry, we got him this time. I cut both of his hands off and he died on the way here."

I pushed my way through the crowds so I could get a better look at what was going on. I could not believe my own eyes, it was Jappel. I lost it, my mind went blank and anger overtook my senses. I quickly ran up to Z and punched him in the face, knocking him to the ground. He got back up and told the guards to stand down.

"It's my turn, Marco, I am going to kill you!"

"Try it, mother fucker!"

We slammed into each other, punching until both of us hit the ground. I got on top of him, punching his face, and he quickly flipped me over, landing a hard right to my nose.

"I think my nose is broken."

I grabbed his right arm, bent it backwards, and slammed his face into the dirt. I stood back up and was taken down by the other guards. Z came running towards me but was held back by guards as well. All I could here was "What the fuck is going on here!" It was Tinzo and he was not very happy.

"He killed Jappel, a harmless person who meant no harm, he was the one who helped save us yesterday."

Z in full anger screamed out, "I killed a thief and then I'm going to kill you! Guards, take them away, put them in holding cells until further instructions."

"Samarra, I am so sorry, why didn't you say anything to either one of us?"

"It was not the right time or place, Daniel. It is not like we have had any down time either to share feelings and shit."

I just held her close to me and let her cry it out.

Fuck, in a holding cell again, my parents should have made my middle name "Inmate"! That thought brought back my memories of my youth and my parents, who just gave up on me. In this world I was living in now I was sure everyone I knew was dead.

"Alright, Marco, quit being so negative, you have to keep it together, you still have a mission."

"Where the hell is Marco, Daniel, we have been looking for him for an hour?"

We began to hear our names being yelled out in panic. We turned around, it was Ellis.

"Ellis, what's wrong?"

"It's Marco, I was told him and Z got into a fight on the compound and now Tinzo took both of them away to holding cells."

"Shit, Samarra, what the hell are we going to do now?"

"Not much, Marco will handle it, we just have to wait on him, hopefully they will go easy on him considering what he did for Tinzo. Ellis, let us take you home so you can relax."

"Thank you, guys, for being there for me. You must really care about Marco, don't you?"

"I do, Samarra, I knew it from the first time I saw him."

I could hear someone coming. "Thank God, Tinzo, it is you, what is going on?"

"I do not know yet, Marco, I put in a really good word for you and explained to the Giver about Z, which he already knows what he is like. He said you still have broken laws, I am here to feed you and when you're done he wants to talk to you."

"Well, tell him I'm not eating and when he is ready I will be there."

"I will, and Marco?"

"Yes, Tinzo?"

"Just be calm and do not get angry, he will not like that, okay?"

"I got it and thank you for the good words, I do appreciate everything you are doing."

"What are friends for?" He smiled and walked out.

Friends, wow, I hadn't had many of those over the years. It had taken me to go to the future and a destroyed Earth to get one, life is crazy like that, I guess.

Thirty minutes went by at least and Tinzo returned to my cell.

"Are you ready? The Giver is ready to see you now."

"Just lead the way. I am ready to get this over with, my friend."

"I am glad, Marco, you consider me a friend."

"It's kind of like a bromance."

"What the hell is that, we're not lovers?"

I started to laugh. "I know, never mind, it is an old expression, you must have never heard it before?"

"Okay, Marco, here we are. I will let you in and I will be outside waiting for you to be done, he wants to talk to you alone."

"Okay, wish me luck."

"I already have."

Tinzo opened the door and I walked in, and the door quickly closed behind me. At the end of the room I could see him sitting in his very large chair and a smaller chair beside him.

"Come here, Marco, we have a lot to discuss."

I walked down to him and he pointed at the smaller chair.

"Please take a seat. I heard what you did yesterday, Marco, and I thank you for defending the compound and my guards, especially Tinzo."

"Thank you, Giver, that is the type of guy I am."

"I know you are, but why did you and Z fight each other?"

"He killed someone I knew who did not deserve to die."

"Why do you feel that way? The dead one was a thief and stole from this great community."

"He did it to survive, he was small, he didn't eat much, he also gave us shelter so we would not die when he didn't have to. Yesterday he saved Tinzo and me."

"So I have also heard from Tinzo as well. The rules for this compound are very clear, he was a thief. If he would have asked for help he could have been a part of this community and had all the food he needed. He choose not to and that in itself was his mistake."

"So killing someone is not a crime?"

"He killed him over some vegetables. Marco, you do not understand, we need order here, these humans need to be taught how to live again. I understand your old laws but they do not apply in today's society. So now I have an issue and what to do with you and Z, there has been many laws broken. Both of you are at fault for many things but yet I do not want to lose either one of you. I have high hopes for you, Marco, you smell of potential. Your relationship with Ellis is also very pleasing to me, the two of you make a wonderful breeding pair. I think you can also teach the humans to let's say be easier managed. Most humans are raw and uncivilized. You are as well but more civilized because you're not from here, so to speak. Building the humans up to be more civil is my goal. In my head I was thinking you want them more civil so they're easier to accept life for what it is under your control. Here is the option I have to fix this unusual situation we are currently under. There can only be one of you. Neither one of you will ever be able to work together. Thus creates conflict and a unstable atmosphere that is not productive to this community." He paused with his long black skinny fingers twitching in the air. "So here is my solution to this problem and it will be up held. Tomorrow is the day before work, the execution of the prisoner has been postponed until further notice. So tomorrow at midday you and Z will enter the pit of no return. It is very simple really and very charming of a place to die. The pit of no return is a dug-out pit on the compound about ten feet deep and twenty feet wide. In the pit are wooden sharp spikes sticking out in all directions. You will have no weapons, neither one of you. During the battle at random there will be a total of four mud people released into the pit as well. If the two of you are still alive there will be two drifters or crazies, whatever you like to call them, thrown into the pit as well. These men will be fighting for their lives as well and their release. Now saying that, Marco, if you should live you will be my righthand man and in full control of the guards. Do we have an agreement, Marco?"

"We do, Giver, and thank you for your understanding."

Tinzo walked in.

"Take Marco back to his holding cell, make sure he eats and drinks well, he will need it for tomorrow."

"Yes, sir, Giver. Come on, let's go, Marco."

We left the room.

"Marco, are you okay?"

"Yeah, I guess I have to fight Z in the pit at midday tomorrow."

"Shit, Marco, no one survives that!"

"Well, I have to, do me a favor."

"Anything, what is it?"

"Tell Daniel and Samarra but not Ellis, keep her away from the pit even if you have to send Lenetta over there to distract her. Tell Daniel and Samarra not to do anything, just let it happen, if something goes wrong tell them they know what they have to do stick with the mission!"

"I got it, Marco. I will send for someone to get your food."

"Thanks, Tinzo, take off and go."

I sat there for a while just thinking of how in the hell I got myself into such a predicament. It really did not matter now, the fact of it was I had to get myself out of it.

Some time passed by and Ada brought my dinner in a little earlier than the normal time it was to be served.

"Hey, Ada, it is nice to see you, it has been a little while."

"Yes, it has been, Marco, but I am a little upset with you."

"Why is that?"

"Why did you get into trouble? You had it made here, why would you screw things up?"

"It is not all my fault, he killed someone who was innocent. Jappel was his name, he helped me and my friends out, gave us shelter and food, and did not expect nothing in return."

"Why, Ada, was he not given the chance to defend himself? Now I have to fight for my life tomorrow in the pit over stupidity and ignorance against a man who cares nothing about human life at all. Do you see where I am going with this?"

"No, I do not, what are you trying to say?"

"Everything that is going on here at this compound is not the human way, can't you see that? Z killed someone unjustly, Ada, and now I have to fight for my life defending myself against a murderer. Babies disappear from here. The Giver is going to bring his people here and when he does they will have complete control. While all of you work to make their lives better you are all slaves and food!"

"Hush, Marco, you are going to get us all killed!"

"Ada, why are you so upset? Isn't the Giver kind and honest?"

"Stop it, leave me alone!" She ran out of the door crying and just left me there with just my thoughts. I hoped I got through to her, maybe she would see the truth.

I left Marco and quickly went looking for Daniel and Samarra, they needed to know what was going down. I could not find them in the streets so I headed over to where Marco and Daniel were living. I knocked on the door very loudly and Samarra answered the door.

"Hey, guys, we need to talk, we have a problem."

Daniel rushed to the door. "What is going on, Tinzo?"

"It's Marco, we need to talk."

"What has happened to him?"

"Marco had got into some trouble earlier today."

"We know, Ellis told us but we do not know the full story."

"Z brought somebody in from the outside walls who had been stealing crops and Z cut off both of his hands. By the time Z got back the guy bled to death."

"Who was it?"

"I cannot remember the name. Marco told me but he was a very small person, kind of deformed looking."

"Fuck, Samarra, it had to have been Jappel. Marco and Z got into a fight in the compound streets, I had to take both of them away to holding cells. I took Marco to see the Giver, he wanted to have a private discussion with him. When I picked him up he told me at noon tomorrow him and Z have to fight to the death in the pit of no return. Look, you two, the fighting in the pit, no one survives, it is a death sentence."

"Daniel, we need to get him out of there tonight!"

"No, Samarra, you can't."

"Why the hell not, Tinzo!"

"Here is the message from Marco. He said keep Ellis away from the pit and if something goes wrong to stick with the mission."

"Fuck, Daniel, fuck this shit!"

"Calm down, Samarra!"

"Easy for you to say, Daniel, we should get him out of there now!"

"No, Samarra, we have to listen to his orders, he is the captain!"

"Captain of what?"

"You do not know, Tinzo, I am sure you do since you have been around the Giver all this time?"

"No, I do not know what the hell you're talking about."

"We don't have time right now, Tinzo, all I have to say is the Giver is a liar and all of you are pawns in his game."

"Samarra, shut up, not now!"

"Leave me alone, Daniel!" Samarra rushed off, ran into the bedroom, and slammed the door.

"Sorry, Tinzo, I will explain later and if God willing Marco will explain all of it to you."

"Who is God, Daniel?"

"Never mind, we will talk later, thank you for telling us what is going on. I think we need to make Samarra go to Ellis' house and keep her company and hopefully the two of us will be by the pit when the fight begins."

Samarra stayed at my place that night, we were taking a risk but thus far no one had been checking up on us. We talked a while, Samarra was getting better but I also thought her hormones were starting to get the best of her. I held her very closely to me, she finally calmed down enough to rest and go to sleep. I looked up at the ceiling and for the first time in my life I reached out for God and prayed.

"This is not what you created for us or do you want this world for your people. Show mercy on us all." I could not believe I was praying and then quickly without warning I drifted away.

It was late, I could not sleep, my thoughts stayed on the future, or should I say the past, hell, either one is correct. I had to win tomorrow, I just had to, this could be our way out for all of us. I heard a noise, it sounded like someone was approaching my cell. My name was being called, it was the Giver.

He approached my cell very stealth like with his movements. "Marco, I can smell your fear and anger, you are very nervous and have a lot of anxiety in you."

"Wouldn't you if you had to fight for your life tomorrow?"

"My kind does not fear death, when we die it is a gift and we are lifted up beyond all the stars and planets and live with Lan-Ta and others who have passed before us."

"Who the hell is Lan-Ta?"

"The god of everything you see, hear, touch, and smell. When death comes for someone, Lan-Ta embraces them and we all become one with the universe. The point is, Marco, do not fear death or you won't be scared or angry anymore."

I almost began to say something but I just kept my mouth shut. "Giver, are you going to be at the pit tomorrow?"

"No, the sun is too hot but I will be eagerly waiting to find out the results. I actually hope you win tomorrow, Marco, you have great potential to be a leader. You understood what humanity was like before and you can help mold them back to being submissive and somewhat more civilized. You and your friends can help me change the minds and souls of the people, we can do this together as equals and Marco, there will be many great rewards for you and your future. A lot will change around here soon, Marco, and I mean sooner than you think. I suggest you embrace the change while you can. Oh, before I leave just wanted to let you know Z has a badly strained muscle in his ribcage on the right side of his body. I suggest you use it to your advantage."

"Why are you telling me this, Giver?"

"Goodnight, Marco, may Lan-Ta be in your favor tomorrow."

He left as stealthily as he came in. What in the hell was that all about? I heard more steps approaching the cell, who could it be now? It was Ada, she stood in front of the cell with her head partially bowed.

"Ada, are you okay?"

"Yes."

"Do you want to talk?"

"Yes."

"Ada, I am not mad with you, what is wrong, why are you here?"

She began to cry.

"It's okay, I won't tell, what is wrong?"

"Everything, Marco, everything. I know he is not good, I know things are not right here."

"Ada, calm down, don't talk too loud, you do not want anyone to hear you!"

"I saw something, Marco, I did with children and some adults."

"What did you see, Ada, tell me."

At that moment two guards came rushing in, grabbed her and dragged her by her hair out of the room. I could hear her screaming and crying, then she was gone. I yelled out to them let her go, she was a woman! One of the guards walked in, looked at me, and told me to shut my mouth, that she was sick with some kind of strange flu and she was out of her mind. The guard walked out and I just screamed to the top of my lungs, lay down on the floor, and fell asleep.

As I slept I kept having dreams or visions flashing through my head. One minute I saw Jappel lying dead on the ground with no hands and the next visions of fighting cave people while freeing Samarra. Flashbacks of what Earth used to be like before we arrived in this future state of hell. Flashbacks of my early years going through training and the memory of my parents not being there after graduation. Bombs exploding, people starving, young children dying from disease and hunger, the world was dying, it jolted me out of sleep. I was pouring a cold sweat but now I felt alive again, the mission must succeed!

I woke up with a peaceful night's sleep with Samarra lying in my arms. It felt a little strange also, but honestly with what was going on I had never been happier in my entire life. I lay there and stroked her hair and realized this was the quietest I had ever heard her and I began to laugh. My laughing started to wake her up, she began to stir and she flipped over and looked at me.

"What the hell are you laughing at, dick, it's early!"

"Good morning, baby, just admiring your beautiful face."

"I guess you want sex now right?"

"Well, if you're asking?"

"Daniel, give me your best five and then this chick needs breakfast."

"Yes, ma'am!"

Samarra and I went to breakfast, both of us were worried about what could happen today.

"You know, Samarra, if something happens to Marco it is up to us to finish the mission."

"Daniel, I knew you were all brains but thank you, baby, for letting me in on that little secret."

"Damn, can you be a little easy on me, I am stressing out?"

"Oh, wow, Daniel, it sounds like we are married now. I was joking, and Daniel, and I do understand, no matter what we will get through this. Look, can you hang out with Ellis today so she does not find out what is going on?"

"Not a problem, we can have girl talk, I am sure she is still upset."

"Do you even know what girl talk is?"

"Of course, dick, I hear you and Marco doing it all the time."

"God, I love you!"

"I love you too, Daniel!"

I woke up early that morning suddenly with the sounds of someone calling my name.

"Wake up, Marco, time for your breakfast, the Giver wants to know what kind of food you want before the fight?"

"I want meat and vegetables loaded in carbs, bring some bread with it."

"I will let him know, Marco, and good luck out there today."

"Thanks, and by the way ask him what happened to Ada. I am really concerned about her situation."

"Okay, I will, breakfast will be here soon."

Breakfast came very quickly. I was so nervous about the day I really did not feel like eating but I forced myself to. I lay around resting most of the day until I could see the sun getting close to being high in the sky through the tiny window. At that point I got up, started stretching and mentally preparing myself for combat.

"Okay, Daniel, I am off to Ellis' house."

"Okay, give me a kiss. Samarra, be careful, do not converse with anyone, okay? I am sure with everything that has gone on with Marco some people may be suspicious of us."

"Daniel, I understand, give me one more kiss and you be careful yourself, please let me know what's going on as soon as you can."

"I will, love you, see you soon."

I headed out to Ellis' house, the streets began to get pretty crowded, I think people were coming out in droves to see the big event. It was amazing to me to see so many people excited about watching two men fight to the death. I kept hearing a particular voice yelling out of the corner of my ear. Where in the hell was that voice coming from? I kept looking around and could not pinpoint the location.

"Hey, stupid, look behind you!"

I turned around and saw a man shackled by his legs and hands to a post. He was badly sunburnt and smelled like shit.

"What do you want!"

"I know you, I do know you!"

"You do? Funny, I do not know you and I am taken, so if that is what you're after forget about it, dick!"

"Your boy talked to me the other day, told me some shit!"

"Who would that have been?"

"You know, Marco!"

"How do you know Marco?"

"I was sent by Eve to kill all of you."

"Looks like you suck as an assassin, my friend! See ya, got to go!"

"No, wait, please wait!"

"What do you want? Stop wasting my time!"

"He told me things about what was going on here, he wanted me to help him talk to Eve about it!"

"Do not know anything about that, but I will find out in the meantime, dick! So the next time you see me, be a little more respectful, you got it!"

"I do, please talk to him soon, I am willing to help!"

"That or you're either desperate and like most men you will say anything to bullshit a woman!"

"No, please, I'm not, I swear to you! I will get back to you."

"By the way, failed assassin, what is your name?"

"It is Raz."

"Sounds like something I would name a pet rat."

"Maybe you would, but look, my friend Brinn died at the hands of these people and it haunts me every day."

"So sorry, but not really, what is your point!"

"Look, I did not know the full story and neither does Eve, please just let me help!"

"We'll see, I will get back with you, I don't know nothing at this point and I have shit to do, gotta go!"

"What is your name, pretty lady?"

"None of your concern!"

I finally got to Ellis' house, she was on the front porch when I arrived. She greeted me from afar as I approached the home.

"Hey there, Samarra, what brings you here this time of day?"

"Just a visit, figured we could hang out for a while, if that would be okay with you?"

"Anytime and always, Samarra, but I already know about the pit, no need to lie to me about it!"

"I'm very sorry, Ellis, I was not trying to lie, I just did not want you to worry, I am so sorry!"

"It is okay. Tino's wife told me, I am not mad, I am just scared."

"All of us are, Ellis!"

They began to hug.

I left right after Samarra did. The sun was getting high in the sky and the streets were getting very crowded on the way to the pit. I was almost there when Tinzo bumped into me.

"Hey, Daniel, how are the two of you holding up?"

"As well as we can, what's going on with Marco?"

"Last I saw he was warming up and preparing for the pit."

"I sent Samarra over to Ellis' house to keep her distracted."

"Good, I have to go back and bring them to the pit soon."

"What time is it going to start?"

"About twenty minutes. Daniel, hold tight and do not do anything stupid, no matter what happens."

"Don't worry, we got this!"

"Oh, Daniel, by the way, I know everything about what is going on, Lenetta told me. Her and Ellis talked so do not worry, I am on your side!"

"Thank you, it means a lot! Tell Marco good luck from the both of us!"

"I will, see you soon."

"So Samarra, do the three of you actually think you may be able to reverse everything if you go back?"

"We do, at least we can try. I cannot promise it, but no one should have to live their lives this way, Ellis, no one."

"Can I come with you guys when you go home, it would be smart if you brought someone back with you that can speak firsthand about what has happened to the world."

"I am not sure, that would have to be Marco's call, he is in charge of the mission."

"I understand. I myself would love for you to come back with us, you make Marco happy and usually he is a dick."

Both of them started laughing.

The Pit

Tinzo came to my cell.

"Marco, are you ready, it is time."

"About as ready as I am going to be."

"Z is already at the pit waiting."

"Have you seen Daniel and Samarra?"

"Yes, Daniel is at the pit and Samarra is staying with Ellis."

"Good, good."

"Look, Marco, I do not know what to say in a time like this, but I back you one hundred percent and if you live we will all get out of here together. I mean it, Marco, I am out of here and so is my wife."

"Where will you go, Tinzo?"

"Anywhere but here, I will figure that out later."

"What has happened to Ada?"

"I am not really sure, I do know she is in lockup but I have been working other security details so I really don't know more than that."

"Okay, Marco, let's go."

"Lead the way, Tinzo, let's get this over with one way or another."

Tinzo led me down the streets, my hands at this point were still shackled and I could feel the sun's warm rays hitting my body. The air was dusty and I could hear a lot of chatter from the people on the streets. I was getting boos and cheers and spit on by others as we approached the pit. Tinzo had to shove a woman to the ground who tried to hit me with a stick. We had arrived and I was very overwhelmed when I saw the pit for the first time. The pit was bigger to me than what they said it was and was full of wooden spikes coming out of the walls. The seating was amazing, it was just like a hockey arena with rows and rows of seats and the noise from the crowd was insane, I could hardly hear myself think. Tinzo led me into the lower decks of the pit to my waiting room.

"Let me take your cuffs off, Marco, I will be the one to take you out and another guard has Z. When they are ready they will start beating them drums and then will go. Look at me, Marco, remember, they will mix water people and crazy people into the arena at different times, everyone has a stake, all of you want to live so mind your surroundings at all times!"

"I will, Tinzo, and thank you for being here for me, I mean it!"

"Not a problem, and Marco?"

"Yes, Tinzo?"

"Kill that son of a bitch and let's get out of here!"

"I will fight to the death," and we gave each other a hug.

The drums began to beat and my stomach got weak. I bent down, grabbed some dirt, and rubbed it through my fingers, I was sweating so bad. We walked out into the pit and the roar from the crowd was insane. These people were waiting for a bloodbath, it was shocking. I saw Z on the other side of the pit, he stared at me like a wild animal who had not eaten in a long time. I was thinking with my training from the military I might be able to surprise him with moves he had never seen before. At the same time he had been fighting his whole life in this crazy world. Either way let's go, there was no turning back.

A man came to the center of the pit and ordered the crowd to be silent. He began to speak. "Today is a day like no other! Two men guilty but no way to tell who must be punished! The Great Giver said let fate decide the outcome! Whoever shall win today will be free and the loser will be guilty and dead!"

The crowd exploded in cheers and clapping. He raised his hand once again to silence the crowd.

"Either way justice will be done and all will be restored as it should be. This act of sentencing has been approved by the Great and fair Giver. We thank the Giver for his knowledge and compassion, all hail the Giver!"

The crowd exploded, screaming the Giver's name, praising him like some kind of god.

One last time he settled the crowd. "Enjoy the show today, my friends, tomorrow starts work again. On my signal let the fight begin!"

My mind and my heart were racing. I could not believe the mind control he had over these people. A guard entered the pit with a grazier and handed the announcer a sword. The guard shoved the grazier to the ground. The announcer raised his sword and slammed it down on the neck of the grazier, decapitating his head. He pulled his sword back up into the air and screamed, "Fight!" The crowd exploded with excitement and the noise was overwhelming. We moved to the center of the pit, staring at each other's hands up in fighting positions. He charged me full speed, I swept his leg, he tripped and fell down but got up very quickly. The crowd was roaring. He charged again, this time we locked bodies and I slipped around him and put him in a chokehold and quickly brought him down. I was squeezing him like a python trying to make his pass out, but he was fighting every second of it. He was freakishly strong and my arms were getting tired. Out of nowhere I felt extreme pain, he had bitten my arm and I had to let go. He quickly jumped on top of me, slamming my face in the ground not once but twice. He tried for a third but I used one of my hands to stop the momentum, then I came back up with a headbutt that caught him in the chin. He stumbled back and fell awkwardly to the ground. This time I pursued him running, he quickly got up and tackled me in the midsection. We hit the ground and the fucker bit me again and I slammed my right fist into his ear. We rolled on the ground, exchanging punches when I noticed two mud people coming towards us. I quickly gouged his eyes hard with my fingers and he rolled away from me. I stood up and one of the mud people tried to grab me, we locked arms and I shoved him hard and fast into one of the spikes on the side of the wall. My left leg gave way. Z had kicked me in the back of my leg and I went down like a sack of rocks. The other mud person found great interest in me when I went down and started creeping my way. Z just sat there laughing, trying to catch his breath.

"I told you, Marco, I was going to kill you! I told you!"

I guessed he was not watching either but a crazy was let loose and Z was hit in the back of the head and they went down fighting. I knew where Z had hit me only temporarily paralyzed the leg for thirty seconds to a minute, but that was all it took for the other mud person to be on top of me. I was sliding backwards as fast as I could toward the wall to get away from it and give my leg a chance to come back. I backed up to the wall in between some spikes and grabbed one of the spikes for leverage. As it approached I put all my arm strength for leverage. I kicked its knees with my right leg and it stumbled forward face first into a spike. At that same moment the spike I was using for leverage broke and snapped off the wall. I looked down at it, quickly grabbed it up, and put it in my pocket. I looked over at Z, he was on the ground but still moving. The crazy saw me walking that way and started running at me full speed. I leg swept him, jumped on top of him, discreetly pulled out the spike, and jabbed it through his skull. By this time Z was standing up staring at me both of us were covered in blood.

I yelled out to him, "Z, it does not have to end like this! You could help us!"

"I am not helping you do anything! You're weak, Marco, just like the old Earth and like your friend Jappel, none of you deserve to live!"

At that moment another mud person and crazy was released into the pit. The mud person was moaning and growling, it was hungry. The crazy person just stared at us, trying to make its mind up on his next move. He was bigger than usual and my body was starting to give up. In the center of the pit the ground gave way in the shape of a circle. A person started to rise from the ground and then I could see it was Ada, her hands were cuffed and she ran through the pit screaming in fear. She drew attention from the mud person with her screams and looked at me.

"Go ahead, Marco, save the weak. I know that is what you are thinking!"

He was right, the mud person was focused on her. I started running towards Ada when I was tackled by the huge crazy. His weight was over the top and he was crushing me. Z took that to his advantage and started kicking the crazy in the ribs to weaken him down for himself. The crazy got off me, I lay there in pain for about a minute. Slowly I got back up and noticed the other mud person was dead against the wall. I turned and looked, the crazy's huge back was in my sight. I pulled out my spike and drilled it through the back of his head. As he fell down to his knees and died I saw Z holding Ada from behind.

"Z, stop, you do not have to do this!"

"But I must, Marco, there is no other way!"

"There is, Z, we can all leave together, the three of us, there is hope in the world!"

"You know nothing of hope. I will show you hope, Marco!"

Z quickly snapped Ada's neck and she fell to the ground, completely limp.

"Z, you fucked up, I will fucking kill you now!"

Once again it was just the two of us and I was fucking pissed and sad all together.

"You want to kill me, Z?"

"I already have told you that you're weak, you do not deserve to live!"

"So kill me then, pussy."

I slid the spike out of my pants and turned my back to him.

"What are you waiting for, coward, kill me, I don't have all day!"

I dropped down to one knee and he slowly approached me. He grabbed my head, he was going to try and snap it. I quickly grabbed his arm, slung him over my back, and he landed in front of me. One quick and powerful thrust and the spike landed into his throat. I twisted the spike all around, his body was jumping around like a freshly killed chicken. His head came off, I picked it up by his blood-soaked hair, stood up, and raised it towards the crowd, giving all sides of the pit to see it. The crowd erupted in cheers and boos. I raised my hand to settle the crowd. The crowed slowly got quiet enough for me to talk.

"I tried to save his life as well as Ada's, but look what happened! This is not what life is supposed to be like! There is hope and mercy, all of you are living a lie! You have been fooled by the Giver! It wasn't always like this! All of you are food to the Giver and his people! Wake up, this is not real, it is just a way for him to buy time to get his people here and soon all of you will be dead!" I dropped to my knees and blacked out.

Hours or so later I woke back up in my cell, no one was around and through my little window I could tell it was nighttime. I could only remember bits and pieces but I did know I killed Z. And then I saw Ada walk up to the cell.

"Hey, Marco, I hope you are doing okay?"

"I'm fine, I think, what did they do to you after they took you?"

"You know, Marco, the usual, do you need food or water?"

"Not right now, Ada, thank you, though. Ada, are you safe now?"

"I am, Marco, thank you for asking, my life now is better than I could ever imagined."

"What happened today, Ada, I am not sure what is going on, my mind is fuzzy right now."

"I am sure it is, you went through a lot today and thank you for everything you did. You started a movement today, Marco, you really did."

"What movement are you talking about?"

"The one to the truth, Marco, get some rest, you will need it, and I will see you again."

I must have fallen back out again and was awoken with Tinzo in my face.

"Hey, Marco, are you okay?"

I did not realize where I was at, I could hear him but really couldn't put things together. Again I must have blacked out.

"Marco, it's Tinzo, wake up, man, we have to talk."

Then I saw Ada hovering above me, she looked more stunning than I remembered and she had a peace about her that overtook my emotions.

"Marco, please, I need you to get up now, you have things to do." She smiled and she was gone.

I arose from my bed, gasping just like I had come up from the water.

"Thank God, Marco, you are up, we need to talk."

"What do you want, Tinzo, I was just talking to Ada?"

Pain and more pain was felt all over my body. I felt worse than a college kid after a frat party. What the hell, as I lay there I started having flashbacks of the pit starting to slowly come back to me. I remembered sticking the spike through Z's neck and visions of mud people hitting me hard. Then the worst, I saw Z snap Ada's neck and she fell on her knees in slow motion. My heart broke, such an innocent young woman losing her life way too early. I could see the fear and confusion in her face over and over again, my stomach began to get sick and tears rolled down my cheeks. My God, this could not go on any longer.

"Hey, Marco, how are you doing?"

"As bad as I look, Tinzo, I am not doing very well!"

"I know, I have some pain meds that will help you and let you heal quicker."

"I trust you, let's have them, I need it!"

"I am going to give you a shot in the arm, it should help you for the rest of the day." He punched the shot into my left arm and it hurt like hell! "Sorry, Marco."

"It is okay, everything hurts anyway."

"I'm sure it does, buddy, but you're alive and that is what counts."

"I guess, why am I still locked up?"

"After your speech at the end of the fight, the Giver did not trust you and wanted you back here until he knew what was going on. I told the Giver that you were just delusional and out of your mind, that the fight was brutal and that you did not know what you were saying at the time. He trusts me, Marco, I told him about our talks of you becoming a big part of this compound and lied, saying how much you believed in his work for humanity that you had come around. He believed me, that is why you are still alive, he wanted you executed!"

"Now I owe you, Tinzo!"

"No, you don't, we owe it to mankind now."

"Well said, thank you again, my friend."

"I am going back to him and report you are okay but hurting to see if I can get you released. He is going to want to see you, I am sure, so you have to play the game."

"That won't be a problem."

"I will be back soon, you rest and I will send someone with food and water."

"Thanks, I need it, especially water."

I sat there and wondered how Daniel, Samarra, and Ellis were holding up. I missed them all.

An hour later Tinzo came back to my cell. "Alright, Marco, he is ready to see you now, are you ready for this?"

"I am, ready to get the hell out of this nightmare."

"Remember, play the game."

"I will, don't you worry."

We walked very slowly down the long hallway, the medicine was finally starting to kick in and my body was starting to relax a bit but walking was still not easy. We arrived at the door and Tinzo knocked very hard. Two guards opened the door and escorted us in. The Giver sat on his throne and with his long skinny crooked figure motioned us to him.

"Take a seat, Marco, looks like you're having a hard time standing."

"Thank you, Giver, that would be nice."

"First of all, well done at the pit, everyone was talking about your leadership and warrior-like skills. I am even more impressed than I was before and that usually never happens."

"Thank you, Giver, for the kind words, I did my best."

"Indeed you did but one problem, though."

"What is that, Giver?"

"Your speech at the end, do you really believe what you spoke?"

"I do not even remember what I said, Giver, this is all news to me."

"Well, Marco, yes, I harvest humans but so do humans themselves. It is rough times for both of our kinds, we do what we need to survive, that is living. I also know young Ada was thinking the same way and maybe in your delusional state you just repeated what you had heard. The guard told you she was ill with a strange flu that made her unstable. Does this make sense to you, Marco?"

"Perfect sense, Giver, my brain shut down at some point during the fight, this is all new to me."

"I understand very well about the human anatomy and especially the mind, it is very tricky and easily influenced. I also have the word of Tinzo, whom I trust without a doubt, and he says you are a good man. What do you say, Marco?"

"I agree, Giver, I am a good man and things are becoming clearer, I want to be a part of this compound and do good for everyone."

"That is good to hear, I want that as well, so here is your first opportunity to prove you are telling the truth."

Two guards busted through the door with an older man in chains, he was scared and trying to wiggle away from them.

"This man, Marco, has been sentenced to death. I will spare him the pain of letting the mud people slowly eat him to death. Your first act of contribution to this compound is to execute him by cutting his head off with this sword. Marco, I am showing compassion as you want people to do but still upholding the compound's rules and regulations."

"What has this man done, Giver?"

"That is not your concern, your job is to carry out my orders for the good of the compound."

The two guards quickly put him down to the floor and another guard brought me a sword. The Giver stretched out both of his arms and opened his hands. Inside his palms were two black balls that were shiny and smooth. He dropped them to the floor and they began slowly rolling towards me. As they rolled they began to change form until they were almost to me. I raised my sword in defense, not knowing what the hell they were. They transformed in an instant and was an alien species almost like the Giver but different. Their bodies were very similar to the Giver's but they were protected by some sort of a biomechanical suit. I had never seen anything like it before. They did not speak and nor could I tell what their emotions were.

"Let me introduce you, Marco, these two came with me from my planet. They are what you would call my special elite forces. We have many special forces like them back on my planet but I only needed two for now. No weapon on this planet can penetrate their suits, nothing on this planet can outrun them, they never tire out. No human can match their strength or match their reflex abilities. In other words they are the ultimate warriors and will only be used in extreme circumstances. They are trained to act, not feel, and they are relentless and fearless as well. This is something you should know in the event you should see them later during your duties." The Giver opened his hands once again, they began to break down and rolled to him, bouncing off the floor into his palms. He closed his hands and reopened them and they were gone. "Are you ready to fulfill your duties, Marco?"

Inside I was praying, Dear God, forgive me, but many lives were at stake. The man began to scream for mercy.

"On the count of three, Marco, take off his head! One, two, three!"

My sword came crashing down and then it bounced quickly out of my hand so hard it made my wrist numb. I stood there in shock and looked down at the man. The Giver had shot something long and thin from his finger, it could not have been barely an inch thick. It was so tough and durable, I did not even scratch it. As quick as it was shot out it went back in even faster.

"Well done, Marco! Guards, take the prisoner back to his cell. I will figure out what to do with him later."

"Yes, sir." They dragged the man off through the back doors.

"Marco, you and Tinzo are going to be head of the guards, you will train under Tinzo. I knew you would be valuable to this compound."

"Thank you, Giver, I am honored to have this opportunity to serve everyone in this capacity."

"Do not let me down. I am the Giver most of the time and I have another side called the Taker, you do not want to see that side of me."

"Understood, I won't let you down."

"Take today off and rest, you will start work with Tinzo tomorrow."

"Thank you for the rest, I really need it."

"The sword is yours, Marco, and Tinzo, also give him the double-sided tomahawk as well."

"Yes, sir."

"You two are free to go but first, Marco, you will need your security clearance sign so you can have full access to the compound."

A man walked out dressed in a lab coat and carrying a long black object with a round ball at the end.

"What is it, Giver?"

"Do not worry, it only hurts a second, it is your security clearance mark you must receive. Tinzo, show Marco yours."

Tinzo lifted up his sleeves and there it was.

"See, Marco, only my elite carry the symbol."

The man walked up to me. "Okay, Marco, this is going to hurt pretty bad for a few seconds but as soon as it is done I will apply some cream to it and the pain will be gone, understand?"

"I do, let's get this over with."

He stood a foot away from me with the long stick and placed the round ball against my arm. "Okay, Marco, on the count of three we are going to do this, are you ready?"

"I am ready!"

"One, two, three!"

The ball tip began to spin in all sorts of directions, changing its speed constantly and then it suddenly stopped. The ball was no longer round, it was in all different unusable designs. It exploded into my arm at such a fast rate it took me by surprise. I yelled out in agony and dropped to my knees on the floor. I began to throw up from the pain and the man in the lab coat applied the cream and the pain was gone, I could not believe it!

"Wonderful, Marco, you are free to go and enjoy the rest of your day and if you need anything you report to Tinzo."

"Thank you, Giver."

Tinzo and I were free to go and we left the Giver and headed out to the compound.

After Marco and Tinzo left the Giver summoned over one of the guards. The guard walked up to him and knelt on one leg.

"Yes, Giver?"

"Keep a close eye out on Marco, if there is anything strange you only report to me."

"Yes sir, Giver."

Tinzo and I got out into the compound, it was nice and relaxing to be outside in the air.

"How much longer is everyone working for the day?"

"About two more hours, you did good in there, Marco, I was very impressed and I think the Giver was also!"

"Thanks, I hope he was, it will make my job easier."

"Okay, Marco, I have to get back to work, you relax or do what you need to, I will see you tomorrow. I will tell Daniel in the field you will be home when his workday is over."

"Thanks, be safe."

"You do the same."

I strolled around the compound very slowly. I still hurt pretty bad but I enjoyed the air. As I walked past certain people some of them smiled, called me by my name, and others just stared. It felt good having weapons on me again, it was just a security thing is all. I walked around the corner and lo and behold chained up was Raz. Our eyes met and he began to speak.

"Well, look at the big dog on the block now, you must be one hell of a bad ass from all the talk I have heard on the streets."

"Not really, fortunate I am alive. Did your girl talk to you about me?"

"No, I have been a little busy! She won't listen to me, I am in and I want to help you and your mission. I can talk to Eve and make her understand what is going on, she trusts me very much, we have worked together since all of this started."

"How can I trust you, Raz, you tried to kill all of us!"

"I did not know the truth, Marco, I do now, I have seen the animals out at night. They put me inside at night but there is a full protected window, those things look at me all night, they want to kill me! These people here do that to me to torture me, fuck with my mind and spirit to break me down before they kill me! When I saw these animals there has never been anything like this on Earth ever! Eve does not know and she should and we can tell her together!"

"I am going out on a limb for you, Raz! I will trust you but if you do me wrong I will kill you and you will wish one of these things got you before me, do you understand!"

He laughed at me oddly. "Marco, are you okay?"

"No, would you be?"

"No, I guess I would not be. When will you get me?"

"Not sure but soon, you hold tight, I will keep my word to bring you back and you better keep yours!"

"I will, I will, thank you!"

I walked off and headed to the local school house just to peep my head into the door so Ellis would know I was okay. I approached the school house, walked up the steps, and peeked in. I watched her for thirty seconds, she was so intense about her teaching and the students, I was in awe of her! She glanced my way and did a double take. She dropped her book and came running, it startled the students and she jumped into my arms! She landed kisses and hugs, I loved it.

"But please be gentle, I am still hurting!"

"I am sorry, Marco, I am, but I heard you had survived and I am so in love I cannot help it, just hold me! I thought you were dead, Marco, I really did!"

"You and I both, Ellis!"

"Stay with me tonight, Marco, please!"

"Not tonight, I have to talk to Daniel and Samarra but I promise the next night I will!"

"I understand, it just gives me one more day to impress you with a new meal."

"I love the sound of that! Okay, Ellis, I will let you teach and I will see you tomorrow after work."

"I cannot wait." She smothered me with kisses and hugs.

As I left the school house there was a guard outside across the street standing at the corner. As I walked down the steps he just looked at me and he raised his hand to wave to me.

"Good day, Marco, you need to get some rest."

"Believe me, that is where I am going right now."

"Okay, good day to you, sir."

I headed back to Daniel and my room, quickly stripped my clothes, and lay on the bed and just passed out!

Hunger Pains

I woke up to Daniel and Samarra rough housing in the bed.

"Hey, hey, stop it, damn, guys, I am still sore as shit!"

"Sorry, king bad ass. I have to say, Marco, I will not ever call you a pussy again."

"Thanks, Samarra, that just makes me feel so warm inside coming from you."

"Get dressed, Marco, it's chow time."

"Oh, shit, Daniel, thanks, I would have slept through it."

I got dressed and we all headed for the chow hall. Nice selection of food, we filled our plates and headed to a table.

"Look, guys, let's just eat here, we will talk back at our place, it's time to make a plan. I want us out of here in 72 hours."

"Sounds good but hush your mouth, this pregnant woman is hungry!"

We all began to laugh.

"Stop it, Samarra, it hurts my ribs to laugh."

"Sorry, pussy, woops, I meant Captain Pussy."

"I have to say, Samarra, for once and do not get too excited, I did miss your mouth for a minute."

As we headed back to our room I watched Samarra stuffing food into her pants. Daniel and I just stared at her in disbelief.

"What, what! What are you two dicks looking at?"

"Can we just get back to the room, for the love of God, Samarra?"

"Geez, I'm coming!"

Finally the three of us got back to the room and sat down at the table.

"Before we begin, Samarra, can you please remove that piece of meat from your teeth, I can't think."

"Damn, Marco, what is your problem, did you take too many shots to the head?" She wiped here face and began to get serious.

"Look, guys, tomorrow I start a new job, Tinzo and I are head of security." I lifted up my sleeve and showed them the brand mark I was given. They both looked at it.

"What does it mean, Marco?"

"Not really sure, Samarra, other than just a clearance mark."

Daniel piped in. "I do not know what it means but on his planet it must have a meaning. There are way too many designs on it just to mean security. On top of that, Marco, those symbols and marks are intriguing."

"Agree with you, Daniel, who knows and we may never know the answer. Tomorrow with my new clearance I will start investigating all areas of opportunity that may help us get out of here. You guys just play the role and do what you do. Tinzo is on our side, he will be an great asset as well."

"You fully trust him, Marco?"

"I do, Samarra, he has saved my ass more than once and besides, if he wanted to we would already be dead. Tinzo and Lenetta want to leave when we do. Oh, yeah, Samarra, did you talk to Raz, the prisoner in the streets?"

"I did, he said that you and him had talked, I did not trust him, I think he was a wack job."

"Damn, Samarra, I told you not to talk to anyone!"

"Relax, Daniel, I am a full-ass-grown woman!"

"I know you are but you're hard headed as hell!"

"Stop it, you two, we do not need this, we have goals to meet. You two better leave, you're almost late for work, I am going to try and relax, I will see you later."

Role Play

I was up early, met Tinzo for breakfast before we started our workday.

"How do you feel, Marco?"

"Pretty good, just sore as hell but better."

"Good to hear, I am going to show you all around the places we are allowed to go. The two of us have full access inside and outside of the compound. You will need this to start your day." He handed me over a handheld radio very primitive to what I was used to using. "Be careful of what you say on it, all the guards can hear the chatter."

"Got it, thanks."

"As soon as you're done with breakfast we will leave."

"Sounds good, let's go."

"First stop, the Ag-Wazs."

"You know, Tinzo, I don't think I can stop being amazed by these creatures no matter how many times I see them."

"They are amazing, Marco, for sure, but nothing to fuck with."

"I have no doubt about that, my friend."

"So do you know how to stop all of this when you get back?"

"I think so, I met an older man before I got here, claimed to have the knowledge about a man named Abbas Tahan, a terrorist from the Middle East who put a virus in defense computers in a lot of nations. This set off the war of all wars and here we are."

"So how do you stop it then?"

"Easy, Tinzo, squash the bug before it multiplies, he must die and anyone else who is working with him."

"Can this be done?"

"You bet your sweet ass it can!"

We left the building and walked back outside.

"Across the street in that building is where all the workers' tools are stored. Let's take a look inside."

Tinzo unlocked the door and we stepped inside.

"What exactly are you looking for, Marco?"

"Something like bolt cutters to break chains."

"Nothing like that here but we have a flame unit."

"What is that?"

Tinzo pulled it out, pressed down a lever, and a hot sharp flame came out.

"Oh, shit, man, this is what we called back home a welder's torch."

"Is that good?"

"Hell yeah, Tinzo, this will burn metal pretty quickly. Can I take this, Tinzo?"

"You can but at the end of the day the guards account for every tool in this building, security you know."

"Understood, I need it after lunch, I have a plan."

"Whatever you need, just remember if you get caught it will be death for you."

We left the shop and walked a bit.

"Over here, Marco, to your left is a sick room or trauma room for workers or guards during the day if there is an accident or anything else. As you can see there are a lot of small shops here where people make things we need for the compound such as wood products and people who prepare meat and spices for consumption. Down that way further south is all housing, we patrol those areas as well except for at night, as you know the Ag-Wazs do that."

"So, Tinzo, let's go outside the compound, I would like to get a lay of the land if you don't mind."

"Not a problem, let's go this way. As you can see we have a lot of workers in the field and a lot of mouths to feed."

"What are you growing out here?"

"Some traditional crops like corn, some peppers of different kinds, and other stuff that came from the Giver's planet that could grow here. Some of the crops here are also grown for medical purposes as well."

"Interesting."

"As you can see when the workers hold up their hands the bag is full. You have to go pick it up and give them a fresh one and take the full bag to the cart so it can be carried in at the end of the day. The new crops from the Giver's planet grow very quickly here so there is always work to be done."

"What do they do when the weather gets cold and the crops are no longer growing?"

"It does not get cold anymore, Marco, the coldest day we had was 70 degrees."

"Wow, that is crazy."

"Yes, it is, we have a huge problem with skin cancer here and just the radiation in the air makes people very sick and in time they die."

"What is past the compound going north?"

"The more of the same mud people, cave dwellers, stragglers, and your all-out crazy folks, it's a landscape of death. The compound is relatively safe, that's why people stay here, not much of a need to leave unless you have a death wish."

"But now, Tinzo, you are ready to leave?"

"I am, either way we are going to die, I just hope you can stop this madness, the world is worth saving if there is even a small chance."

"Look, Tinzo, we are working on it, I promise, I have a few ideas to start with but I will need a little more time."

"Would you be able to stay at our house tonight, Lenetta wants to talk with you?"

"I would love to but I promised Ellis I was staying with her. Tell you what, though, ask Lenetta if you two want to stay at her house we can all have dinner and talk more."

"Do you think she would mind?"

"Not at all, four heads are better than three, am I right?"

"So true and your head still looks a little swollen to me."

We both started laughing.

"Hey, Tinzo, can you go tell Daniel what we are doing tonight and that I will talk to him tomorrow, it may be better if you go to keep the suspicion off of me. While you are doing that I am going to officially introduce myself to the rest of the guards."

"Sounds good, I will meet you for lunch."

I started introducing myself to the other guards, they were pretty eager and willing to talk to me. Most of them were amazed of the day at the pit and believe me so was I. There was one that really did not care to get to know me, his name was Trammer. Not a very friendly guy and seemed to have a personal grudge against me. Maybe him and Z were buddies, who really knows or maybe he just thought I was an asshole. Whatever it was I really couldn't care less, I was here for a reason not a congeniality contest.

Tinzo and I met for lunch.

"So what did you think, Marco?"

"A perfectly planned takeover of the world," and we began to laugh.

"Tinzo, do you know anything about any weaknesses the Giver may have?"

"What do you mean?"

"What could kill him?"

"I do not know, Marco, his body is very foreign and he sure does not explain to us anything. One thing I know is his planet was mostly dark and very little light. He can come outside during the day but not long, usually just a hour at max. He typically sleeps a lot during the day but I have seen him up at all hours."

"What is up with Trammer?"

"Young, dumb, eager to please, why you ask?"

"He was very standoffish today."

"Probably nothing more than he thinks you took his job, you know how young people are, they forget you do not receive things without working your way up first."

"Maybe, we will see."

"I told Daniel and Samarra so they are good. Lenetta and I are meeting you at Ellis' house after work, Lenetta confirmed it with Ellis to double check if it was okay so now it's officially a double date night."

We began laughing. On the way out from lunch I grabbed a few items I needed for the night. One was a can, the other was a six-inch tube and a two-inch piece of steel.

"You ready to make your rounds, Marco?"

"Let's do it, won't be long before quitting time."

The Bee's Knees

Quitting time was at hand, the tool shed was locked up and the sun was getting ready to set soon. Off I went to Ellis' house to join my love and allies. As I approached the house on the front porch I saw Ada, she was smiling and sitting in a chair. The front door opened and as quick as I had seen her she was gone. Ellis came outside, wrapped her arms around me, and gave me a powerful hug and a kiss. I could feel the love and was never this happy. I had never in my life experienced love like this, it was magical to me and I could not get enough. She began to cry and rubbed her hand through my hair. I felt calm for the first time in my life like nothing could ever go wrong.

"I love you, Ellis, I have missed you so much, I have been waiting for this moment which has felt like forever to me."

"Me too, Marco, please come inside, I love you too!"

Tinzo and Lenetta had big smiles on their faces, they were happy for the two of us.

"Okay, everyone, emotional time is over," Ellis yelled out, "it is time to eat."

We all laughed and headed to the kitchen table. All of us dug into our food and we began to tell jokes and had great conversation. It was great, I really needed this, it had been a long time since I could kick back and just relax.

Lenetta broke the conversation into a new direction. "Marco, any plans on how to get out of here?"

"Still working on it, just getting a lay of the land and hopefully go from there."

"Hey, honey, I had talked to Samarra and expressed interest with going back with you guys to help explain what was happening."

"Ellis, I don't know, that could be putting you into danger."

"I know but I want to, I cannot be without you anymore."

"Let me think on it and we will talk about it later."

"Okay, but do not let me wait too long, okay?"

All of us started to laugh. I got up to go to the kitchen for some water when something caught my eye through the window. I did a double take and whatever it was it was gone.

"Tinzo, is there any guards still working right now?"

"Not usually, it's almost dark but they may be finishing up with something, why?"

"Not sure, I thought I got a quick glance at someone out of the window."

"It's just stress, Marco, come back to the table and relax."

We finished dinner and headed into the living room and took a seat.

"Great dinner, Ellis."

"Thanks, everyone, it is nice having company over, we don't do this often enough."

"Look, guys, I will need all of your help and silence to try and pull this off, I appreciate your faith and trust in me. This will get ugly but in the end it will be well worth it."

"I have a question, Marco?"

"Yes, Lenetta, ask me anything?"

"What will happen if you succeed and the wars never start, will Tinzo and I still be together?"

The question threw me for a loop, at first I just hesitated, I did not know what to say.

"I will be honest, Lenetta, I really do not know but what I do know is that millions and millions of innocent lives will survive."

It was getting late and it was time for bed, we all said our goodnights and headed to our bedrooms. Ellis and I got into the bed, cuddled for a while, and made love most of the night. I woke up the next morning with Tinzo shaking my arm.

"Wake up, man, time to get ready for breakfast and work, sorry, Ellis, for the intrusion."

"Don't worry about it, Tinzo, I need to get ready myself." I gave Ellis a kiss, got dressed, and Tinzo and I headed out for breakfast.

"You know what, Tinzo?"

"What's that?"

"You are the bees knees."

"What?"

"Never mind, just an old saying," and we both started laughing.

I had been a housewife now for many years. I loved my Tinzo. I could not imagine him not being in my life at this point. He had always been a good provider and faithful husband. I had always loved him and supported him throughout the years, even though I had had my concerns about what was going on, but like any wife I stood by his side. I loved the fact he had met Marco and he saw things more clearly and realizing the truth about this place. The thoughts of last night when Marco said he did not know really scared me, he was all I had ever wanted and loved.

The trail of thoughts was broken with heavy knocks at the door. Tinzo probably left something at home, he usually did that from time to time. I walked to the door.

"Who is it?" and no answer.

I walked away and again loud knocking.

"Who is it?" and again no answer. "If you can't speak, I will not open the door."

I started to walk away again when I heard a voice yell out, "Open the door, Lenetta, I am a guard, look out of your window if you do not believe me!"

I went to the window and I knew he was telling the truth. I had seen him before, but I did not know his name.

I cracked the door open slightly. "Can I help you?"

"Yes, you can, we need to talk."

"About what?"

"Life, yours, mine, everyone's, your husband and the wonderful Marco!"

"Who are you?"

"For now that is not really important, but we need to talk, you are in so much shit right now, you have no idea how bad I could fuck all of you!"

"What, why, we haven't done anything to anyone? You are out of your mind, we are all good people here and are high up in the ranks in this compound."

"You may think so, Lenetta, but not anymore!"

"What do you want?"

"Your time and attention and my demands, so you better listen! It is up to you, Lenetta!"

"Fine, let's talk on the porch then!"

"I knew you would be reasonable, and believe me, Lenetta, I am reasonable as well. I would not have given you this opportunity if I wasn't."

"What is your problem, guard!"

"All of you, Lenetta, you let a man come in and take over a place who preaches false lies and says he can fix the world, why is that?"

"What are you talking about?"

"Do not play stupid. I know what Marco was and he is wrong, all of you have been lied to and the Giver is a good person, don't you understand that!"

"To begin with, guard, don't you understand he is not a person!"

"Shut your mouth, Lenetta, whatever he is makes no difference!"

"No, you're wrong, it does, and our best interest is not with him, it is his own peoples!"

He grabbed my face and squeezed very tight, "Do not make me kill you today, dammit!"

"Let go of me now or Tinzo will kill you as quick as he can."

"You tell Tinzo a guard stopped by today, you have two days to get all of your shit together or I will be back and this will not end well, I promise!"

"I am not scared of you, do what you must and so will we!"

"Fix the problem, Lenetta, now, if you don't I promise you your death will be very painful!"

I dropped down to the ground crying and he walked away.

After breakfast Tinzo and I split up and began our workday. I left the compound gates riding a four-wheeler out to the fields for patrol duty. There was a few mud people coming out of the woods, they seemed to be getting more and more desperate for food. I quickly got to them and cut their heads off with my sword before they got too close to any of the workers. I saw a bag being held up. I drove closer to the worker and it was Daniel.

"Well, hey there, Daniel, is everything okay?"

"Great and you?"

"Fine, just trying to figure stuff out. What are they having Samarra doing now?"

He began to laugh. "She is the lunch lady now."

"Well, she does like to eat and soon they will realize they put her in the wrong job. Look, Daniel, tomorrow hold your bag up when I am near, I am going to sneak you a weapon. Just be ready!"

"Not a problem, Captain, I will be eagerly waiting!"

My radio went off. "Hey, Marco, where are you?"

"North Field."

"Come to the West Field now, mud people, we need help!"

"On my way, Tinzo!"

"See ya, Daniel."

I jumped on my bike and took off! When I had arrived Tinzo was already fighting off some mud people. I jumped off my bike, pulled out my sword, and jumped right into the fight. We cleared out the small hoard pretty quickly.

"Tinzo, what is going on, they are becoming a huge problem?"

"They are hungry, they usually stay by the water but food is hard to come by these days."

"Do they have a leader?"

"Are you seriously asking me this?"

"Yes, I am."

"I don't know, I seriously doubt it, they are more animal than human, they just eat."

"I get it but even in the animal world there usually is a leader."

"I do not know, Marco, why don't you just try and talk to one?"

"Brilliant, Tinzo, let's just try that."

"Marco, you are out of your mind!"

"Am I? Prove me wrong."

"Are you serious or are you really mad?"

"Hey, Tinzo, what do we have to lose? Tinzo, just give me this, please, if I am wrong I will admit it, okay?"

"I will help you this time, dumb ass, you better not let me down."

"Thank you."

"Damn, Marco, we will find some after lunch but we need to get back on patrol, we have been gone a little too long now."

We drove up to the gate.

"Where have you two been?"

"Mud people problems on the west side of the fields. Let someone inform the Giver Marco and I have fought off quite a few mud people and the problem is getting worse."

"Yes, sir!"

"Wow, Tinzo, that was a great lunch."

"Indeed it was but I still think you're nuts in believing you can talk to them and carrying on a productive conversation."

"Maybe but you never know unless you try, it is worth a shot, my friend."

"Well, I have only heard them growl and typically they are so focused on trying to eat you the thought of conversation or the ability to speak is unlikely."

"That is why, Tinzo, I am bringing food with me and maybe some restraints."

"This isn't going to be good."

"Hey, have a little faith."

I took a couple of deer steaks from the kitchen and loaded them up in one of the sacks that was used in the fields.

"Okay, Tinzo, are you ready?"

"About as ready as I am going to be. Marco, didn't you say you needed something out of the workers' tool room?"

"Yes, but not today, a slight change of plans for now."

We took off past the compound gates at full speed and stopped at a creek about a mile away. It was a relativity small creek but a lot of marsh land surrounding it.

"What now, Tinzo, I don't see them?"

"Just start stomping your feet hard and make some noise."

A few minutes later we started seeing bubbles come up from the water.

"Stand back, Marco, one is trying to surface, they are faster in the water by far than on land."

I started to see a muddy head slowly peeking its way up to the surface.

"Once he crawls up on land, Marco, I will grab his hands, lead him off, and tie him up and you can do your little experiment."

Tinzo quickly jumped on it and dragged it to the shore, it was snapping its teeth and hissing.

"Hold him, Marco, I will tie him up!"

Tinzo restrained him tightly and it was not happy at all.

"Your turn, Marco."

I pulled out the deer meat and tore it apart with my hands. Grabbed a stick and stuck some of the meat on it and spoon fed it like a toddler. It quickly began to eat, the more it ate the calmer it started to get.

"Can you talk?"

No answer. It just ate and looked at me very passive aggressively. I brought out the second steak and began to feed it. It was slower to eat but you could tell it loved it.

"Talk to me, say anything, damn it!"

"Nothing, just stares and chewing."

"I tried to tell you, Marco."

"Tinzo, get the sack and fill it up with water and bring it to me, please."

I poured the water on its body and kept feeding it. Out of nowhere I heard the words "Help me." Tinzo and I just looked at each other in disbelief, we could not believe it spoke.

"What is your name?"

"Not understand."

"What do others like you call you?"

"Not understand."

"Who is your leader?"

"What dat?"

I keep feeding it and Tinzo kept putting water on it.

"The one who makes decisions, the one who tells all of you what to do."

"Not understand."

"Okay, okay, okay, let me think on how to word this. Shit, who does everyone people like you talk to when you need food?"

"Wom-Pal."

"That is your leader?"

"Wom-Pal."

"Listen to me, talk to Wom-Pal, tell him I," as I slapped my chest, "want to talk to him. I will bring food," and I pointed to the deer meat, "but he cannot hurt any of us. We can help all of you but we need to have trust between us. Tell him I will bring food tomorrow for him. I am going to give you the last deer steak, when you go back give it to Wom-Pal. We are going to let you go now. I will give you the rest of the food but if you attack we will kill you."

"Wom-Pal food, good talk, okay, I go now."

Tinzo cut him loose. I had the meat in my hand and lured him to the swamp and threw the meat into the water. He went after it and disappeared into the marsh.

Water Play

We rode back to camp, we still could not believe what just happened. We sat on our four-wheelers at the edge of the field in amazement.

"What's next, Marco?"

"Well, I guess I have a meeting with Wom-Pal and see what happens."

"You're still a fool."

"Yes, I know, no arguments there."

"We better get back, Marco, the workday is almost over."

The rest of the afternoon went by very quickly and it was quitting time. We finished up our checks and helped secure the main gate.

"Alright, Tinzo, I will see you tomorrow."

"Yes, you will, my friend."

I began to walk home, still in amazement about what Marco had done, and could not wait to get home and tell Lenetta. I was almost there and I could see Lenetta on the front porch waiting for me. The closer I got, I could see the tears running down her cheeks.

"What is wrong, honey, why are you crying?"

"Tinzo, sit with me, we need to talk, we are in a lot of trouble, I am so scared."

"What, why are you scared, everything is okay."

"No, no we're not, after you left this morning a guard came to the house, he threatened to kill me, he grabbed my face and squeezed it hard."

"What, who was it!"

"I don't know, he said that he knew you and Marco were up to something, that if you didn't get your shit together he was going to tell the Giver!"

"What did he look like?"

"Probably in his late twenties, shaved head and light beard."

"I think I know who it is, probably Trammer! He wanted Z's job and did not get it and now he is pissed. He will not get away with this, I promise, no one lays a hand on my wife!"

"You be careful, Tinzo, you never know what he might do."

"Maybe, but he has no idea of what I can do either!"

We had dinner and went to bed. I reassured her everything would be okay.

"When I leave, honey, lock all of the doors and I promise this will end today."

I headed out of the door, headed to breakfast to meet Marco.

"Hey, Tinzo, did you have a good night?"

"Not really, do you trust me?"

"You know I do, why are you asking?"

"No questions, just follow my lead today."

"Okay, is everything going to be okay?"

"It will be, I am bringing a guest with us when we go see Wom-Pal."

"No, you can't."

"Yes, Marco, I can, please just trust me on this."

"Okay, Tinzo, I trust you, you're just creeping me out a bit."

We both went to work and went our separate ways. The day went by very slowly, wondering what in the hell Tinzo was up to, but I did trust him until he gave me a reason not to. Finally it was lunchtime and we sat down to eat. Tinzo brought another guard with him.

"Hey, Marco, I want to introduce one of our newest and rising stars on the compound, his name is Trammer."

"Good to meet you, Trammer. Tinzo has mentioned your name a lot, you must be a top-notch guard."

"Thanks, it is good to meet you too. I told Trammer on the way over about helping us out with your experiment and theory that mud people can talk."

"That would be great, would love a good extra pair of hands."

"Marco, I hear you are a time traveler?"

I began to laugh. "Where did you hear such a thing?"

"Oh, just around."

He looked irritated at me and I knew Tinzo did not trust him by his expression.

"You should not believe everything you hear, son, word of mouth is the same thing as a lie, you know?"

"Maybe, but who really knows."

Tinzo jumped up from the table. "You boys ready? We have an experiment to get to."

"I am ready, Tinzo."

"How about you, Trammer?"

"I am, let's get started, I am getting bored."

"Marco, do you have the meat?"

"I do, let's roll."

We headed out of the gate on our four-wheelers and Trammer rode on the back with Tinzo. I could tell something bad was going on and by the look on Tinzo's face he was not playing around. We had arrived at the place where we had talked to the mud person the day before. I got off my four-wheeler and started stomping the ground and making noises.

"This is stupid and dangerous!" Trammer yelled out.

Tinzo quickly turned around and hit him with his baton and he hit the ground. "Help me tie him up, Marco."

"What is going on?"

"Just tie him up, trust me!"

We tied him up to the base of a tree, he was still somewhat out of it from the smack to the face. The whole swamp began to boil with bubbles. I was getting nervous, it looked like hundreds were trying to surface. Five, ten, fifteen heads started to arise from the muck, I was losing count. In the center of it all I could see something very large coming up to the surface. The head broke the surface, it was the size of a large boulder, and then the arms surfaced, which reminded me of frog's feet. It just paused, stared at me with those black large round eyes that were on the side of its face. Mud and slime like an eel dripped from its body. Then it began to speak. The voice was raspy and wet but very easy to understand.

"Me Wom-Pal, you have food, we talk?"

"I want to talk to you in peace. I am Marco. I lived here on Earth before everything went bad."

"What Marco want with me?"

"Your help, Wom-Pal."

"You want help, no one helps!"

"I do, I know what things were like before the big war. First this is for you," and I threw in a deer steak.

He descended back into the swamp and was gone, two seconds later he quickly resurfaced like a bass and attacked the steak.

"I have a ship, Wom-Pal, I am trying to get back to stop everything that has happened to the planet so none of this exists."

He laughed, spit out some phlegm, and asked for more food. Tinzo gave me another steak and I threw it to him.

"What you want from Wom-Pal? And how will it make Wom-Pal people better?"

"You help me, Wom-Pal, together we can produce more food so everyone can eat. We should not be killing each other for it. And Wom-Pal, the one who runs the compound is from another planet who are trying to make all of us food for his kind that are trying to rule."

"You are a liar!" Trammer screamed out.

"No, Trammer, sorry for you but you have been lied to! The Giver will kill you both for this!"

"No, he won't, Trammer," Tinzo replied. "Because today, Trammer, your life is over!"

Wom-Pal asked, "What you want me to do?"

"Fight, Wom-Pal, with everyone you have!"

"Wom-Pal can see the beast that run at night, very bad and kills Wom-Pal's friends!"

"Bite them first, Wom-Pal, your bites will make them sick, you can feed on them and help us escape! Not tonight, Wom-Pal, but can you get everyone you have to arise at dark and attack the compound the next night."

"Why Wom-Pal trust you?"

"I need your help badly to save all of us, and I am giving you the food in a peace offering that I know you need so badly!"

"Wom-Pal like food but we need to be close, come in the water with Wom-Pal to be in trust with Wom-Pal!"

"No, Marco, do not do it," Tinzo replied.

"Wom-Pal, I trust you to keep your word." I threw my weapons to the shore.

"Come to Wom-Pal and friends."

I slowly walked into the muck, they gathered around me growling and hissing. Wom-Pal drew closer, his face was in front of mine. Wom-Pal's tongue licked my forehead with his long slimy tongue.

"Wom-Pal likes you. Wom-Pal will give you a chance."

"So you like me, Wom-Pal?"

"You leave in peace, Marco, for now, Wom-Pal is good!"

I walked out of the marsh covered in slime and followed by the rest of the mud people.

"Thank you, Wom-Pal, not tonight, but the next night attack the beasts of the night with everyone you have, please."

"Wom-Pal will, where is Wom-Pal's food?"

"Bring him to me, Tinzo!"

"Yes, sir!"

"No, no, you can't stop, I am sorry, no, do not do this to me!"

"Sorry, my friend, you are on the wrong side of history!"

"Wom-Pal loves the smell of live meat. Wom-Pal and others eat good now!"

"Indeed you will!"

I dragged him to the bank. They quickly swarmed him, bit him, and disappeared into the swamp!

"How was that, Tinzo?"

"Good job, Marco, I will inform the guards Trammer was killed by mud people in a surprise attack."

"Good, let's get back, revolution day has begun."

After work I decided I was going to stay at Ellis' house for the night. She met me at the door with open arms and lots of love.

"Ellis, I want to let you know things are about to quickly change around here and hopefully the world as well."

On my way home it was getting dark quickly and I could not wait to tell Lenetta the news, that she did not have to live in fear anymore. The closer I got to the house, I could see the door was hanging off by its hinges. I ran as fast as I could up the steps, sword out, yelling her name! I went yelling from room to room, searching! I ran into the kitchen and there were three guards leaning against the counter.

"Where is my wife!"

"Not here, Tinzo, put down your weapon!"

"No, where is she!"

"You, Tinzo, are under arrest for conspiracy against our leader!"

"No, I am not, and where is my wife!"

"She is being held as a prisoner by the Giver, guarded by his elite forces. You really screwed up, Tinzo, and sad for you but you're going to have to pay. Now it is time to take you in."

"It's dark, no, the Ag-Wazs are out! Not this time, let's go!"

"Put your weapons on the ground, we do not want problems, think about your wife's safety, Tinzo!"

I put my sword and my knife on the ground, dropped to my knees, and put my hands behind my head. I was rapidly swarmed and tied up. The picked me up and shoved me around the streets of the compound. We arrived at a building, it was so dark and my eyes had not adapted yet, so I was a little confused of where we were. They pushed me forward and I was led to a holding cell, and they shoved me in.

"We will be back for you when the time comes."

An hour went by and they returned to my cell.

"Alright, Tinzo, time to go, let's go see your wife."

"Is she okay?"

"She is, Tinzo, the Giver is not a mean person, you know that."

They grabbed me up from the floor and took me out of the cell. One of the guards put a hood over my head and we began walking.

"Where are you taking me?"

"We already told you, Tinzo, to see your wife, just shut up for now, I am tired of all your damn questions!"

We were outside of the compound and were walking into another building. They escorted me up two flights of steps and we came to a sudden stop. The hood came off and in front of me was the Giver, Lenetta, and the two elite guards from his planet. I yelled out to Lenetta but she would not speak, she was very drugged.

The Giver turned to the three guards. "You have done well, my loyal servants, you can go now and enjoy your evening, I will take it from here."

"Thank you, Giver, goodnight," and they exited the building.

"Tinzo, what am I supposed to do with you?"

I could not speak, I was in shock.

"You I trusted and you have really screwed up badly. I am a Giver, not a Taker, yet you put me in a bad predicament! Now I have to make a choice, what to do? You know, Tinzo, what you have done, you are smart and so am I. You had everything, Tinzo, why would you screw that up, especially over a lie? I thought even you were smarter than to fall for a lie, Tinzo. Your wife spilled her guts tonight, admitting there was a conspiracy against me and that you and Marco were planning an escape. Is that true, Tinzo?"

"No, she must have been just scared and told you what you wanted to hear."

"Interesting answer, but she was under medication that made her tell the truth. So that is your first lie tonight. The one thing she was honest about was she did not know how the escape would be conducted. I also know that Ellis is in on this as well, and that is a real shame, I really liked her but Marco poisoned her mind just like he did yours, and for that there must be justice!"

"What justice is that, Giver?"

"Your choice, Tinzo. You can tell me the plans to escape since apparently you and Marco are such good friends. Or you can make the choice on who dies, you or your wife!"

"I do not know of any plans, Giver, I don't!"

"I thought you would say that. So choose, Tinzo, which one shall die so the other can live? I asked you a question, Tinzo, what is your answer?"

"Kill me, Giver, Lenetta is innocent!"

"Once again I figured that would be your answer, but it cannot be that easy, I am afraid. I own you, Tinzo, and Marco and everyone on this compound and yes, you will all be food!"

The Giver's elite guards began to make strange noises. I assumed they were laughing at me.

"You were loyal to me. I could have spared some of you, but now you have to pay." The Giver yelled out, "Turn on the blacklights."

We were above the Ag-Wazs and they were ready to leave their enclosure, all of them pacing and growling, full of anxiety. The two guards grabbed me, they were so strong I could not move.

The Giver turned to me and said, "This is for your unloyalty!"

The Giver dropped Lenetta into the pit and instantly she was swarmed by the Ag-Wazs. I saw her being torn apart, and they held my face so I had to watch. I began to vomit and screamed out in sadness, they released me and I dropped to my knees. Puke was rolling down my face when he grabbed me by the cheeks.

"Look me in the face, Tinzo!"

I slowly lifted my head.

"You brought this upon yourself with your friend Marco, I will deal with the rest of them later. You are mine, Tinzo, I won't kill you but you will wish for death soon enough, if you want to redeem yourself you will figure out what he is up to by tomorrow or I will kill all of you! I do not usually give second chances, but you know we go way back. You sleep on it tonight, you have work to do tomorrow."

I could not speak, I was just there, mentally and emotionally broken.

"Take him back to his cell!"

"The attack will start tomorrow night, Ellis."

"Really, how, no one gets out at night?"

"The mud people have made a deal with Tinzo and they are going to start the attack first on the Ag-Wazs."

"Really?"

"Yes, they are and then when hell breaks loose we will go from there. Just be prepared, Ellis, when it starts you can come with us."

"I do, Marco, I really do, but get your rest, sounds like things could get crazy. Marco, no wonder I love you so much."

"Why is that, Ellis?"

"You are a very caring person who loves life."

"That is me, Mr. Compassionate," and we both began to laugh.

"Where the hell is Marco?"

"Not sure, Samarra, but my guess would be at Ellis' house."

"Well, we need to know what the hell we are doing, I am starting to get sketched out."

"Relax, he will let us know, we just have to be prepared, things will be fine."

"You are my rock, Daniel, but I swear I want to kick Marco's ass."

"Hush up, girl, give me some loving and less talking."

"Humm, I like that aggressive side of you, it turns me on, bad boy."

Both of us began to laugh.

"So when we get back am I going to be the baby's daddy?"

"Only if you want the job?"

"Well, I am giving you my application, if that is alright with you?"

She smiled at me and we kissed.

Morning came very quickly, and I headed out for breakfast but today I did not see Tinzo anywhere. It made me a little nervous, but he probably overslept or had something else to tend to. I rode on my four-wheeler and headed out towards the fields. Daniel signaled for me. I rode out to him and picked up his bag, left him another with a surprise in it, we did not speak and I moved on. I rode back to the compound and went over to the main kitchen area.

"Anyone have any security concerns or issues today?"

"No, sir, we are all fine, thanks for asking."

I brought in a bag of goods from the field, in the bag was a ten-inch stick whittled down with a sharp point at the end. Samarra took the bag with a smile and we moved on. The day was going quickly and it was lunchtime. I headed back to the compound and Tinzo was in line.

"Hey, buddy, where were you this morning?"

"Overslept!"

"Are you okay, you look horrible, are you sick?"

"No, leave me the fuck alone, Marco!"

He was very loud and annoyed acting.

"Hey, man, what is wrong, you can talk to me?"

He left without a word so fast, I tried to catch up with him but he was gone. It was time to go back and work in the fields. I saw Tinzo in the south fields monitoring things. I drove over to him. I was worried about him, something was not right.

"Hey, Tinzo, I am sorry if I am bothering you, but something's wrong, you're not yourself."

"Just great, Marco, and you!"

His voice was angry, his face was swollen, and I could see tears in his eyes.

"Can we talk freely, Tinzo?"

"About what, Marco, what the fuck do you want from me now!"

"Tinzo, hey, man, I am your friend."

"No, you're not, Marco, you just fucked me every way a person can."

"What, hey, what are you talking about?"

"You killed my wife, mother fucker!"

He came after me with a knife, very pissed off with vengeance in his eyes.

"Stop, Tinzo, no!"

He flung his arm at me with the knife in it. I grabbed his arms, we both struggled and went down on the ground, rolling around. The workers in the field stopped and watched the show. He rolled on top of me, trying to push the knife into my head.

"Don't do this, Tinzo, I beg you."

I used my right hand and dug out his eye sockets with my fingers. He eased up a bit and I slammed my right hand into his head. He fell over to the side but quickly got back up and ran at me full speed. I did a leg sweep on him, tripping him up, he fell to the ground and the knife went flying off in front of him. I jumped on him and put him in a submissive chokehold.

"Ease down, Tinzo, I am your friend, I will not hurt you but you have to stop fighting me."

He kept on struggling and I had to tighten my grip.

"Dammit, Tinzo, we are friends, stop it!"

He began to ease up and then he broke down completely and began to cry so hard he just went limp. He was a man severely and emotionally destroyed on the inside.

"What happened, Tinzo, please tell me, I am here for you."

Eventually he began to speak a few words at a time. "She is dead?"

"Who, Tinzo?"

"Lenetta."

"Who killed her, Tinzo?"

"Giver, the Giver."

"What, why?"

"He knows about all of us now. He, he…."

"What, Tinzo?"

"He fed her to the Ag-Wazs and made me watch." He began to lose it again.

"Oh, God, Tinzo. Oh my God, I am so sorry, so sorry!"

I pulled him up to me and just held him, trying to give him some comfort as much as I could. Eventually he rolled over and stood up. He stuck out his hand, I grabbed his hand with mine, we shook and gave each other a hug.

He looked at me eye to eye. "So, Marco, what are we going to do now?"

"We are going to war and it starts now!"

Over It

"Okay, look, Tinzo, I am going down where we met Wom-Pal and get them to attack in huge numbers, all they have, we cannot afford to wait until tonight or we all will be dead! I want you to go tell Daniel the fight will start soon. Then go let Samarra know the same so she will be ready. Take Samarra to the workers' tool room and get the fire tool so she can cut the prisoner Raz free, but only do it when things get crazy. After I leave the mud people, I will come to the compound gates and tell the guards there is an uprising of mud people coming from the east side and we need everyone there ASAP. That will give the mud people plenty of time to get here since they are coming from the opposite direction. I will destroy the box that opens up the main compound doors so they cannot be shut. Are you up for this, Tinzo?"

"I am, I want revenge for Lenetta, someone has to pay!"

"You're a good man, Tinzo."

We hugged again and he took off towards the fields. I rode at full speed to get to Wom-Pal. I arrived, jumped off my bike, and stomped around the water's edge and threw sticks and rocks to draw attention. The water began to bubble and within minutes several of them emerged.

"I need help, tell Wom-Pal the war starts now. I know the sun is up but things have changed, he is going to kill us all! Please tell Wom-Pal to bring everyone he has to the fight, it starts now!"

They began to descend back into the swamp and I got back on my bike. I rode back at full speed and got back to the compound gates. I ordered the guards to go fight, that we had a major issue going on with more mud people than I had ever seen. They looked stunned. One of them yelled out, "We cannot abandon our posts, sir!"

"I am ordering you to! I am your captain, do as I say or all of you will be locked up, I will command the gate!"

They grabbed some horses and took off through the fields. I picked up a very heavy rock that was lying around, climbed up the stairs to the compound gate, and smashed the control panel. A couple of hard hits and I could see a little smoke and sparks, that should do it.

"Samarra, Samarra!"

"Hey, Tinzo, what's up with you?"

"Look, the escape is starting, Marco wants you to come with me and get the fire starter so you can cut the prisoner Raz free!"

"But he said not to unless the shit was hitting the fan?"

"Well, the shit is starting to fly, let's go now!"

"Samarra, where do you think you are going, it is not break time?"

"It is fine, the Giver wants to see her, I am escorting her there."

"Okay, Tinzo, how is Lenetta?"

"Good, thank you for asking, Janet, I will have her back soon."

"Not a problem, have a good day."

"You do the same."

We ran down the street to the workers' tool shed as quickly as we could. It was an odd feeling to me, the weather was not as hot as usual and no one around realized the shit was about to hit the fan. My mind raced just like it did when me and Lenetta were on our own, surviving from day to day. The world was here one day, then the next it was gone, maybe we could make it right this time.

"Stay out here, Samarra, and I will get it and be right back."

I sat outside of the tool room waiting on Tinzo. I was very nervous. I knew at that very moment it was for all or nothing no turning back. I began to think about Tanya and hoped if we succeeded this world would be nothing more than a bad dream.

Tinzo popped his head out. He had the fire starter and also a machete. That was great a knife and a machete, what could be better.

"What the hell is that, Tinzo?"

"It is called a sickle, for cutting large grass down, you can give it to Raz."

I got back on my four-wheeler and quickly drove down the streets of the compound, heading towards Ellis' house. I pulled up, jumped off my bike, and began yelling for her.

"Ellis, Ellis!"

She quickly flung open the door. "Yes, Marco, I am here, what is wrong, are you okay, I was just on my lunch break?"

"I am fine but the escape is starting, we need to go now, the Giver is on to us and Lenetta is dead."

"What, how, why, it can't be, Marco, it can't be true!"

"I am sorry, Ellis, it is true and the attack is starting, we need to go now!"

"I can't, Marco, I can't."

"What, what are you saying, you were the one asking me if you could go with us, so what is wrong?"

"I cannot explain it, Marco, I am so sorry, I can't."

"Why, do you not love me?"

"I do, Marco, so much, you have no idea, but you deserve better than me."

"What? What the hell are you saying, Ellis, I love you!"

"I know you do, Marco, and that is why I am staying, I do not deserve you."

"That is crazy talk, let's go!"

She became angry and in a stern voice started to shout. "No, Marco, I am not leaving, I deserve this, when you return find me, you know my name and I was a teacher, do what you must and please forgive me, Marco, and always remember this was real love and never forget that."

"I do and I will find you again, Ellis, I promise we will be together one way or another."

She began to cry, we hugged and kissed, she kept on asking for forgiveness over and over, I just ignored her and held her tight. I did not want to let go but I had to leave soon.

She pulled my head down to her and softly whispered into my ear, "Please find me, Marco, and forgive me, you must go now, it is dead line earth, go save it."

"I will find you, Ellis, I promise you, that shit is going to get bad, go inside and lock your doors and windows."

We looked at each other, deep into one another's eyes, and we began to kiss again. She pulled back slowly, held my hands, and looked deep into my soul.

"It is time for you to go now, Marco, you have a job to do."

"I know, I love you, Ellis, do not forget me."

"Never, you have changed my heart and soul in ways you will never understand. I am a better person now and thank you, Marco, I could never repay that."

I hopped on my bike and she called out my name.

"Marco, I was in California at the time, you will find me there."

I blew her a kiss and rode off on my bike, headed back to the compound gates when something got my attention. I stopped my bike and looked to my left at the wooden walkway by the street. I saw a very familiar face standing there. She was all in white and she shined like a diamond among the coal. It was Ada, she was smiling and then she began to speak.

With a great big smile on her face she looked at me and said, "The revolution has begun, Marco, now it is your turn to try and save all of humanity."

I tried to speak but I heard a lot of screams coming from all directions. I turned around, trying to find out where all the noise was coming from. I quickly turned back around to her to speak and she was gone.

I drove off and ran in to Tinzo and Samarra.

"It's time, Samarra, free Raz, we will stand by while you do it, I think the mud people are very close, I can hear a lot of screaming."

We got to Raz and he was begging us for help.

"I told you, Raz, I would, we need to work together."

A few quick burns and cuts and Raz was a free man.

"Look, Samarra, you and Raz take my bike and go find Josh, the leader of the tree people, tell him what is going on. Tell him to get all the fighters he can get together and meet us at Eve's. Raz can help tell the truth about the Giver to her. Tell Eve to have her defenses up, we may need her help to survive."

"You sure, Marco?"

"Yes, I am."

Raz grabbed my arm firmly. "I will not let you down, Marco."

"Thanks, Raz, and make sure you take care of our girl."

"With my life I will!"

They took off, leaving a dust cloud in the air.

Tinzo and I began running down the streets of the compound and eventually found Daniel.

"Where is Samarra?"

"She has left with Raz to inform Josh what is going on."

"What, you let her go with him!"

"Yes, Daniel, it will be okay."

"It better be, Marco, I will hold you personally accountable."

"Not now, Daniel, we don't have time for this shit!"

The screaming got louder and longer and there were many workers running for their lives back into the compound walls. All of us ran up to the compound gates to see what was coming. I could not believe my eyes, there were at least a thousand or more mud people coming this way. Now they were only yards away from the main gate and there were a few guards trying to shut the walls, but to their surprise it was broken. One of the elite guards came running out to see what was happening. He began to fight and with his speed and strength took many of them out. During his relentless attack he had been bitten and started to fall prey to the venom. He gradually collapsed and was swarmed, his biomechanical suit was ripped apart like a turtle shell, and he was eaten alive within minutes. It screamed in a high-pitch noise and all I could see was mud people covering his body like ants.

We heard an alarm go off, and we knew instantly what that meant! It was the alarm of the Ag-Wazs cage, they had been released. They were slow to come out into the light, but hearing the screams and panic got their killing instincts flowing.

"Um, Marco!"

"Yes, Daniel?"

"Turn around and look, we have major fucking problems now!"

Shit, now we could see them clearly, they were pissed and confused.

"Shit, Marco, what do we do?"

"Well, for just this minute be very still."

All at once the Ag-Wazs began to go into a frenzy, attacking and mauling people on the streets. It was horrible to watch and hear, there were a lot of innocent people dying. The hordes of mud people began to spill in like water through the main compound gates. The Ag-Wazs began to attack and the mud people filled the streets. It was a battle like no other. Mud people and Ag-Wazs fighting each other alongside residents of the compound, the death toll was rising quickly for all sides. The Ag-Wazs were relentless but the mud people's venom was starting to take effect. I fell to my knees and everything just went into slow motion. I watched Ag-Wazs biting heads off of mud people and ripping them in half with their jaws. Mud people in numbers overtaking Ag-Wazs and eating them alive. I heard a voice in the distance.

"Marco, get up, don't stop, the world needs you."

As I gazed into the horrific battle scene there she was again, Ada. I reached out my hand to her and I instantly snapped back into reality.

"Hey, let's go to the horse stables now and hope some are left so we can get the hell out of here!"

Our weapons were drawn. We quickly scurried through the streets, the mud people must have listened to Wom-Pal, they paid us no mind. A few minutes later we arrived at the stables.

"Daniel, grab a horse, let's go!"

"I don't know how to ride, Marco."

"Well, this will be a quick lesson, just get on!"

We mounted our horses.

"You ready, Daniel?"

"I guess, but when we get back I want a better contract!"

We began to laugh.

"No shit, buddy, let's get out of here."

We headed out of the stables and rode quickly to the main gate, and Daniel was having trouble controlling his horse. As we got to the main gate an Ag-Waz attacked Daniel's horse and threw him off. The Ag-Waz was about to pounce on Daniel when three mud people jumped on it and began to fight.

"Daniel, quick, grab my hand!"

He stood up, reached for me, and was instantly knocked down to the ground by an Ag-Waz and it was on top of him. I yelled out and distracted him for a bit. I jumped off my horse with my sword in hand. It snarled at me, mucus draining from its teeth and pissed off!

"Hey, fuck face, if you want it come get it!"

Its mouth opened wide and it crouched like it was going to jump. In that moment the Ag-Waz mouth shut, eyes closed, and fell over dead. I was in shock and disbelief. What had happened? I saw a very sharp spear-looking object shot out through its head and retracted quickly. I looked up and it was Wom-Pal. The sharp object had come from his mouth and was sucked back in like a frog.

"Thank you, Wom-Pal, thank you so much."

"You good, Marco, you help me people. We not this way from war, we this way from it!"

"Who, Wom-Pal?"

"Here, dis place no good!"

"You mean the Giver?"

"Yes, Wom-Pal no like, Wom-Pal want to kill him!"

"I know, Wom-Pal, I feel the same, please tell your people thank you so much, I am trying my best to fix things."

"I will, I will, now Wom-Pal must fight and kill, Wom-Pal will always love Marco."

I walked up to Wom-Pal and hugged him. I think it really surprised him that anyone would want to touch him. He might have not been all human since the war, but he still had a human's heart, I could feel it.

"Thank you, my friend, we are leaving, take care of yourself, Wom-Pal, see you in the future!"

"Wom-Pal go too, me need to fight!"

"Daniel, hop on, let's get the hell out of here!"

He reached for my hand and hopped aboard. We rode to the end of the fields and stopped to turn around for one last look. The screams continued but not as many as before, but the fight was still raging and I knew the death count would be high. I felt horrible inside about the amount of innocent lives that were being lost, but the good if we succeeded far outweighed what took place today. It was ironic to me that losing lives actually in the long run saved many more and then my thoughts turned to Ellis.

Raz and I drove hard through the fields and down many trails at full speed.

"Samarra, we should be there soon."

"I hope so, Raz. I still think it may be at least ten more miles, but I am not really sure."

Boom, time stood still, our bike flipped from underneath us and we both went flying and smashing into the ground. My face was covered in dirt, and I looked over and saw Raz slowly starting to move. I heard a bunch of laughing around us, but at this point I could not see anyone.

"What is that, some kind of mechanical horse?"

I got to my knees and yelled out, "What do you want!"

"That's my question, little lady, who are you two?"

"I am Samarra and that is Raz. We are looking for Josh, he is the leader of the tree people, he knows us."

"Well, maybe you are in luck, maybe we are a part of them."

"If you are, get us there quick, it means life and death for us all."

The two of us were put on the back of a cart and the horse took off. Time seemed to slow down but we were alive and thank God my baby wasn't hurt. We arrived at a camp and there were many people waiting.

Josh came out of the crowd. "Samarra, are you okay?"

"Yes and no, the shit has hit the fan at another compound. Josh, there is so much to tell you but I don't have time, we need to tell Eve everything and Marco and Daniel are in danger."

He looked over at Raz. "Why is this asshole with you and where is his murdering friend Brinn?"

"Brinn is dead, Josh." ,

"Good, could not have happened to a better fellow, maybe you will be next."

"No, Josh, he is okay, he sees the truth now, we brought him back to help us tell Eve what was really going on."

Raz dropped to his knees. "I am sorry, Josh, we were all lied to by a bunch of different people, when Eve finds out the truth all will be better, I promise, and we can come together for our better good."

"You better be telling me the truth, Raz, 'cause if not I will kill you myself and piss on your face!"

"I get it, Josh, I understand the trust issue but time is wasting. Josh, we need all of your best fighters and let's go to Eve's now, I will explain everything on the way."

"I trust you, Samarra, and I will get my men ready, just give me a little time."

I told Josh everything, he was in shock and maybe some disbelief, but whatever it was he got off his ass and got his shit going. All of us mounted up and started heading out to Eve's compound.

"I do not trust you, Raz!"

"Well, and you shouldn't, Josh, but I am here and hope from now on we can build up a trust."

"We will see but I doubt it!"

Daniel and I stood at the edge of the field, wondering what had happened to Tinzo. Neither one of us knew he was with us on the way to the stables and things were getting so crazy he was gone.

"He must have gotten separated from us, Marco, in the chaos."

"I'm sure he did. He is a brave, tough man. I am sure he can handle himself but we have to go, we have a world to save."

At full speed we took off on our horses.

I got detached from Marco and Daniel but it was no accident. I had my own mission in mind as well. If I were to have told them they would have just tried and stop me. The love of my life was dead and I had been living a lie under a secret killer. My heart could not bear the pain of it anymore. Her death loomed over my head and so did the lives of so many that the Giver was secretly taking and what he was planning for all of our futures. I just walked through the compound with chaos and death, not really watching out for my own safety. I had one thought and only one in my head, and that was to kill the Giver! I stumbled across another sword on the ground and picked it up, two is better than one. I walked in to an open door to one of the buildings and headed down the long hallway. There were people running up and down in sheer panic. I came into a t-shaped intersection and began to hear loud screaming. An Ag-Waz had gotten into the building and was attacking a woman. I took a left and then a sharp right and I was getting closer to the Giver, I could feel it. The big double doors were to my left. I opened three doors and there he sat, the Giver, with one of his elite guards beside him.

"Tinzo, thank goodness you are alive, you are very loyal and you will be rewarded!"

"Not today, Giver, I am not your slave anymore!"

"What are you saying?"

"Shut up, I am here for one reason!"

"And what would that be?"

"I am going to kill you!"

The elite guard started to come after me and the Giver yelled out, "Stop!"

The guard was eye to eye with me. Then I saw a weakness, better now than never, perfect timing. I slung my sword near its neck, which I was hoping what I had seen was a small enough area to hopefully penetrate the body. I was right, I felt my sword go deep and thick into what felt like mud. I heard loud squealing like a loctus making noise and it dropped down on its crooked legs. I pushed it in deeper and twisted my sword around and quickly pulled it out. The guard collapsed down fully and black thick liquid just poured out everywhere.

"Lucky yet impressive, Tinzo. How is your friend Marco doing these days?"

"I think dead, Giver, just like you are going to be shortly!"

"I did like you, Tinzo, and I was going to spare you when the takeover was in effect but now sadly like Lenetta and many more to come you are going to die!"

"That rule does not seem to apply to you, does it, Giver?"

"Of course not, my species has ruled many planets since life has begun and will continue. I do not mind telling you these things because you will be dead soon."

"Why, why does your species do this to others?"

"The simple answer is because we can and your species made it too easy for us by virtually destroying yourselves. Our takeover is about food planet conditions and our survival. Your goals were simply to destroy one another."

"No, you're wrong, Giver, our species wants to survive, not take over and kill!"

"So Tinzo, really, who is the worst species, us or you?"

"You because you could be helping and we could have helped you, but you chose to be self-centered and it is all about you and what you can take! Giver, you are a liar, you talk about peace working together but you used that to control the minds of the desperate and weak. Just to let you know, Giver, in my eyes you're nothing more than what we say on Earth is a fucking asshole!"

"How do you want to battle, Tinzo, sword on sword?"

"Not a problem, let's go, I am tired of talking!"

"By the way, Tinzo, I have five guards tracking your friends, he will never make it back to the past, I promise!"

Josh did a great job, he rounded up about twenty strong, able men who were ready to fight. I wished we had more but we would take it. They had bows, spears, and a lot of knives with bone handles. Some of them rode on horses, others just ran quickly on foot, but we were on our way to Eve's and I was hoping this would work out. Raz kept assuring me that once he talked to Eve all would be okay, but I was stilled worried. She wanted to kill us and she tried. I did not know if I could ever trust her. Josh was still skeptical of Raz and I did not blame him at all. As we rode I kept noticing he had an eye on him constantly. As we rode I kept hoping that we could reach Eve in time and help Marco with the escape. I was also scared and worried about my Daniel.

"How much longer, Raz?"

"Not really sure, Samarra, should not be much longer, just keep going."

Daniel and I were on the move. Time was precious and we needed to escape as soon as we could. We headed out into the unknown but we knew we were being followed by the Giver's people.

"No matter what, Daniel, keep going!"

"Not a problem, it is getting dark and who wants to be out here at night? Marco, you hear that?"

"What?"

"Stop and listen."

We stopped the horses and heard the sound of engines.

"Shit, they're on bikes, let's go!"

We kicked the horses and they took off at full speed!

I had both of my swords out crossing each other in front of me. The Giver reached to his side and pulled off a small black object. He laid it in the palm of his hand and it began to expand piece by piece until it unfolded in to a full-length sword.

"You will be no match for me, Tinzo, my skills and sword are too much for you or anyone! You may as well just kneel and let me kill you now."

"Not a chance, Giver, my species bows down to no one, especially a freak of nature such as yourself!"

I ran towards him one sword out front and one behind me ready to strike! We collided our swords and the sparks flew. We exchanged blows in almost a rhythmic dance, one blow after another, and then we met sword to sword and pinned each other. His mouth opened and a small eel-looking head popped out full of teeth. Them Marco came to mind. I swept his leg out from underneath him. He fell to the ground and I slung my sword down quickly and slashed the small head of whatever the hell it was that came from his mouth. He grabbed his face with one arm and blocked his head with the other. I slung down my sword on his arm and my sword broke in half. His other arm flew up, which extended a small razor on it and it caught my forehead and he raked it down my face. I stumbled backwards and fell to the ground with my last sword in hand. I grabbed my face and it was full of blood. I stood up with my sword in combat ready position. The Giver sword in hand looked at me.

"You will die a slow death for that, Tinzo, I assure you that!" His voice was muffled, it must have been part of his tongue I cut off.

"Better to die slow, Giver, than to die under your control!"

He let out a screech unlike anything I have ever heard before and he ran towards me with his sword up. Once again we collided into hand-to-hand combat and sparks were flying!

"Hey, guys, I think we are close, everything is starting to look familiar to me now."

"How far do you think, Raz?"

"Not sure, Samarra, but pretty damn close!"

"You heard the man, full speed ahead!"

Ten minutes later Raz came to a stop.

"What is wrong, Raz?"

"Nothing, it is hard to see from here but you see the outline in the distance?"

"Kinda, but is starting to get pretty dark."

"I know but that is it, maybe a mile or so. Hey, Josh, are you good and ready?"

He looked at Raz. "Yes, I have been ready, let's do this, I am getting impatient!"

"Hey, Daniel, they are getting closer!"

"No shit, Marco, but it should not be much further! If we keep this pace up it may be close, though."

"I am up for suggestions, Daniel, if you have any?"

"Well, let's hope we have backup when we get to Eve's!"

"Now I feel much better, thanks, Daniel."

"Anytime, you know that is what I am here for."

In a few hundred yards we saw human-looking figures blocking our path, we quickly came to a halt! A man moved forward with a large club in hand.

"Get off your horses and give us everything you have, including the horse!" The man quickly turned around and heard the engines of the motor bikes quickly approaching. "What is that noise?"

"Death is coming for you and me and everyone else! Let us go and you best leave as well or you will die also!"

"This is our road, no one leaves and your stuff is mine!"

I slammed my sword into his head and kicked the horse into high gear, we broke the line and fled quickly!

"That may help us, Marco."

"I agree, let the assholes kill the assholes!"

Raz lifted up his hand and crumbled his fist. "We are here, let's go!"

I was nervous and I could tell Josh was as well, but we did have Raz and a small army behind us, that made me feel a little better! Raz made a strange combination knock on the door and it slowly began to open. The door opened and there were many soldiers on the other side. They became defensive and so did our soldiers!

Raz stood up and yelled, "Stop! Wait, tell Eve Raz is here in good faith, we need her help! And please, at ease with your weapons, we are here in peace!"

Two guards left to inform Eve.

Knock, knock.

"What is it!"

"Madam Eve, Raz has returned with others, they are armed and he wants to talk to you, they are in the compound."

"What! Who is with him?"

"I do not know."

"You idiots, why did you let them in!"

"Raz said it was important and he needed your help!"

"I am on my way!"

The Giver and I were exchanging blows and I knew I could not penetrate his skin. I was getting tired physically and mentally.

"You give up, Tinzo?"

"Never, only death gives me the right to give up!"

"Then death shall you receive, weak species!"

Our swords collided once again. I was tired and losing focus. I had flashbacks of my Lenetta! I could hear the slamming of the swords but my visions were of her and the love that we had shared over the years. Then reality hit hard. I felt the Giver's sword penetrate my left shoulder and I went down in pain and fatigue from the loss of blood.

He stood over top of me and laughed. "I told you, Tinzo, you were no match and you were going to die!"

"So do not waste any more time and do it, freak!"

"Not with my sword, Tinzo. I will use your friend's weapon we took off of the assassins!"

He pulled it out and aimed at me. I closed my eyes, waiting for the final blow, when the double doors exploded open. It was an Ag-Waz that entered the room! It saw the Giver and headed straight for him in attack mode. It pounced on the Giver and the fight began. I was weak but I could hear Lenetta's voice in my head telling me to get up. I did slowly losing my balance but got myself outside the doors. I could smell smoke coming from somewhere on the compound, lots of screaming and terror filled the air. I dragged myself down the hallway gripping to the wall and found an empty room, walked in, locked the door, and collapsed to the ground.

Eve came stomping down the hallway to the main entry. "Raz, what in the fuck is going on here, answer me!"

"Eve, listen, Brinn was killed, I was taken prisoner! There is a compound of people that are being ruled from something that is not from this planet, he calls himself the Giver! He is harvesting humans and plans on bringing others like him to take control of what is left of this planet. He wants to enslave everyone, Eve, we are all in a lot of danger! Marco and his people saved me, I was in chains and they know I was sent to kill them."

"Damn you, Raz, are you lying?" as she grabbed his face.

"No, he is not, Eve, you know I do not like you or Raz! What he is saying is the truth, Eve, that is the only reason I am here. We have differences, Eve, on how we think but the bottom line is for you and I and everyone else no matter how bad our decisions have been in the past we cannot allow a creature like this to run the planet. Think about it, Eve, we all are victims, it is time we fight together and save what we have, we can work the rest out later but time is short."

"Raz, is what is being said true?"

"It is, my queen, I would not lie to you." Raz looked at Josh and asked, "Can you please drop your weapons?"

Josh stared back at him. "In good faith, Raz, we will but do not let us down!"

"You have my word!"

All of Josh's fighters dropped their weapons and Eve broke down crying.

Eve cleared her face. "Pick your weapons up, we fight for all of mankind, what do we need to do? Samarra, come talk to me, please."

"Sure thing, let's talk."

"Samarra, what is it we need to do?"

"As we speak Marco and Daniel are on their way here, trying to escape, and I am sure there are the Giver's people chasing them. I do not know how many there will be but we need to be ready to help with his escape and defend this place as well."

"Which direction would Marco and Daniel be coming back this way?"

"From the way we sent you three in, they should be exciting toward the back of the compound."

"Eve, can you get your troops ready, they could be here anytime?"

"I can and I will."

I went back to talk to Raz and Josh. "Look, guys, Eve is getting her soldiers ready, she said they should be coming here from the back of the compound, so let's get our people ready, they could be here anytime."

Raz led us to the back of the compound and out the doors. I heard a horn blowing very loudly coming from the compound.

"What is that, Raz?"

"It is a warning for our compound that there could be trouble."

All the soldiers were in lines and Raz, Josh, and I stood in the front. Running out of the compound came between fifty to seventy of Eve's soldiers that fell in line behind us. Eve walked out with an axe in hand and came to the front of the line. She stuck her hand up into the air and brought it down for the crowd to be silent.

"Tonight is the night I ask all of you to look at one another. We are all different in many ways with the exception of one! We are all humans! We do not know how many of them there are. But this I do know. We are going to fight and we are going to win!"

The soldiers all yelled while shaking their weapons in the air.

"Shit, Marco, they are right on our asses!"

"I can hear it, believe me, but it looks like there is a clearing ahead, we may almost be there, I see fire."

"Yeah, or it could just be a bunch of crazies too! Hold on, Daniel, almost to the clearing."

We broke through the woods and hell yes, we could see Eve's compound! Thank God. I could see Samarra and Raz jumping up in down with excitement.

"How many are coming, Marco?"

"Only four I think, Eve, they are on motor bikes, you can hear the engines, most of the guards are all dead, it was a wicked fight at the compound."

The four guards came shooting out of the woods on their bikes and stopped ten feet away from us when they saw all the fighters. One of them got off his bike and slowly approached us.

"Give us the prisoners and we will let you live!"

"No, that is not going to happen!"

"And who are you, woman!"

"I am Eve, the leader of this compound, and you are?"

"None of your concern, hand over the prisoners!"

"There are no prisoners here!"

"If you do not the Giver will become the Taker and you will all be sorry, I promise!"

"You tell your Giver his law and obsession with running a new planet does not exist here or be tolerated!" He began to speak and was quickly silenced by the loud explosion in the sky.

Everyone looked at the sky after the incredible boom, and hovering above the treetops was a bright green light that was hard to look at. It sat there for fifteen seconds and shot off like a rocket towards the stars and disappeared. Everyone was in shock and disbelief of what they had seen.

Eve took a few steps toward them. "It appears that your master has left you and like him you should leave before I have you killed!"

None of them said a word, they hopped back up on their bikes and took off back into the dumping grounds. Everyone was yelling and chanting with excitement.

The Sun Will Rise

The next morning I woke up hurting badly. I could hardly move my arm and even walk for that matter. I opened the door and slowly walked out, being cautious of not knowing what was still going on. I walked through several doors until I reached the streets of the compound. The sun was bright and it was taking my eyes awhile to adjust. When they did I wish I could have taken it back. There was stragglers crying over loved ones and friends, some people just sobbing over what had just happened, not being able to wrap their minds around it. The streets were full of dead people Ag-Wazs and mud people as well. I just kept walking, it was like being in a nightmare I could not wake up from. I was hurting really bad and just fell down beside one of the buildings to rest. I pulled up my knees and rested my head there and began to cry about Lenetta and all the death surrounding me. Many people were dead that should have not had to die this way, I was sick to my stomach. And then I heard a voice.

"Tinzo, Tinzo, is that you?"

I looked up and it was Ellis and I put my head back down and continued to cry.

"Come on, Tinzo, I am taking you back home with me, we need to get you fixed up, okay? Come on now, let's go."

She helped me walk back to her place. She threw some blankets on the floor and I lay down. I kept going in and out of consciousness. I know she was cleaning my wounds. I kept waking up every time she touched them. Finally I woke up for a bit.

"Here, Tinzo, you need to drink some water, please do not fight it, just do it, okay?"

I looked at her. "I thought you were escaping with Marco?"

"No, he told me it was too dangerous, that he did not want to risk it, but he would find me when he got back. I told him where I was."

"Did Marco make it, did he?"

"Not sure, I think so but things got crazy really quickly. I hope he did."

"Me too."

"You rest now, Tinzo, you need a lot of it. I will take care of you now, okay?"

"Thank you, Ellis."

"Not a problem. That is what friends do for each other, you know."

"Yes, they do," and I was out again.

The sun was bright and beautiful that day, it was time for us to leave and try and figure all of this shit out. I walked out the room and walked outside the compound. I looked up at the sky with high hopes for the future.

"What are you looking at, time traveler?"

I turned around and it was Eve. "Just thinking and remembering how wonderful the world can really be and hoping there is a chance to save it."

"I like that thought myself, Marco. I dream about it all the time. You know, Marco, when all of this went to shit you know what I was doing?"

"Please tell, I can't imagine."

She began to laugh. "I was barely nineteen years old."

"You were that age once?"

"Believe it or not I really was. I was on my way to Seattle to try and make it big as a rock star."

"Really?"

"Oh, yes, I could sing and play guitar," she began to laugh. "I got there and actually was doing really well, no big contract yet but I was making it. Then it was all over, my life and the planet and everything about it was gone. What was normal and what I took for granted was gone and it changed me forever! Marco, if you can fix it do it! You just remember to tell them you cannot live and trust technology completely, this is the aftermath, do not put one thing in control of all, it does not work!"

"I understand your point, Eve, and I will. By the way, thank you for helping us last night."

"No, I thank you three. Oh, yeah, Marco?"

"What is it?"

"Sorry for trying to kill you, but it is what it is, am I right?" She smirked and laughed.

"We are good, Eve."

"Good, I will see you three off."

"Oh, by the way, Eve."

"What do you want, Marco?"

"Send a search party to the other compound, a lot of innocent people may be hurt, help them if you can."

"We have already planned it."

"Good, and if you can find a man named Tinzo, if he is still alive, and tell him thank you for me. He is a great man, Eve, and someone you can rely on."

"I will keep that in mind, Marco, and thank you. By the way, Marco, my real name is Trina, not many people know that."

All of Eve's people walked us out to the ship. I placed my hand on the control box and the door slid open. Daniel and Samarra waved to the crowd and they climbed aboard the ship. I turned around and thanked Eve again. She had tears rolling down her cheeks.

I grabbed her and gave her a hug. "The only thing that will stop me, Eve, from fixing this is death, I promise."

"I have full trust in you, Marco, and your word, please don't let us down. I know and I hope to see you in the future or the past, whenever it is." She began to laugh.

I waved at everyone, gave a big thumbs-up to Josh, and climbed aboard the ship. All of us began to check our computers and instruments for the trip back home.

"Marco?"

"Yes?"

"Where is Ellis? I just remembered she is not with you, what happened?"

"She would not come, Samarra."

"Why?"

"I really don't know, she said to find her when I got back. Is everyone ready to go?"

"You just say the word, Captain, we are just waiting on you."

"On the count of three let's do this. One, two, three, begin launch!"

"Yes sir, Captain."

Samarra took us up into the atmosphere and we broke through the Earth's gravitational field.

"Good job, girl, you guys ready for a rough ride?"

"Yes, sir!"

"Daniel, how long until we hit the first hole?"

"Twenty-two minutes, sir."

"Wonderful, relax but stay prepared, no screwups, let's just get home."

As we sat there waiting to reach the first hole it dawned on me all of a sudden what Eve had said, that her real name was Trina. It could not be. I remembered the foul-mouthed young girl on the plane heading to Seattle to become a rock star and I swear she said her name was Trina. Could it have been her or just a coincidence, I did not really know but it had my mind racing in circles.

My train of thought was broken up when Daniel yelled out, "We have arrived at the first hole, Captain."

"Thanks, Daniel. You two ready back there?"

"Yes, sir!"

"On my mark, Samarra, lead us in. Three, two, one."

"Igniting rockets, sir, hold on tight."

Boom, boom, boom, flashes of light led to darkness.

"Good morning, Eve."

"Well, good morning to you, Radan, hope you slept well, you will need all of your energy today."

"Thank you, I did, Eve, and I have the men ready to go when you are."

"Excellent, just remember if they are hostile we will fight but I want to help these people and find this guy Tinzo Marco talked about, if he even survived."

"I have briefed the men on your orders and they fully understand their jobs."

"It is better, Radan, if they trust us, we could be stronger together because you know this Giver will try and come back."

"He may try, Eve, but we are not going to allow that to happen."

"Thank you, Radan, for your understanding."

"We are ready to go, Eve, just let us know."

"Okay, I will be out shortly and we'll go."

We traveled for a half a day until we could see the compound, probably a half a mile away. Little resistance on the way here but our numbers of fighters made others think twice before trying something stupid. It was sad the things I saw, people in the fields acting like wild animals. You really never got used to it, how could you if you still had compassion for human life? I watched two crazy and hungry men capturing a grazier, dragging it off into the woods to be skinned and eaten. In my mind and heart I was hoping Marco would succeed and that none of this would ever be reality.

We arrived at the main gates of the compound and there were many people walking around in a state of confusion and sadness. You could tell some of them were scared when they saw our weapons and others had no fight left to care. Many bodies of all kinds were in piles being burned in the field. The smell was unbearable and it was a visual I would never be able to forget no matter how many lifetimes I could live. We gathered in to the streets of the compound and I asked everyone if they could please gather around, I needed to speak to everyone who would listen.

We came out of the hole and all of us began to wake up. I was pouring sweat like crazy and my throat was very dry and sore.

"Damn, I hate going through holes!"

Daniel yelled out, "I second that, not my favorite."

"Samarra, are you okay?"

"Nope, got to puke, sorry."

We could hear the violent throwing up, then the smell hit.

"Sorry, I do not think the baby likes the ride."

"It's okay, Samarra, hang in there, you can do this."

"Yeah, well, Marco, I am not a toddler."

"Daniel, how long for the second hole entry?"

"About eighteen minutes, sir."

"Okay, guys, relax, we have to do this two more times and then we are homebound."

We all celebrated the thought of going home but it was more complicated than that.

"Marco, it is time."

"You know the drill, Samarra, on my mark. Three, two, one."

Boom, boom, boom.

We took off but this time there was a loud bang and the sound of crunching metal and the smell of smoke and then I passed out.

Many people gathered around us I decided it was time to address the crowd.

"Hello, everyone, my name is Eve and I am here in peace. I have a compound not very far from here, we are a peaceful compound and we are offering peace and security to you. Your leader was unknown to me until now and I know that he had plans to bring his people here and occupy this planet. All of you are welcome to come back with us to our compound. If not we offer you our help to rebuild back what you once had until you get a leader of your own."

The crowd began chatting among themselves. Some people were begging to come back with us and others shouting at us, saying, "What the hell do you really want!"

"Let me tell all of you what I want. I want you to all live and live free. I want all of you to have choices in your lives. I want you to have a great leader who is kind and compassionate, not like your last, who was a murderer and liar. I do not want to be your leader but I do want to help you if you need it. It is time for the human race to rebuild instead of tearing each other apart! We may have differences but that is what makes us humans and it makes us great! Does anyone know of a man here named Tinzo? Step forward, Tinzo, please."

A woman helped him walk to me, he was in pretty bad shape.

"What do you want from me, Eve?"

"Nothing more than to shake your hand. I am a friend of Marco's."

He and the woman were in shock, the woman began to cry and he began to become unstable on his feet. I helped grabbed him.

"Tinzo, are you okay?"

"I am, did Marco make it?"

"He did and they are on their way back. Tinzo, Marco talked very highly of you and I think you should be the leader of this compound."

Tinzo turned to the people and yelled out to them, "What do all of you think!"

The crowd began to scream and yell out his name.

"It is settled, Tinzo, let us work together and fix your compound."

He gave me a hug. "Thank you, Eve."

"It is all about us humans now, Tinzo, let's grow together and live in peace as it should always have been."

"We can and we will. I hope Marco survives the trip home."

"So do I but in the event he doesn't this is a great backup plan for the future."

"I agree."

"Raz?"

"Yes, Eve?"

"Take Tinzo and get him some good medical treatment before infection starts setting in."

"Yes, ma'am, I am on it."

"Thank you, Raz."

The crowd and our group began to mingle and had all kinds of talks about what had happened, the future and just meeting new people.

We came out of the second hole and all of us were in bad shape. Alarms were going off and I could still smell smoke. Our ride was much rougher than usual, if you could believe that.

"Daniel, what is going on?"

"Not sure yet but we do have some structural damage."

"Samarra, Samarra!"

"What, Marco?"

"What is going on!"

"Give me a break, dick, I am trying to stabilize our flight pattern, we're all out of whack!"

"Marco!"

"Yes, Daniel?"

"We have structure damage to the right wing somehow!"

"What do we do, Samarra!"

"Send a distress call, Marco, as soon as we come out of the last hole I am going to have to manually try to fly this bitch in, there is no other choice!"

"Shit, everyone, get ready, we are not dying here, we have come way too far! We are the best in the force, let's light it up!"

"Yes, sir!"

"Time for the last hole, Marco!"

"Okay, Samarra, one last time, on my mark, three, two, one, get us home."

Boom, boom, boom!

"So who are you?"

"My name is Ellis."

"My name is Eve, once again it is nice to meet you. Did you know Marco?"

"I did, actually, he was my boyfriend for the short time he was here."

"Wow, did not know that, I am impressed he snuck some love in there with everything going on."

We both began to laugh.

"Yes, Eve, he is something else."

"So Ellis, what did you do here on the compound?"

"I was a schoolteacher. He left enough children here to teach, gave the appearance that he cared for young humans. The sad thing is, Eve, he took a lot of children away that never came back. I do not want to even imagine what he did with them."

"Took them where, Ellis?"

"Back to his home planet, wherever that is. I would see one of his ships take off in the middle of the night and people would go missing."

"That is awful, Ellis, but things are going to change and he will not ever rule again, I promise! I think Tinzo will be a good leader for this compound, Marco really liked him."

"Okay, Tinzo, lay on the table for me, we have to clean you up, especially that shoulder so you do not get an infection."

"Okay, Raz, give me a second, I am really hurting."

"That is okay, take your time, my friend, we have plenty of it. Alright, let me help you get your shirt off so I can clean your wounds."

"Ahh, shit!"

"I know, I am sorry, it is a nasty wound, what happened?"

"The Giver's sword caught me but the joke's on him, he didn't kill me."

"That is amazing, Tinzo, you fought an alien and live to tell about it, great campfire story."

"Yeah, you could say that," and I began to laugh.

"Don't look at your wounds, just focus on me, okay? These will be some great stories you can tell your grandkids one day."

"That won't be possible, I am afraid now."

"Why you say that, Tinzo?"

"The Giver killed my wife in front of me."

"I am sorry, please forgive me, I didn't know."

"It just happened two days before the battle at the compound."

"You have been through so much, I am overwhelmed of how well you are doing."

"Thanks, I just keep thinking of my wife, it is the only thing that keeps me going."

"So Raz, you have changed a lot from what you were. Marco was very adamant about freeing you to help with the cause."

"I have, I lost my friend Brinn when we arrived at your compound, as you know."

"I do and I am sorry about that."

"Me too, he was not very smart but had a heart of gold and I considered him my brother."

"I understand that feeling."

"Are you ready to be a ruler now, Tinzo?"

"I am, I want what is best for the compound and bring back a normal life to everyone."

"It sounds like you could actually pull it off."

"Well, I will try the best I can, it will not be easy, Raz. I have a question to ask you."

"Fire away, what is it?"

"How would you like to be my second-in-command? I mean, Eve has Radan working very closely with her, what if you were to stay here?"

"That is a very deep question, Tinzo, it just threw me for a loop. I am very honored you would even think of me in that way."

"Well, Raz, I have seen what you have done and in the time of need you have stepped up and shown leadership skills. Just the type of person I need to help me out. Raz, how would you think Eve would react if I brought it up to her?"

"Not really sure but she seems to be getting extra close recently with Radan, so who knows, she may not really care."

"Is it okay with you if I ask her then?"

"You are a leader now, Tinzo, it is your call, the worst she could say would be no."

"Very true, then it is settled."

"Not so fast, Tinzo, I have cleaned you up but I need to give you some pain meds. It is going to hurt, I have to give it to you in the wound but after that you will be thanking me." Raz filled up the syringe and tapped it on the side. "You ready, Tinzo?"

"I am, let's get this over with, I need some relief."

He pushed the needle in, instant extreme pain.

"Shit, shit, fuck, awwww!"

"Breathe, Tinzo, almost done. All done, Tinzo, you can relax now."

"Okay, thanks, Raz, that really hurt."

"I bet it did, my friend. You should feel some relief pretty soon."

"Wow, I can already feel it kicking in." I felt my face begin to sag and I could barely move my limbs.

"What is wrong, Raz?" I tried to shout out but the words never left my lips.

"Since you cannot really speak you are going to die soon. I just gave you three times amount of painkiller that you needed." At this point I was a total vegetable who could only hear my own thoughts. "You see, Tinzo, I was born to be an assassin, that is what I do. My goal and job in life is to kill and survive no matter how I have to do it. All of you should have left me to die, that was all your mistakes. I would never be your second, I am always first! I will control this compound, I am no one's number two, not even to Eve! Tinzo, it is time for you to see your wife again, you should be thankful!"

Raz pulled out another syringe, filled it up, and stuck it into Tinzo for the second time. Tinzo's eyes became wide open and he suffered a major heart attack.

"No one defies me ever and a little payback for Brinn. I will be the only leader of this compound, there will be no other choice!"

"Eve, Eve, help me, damnit, I need help now!"

Eve's guards came running.

"What is wrong, Raz?"

"I was cleaning up Tinzo and he started shaking like crazy and I think he is dead."

Eve and some more soldiers walked into the room and saw Tinzo had been cleaned but he was dead.

"So what did you do, Raz?"

"I cleaned him, gave him a shot of pain meds, and he started flipping out all over the table and then he just died."

Eve just looked around the room, you could tell she was upset. Eve bent down in front of Radan on her knees, looked up at him, and said, "You know what you have to do, so do it!"

He looked at her, turned around, and cut Raz' head off!

"Thank you, Radan, that is the one thing I like about you, besides being smart you can read my mind as well."

"My allegiance lies with you, Eve."

"I knew that Marco thought very highly of Tinzo and so did I, I was very sorry and upset that one of my own did that to him. We have a lot still to learn about human behavior and forgiveness. My friends, this is an example of that and things need to change. Raz was a product of his environment and bad upbringing, which now has led him to his death."

Ellis walked in through the door and saw Tinzo dead on the table and Raz' head lying on the floor next to his body.

"My God no, no! Why did this happen, why!"

Eve held Ellis and escorted her out of the room to comfort her.

All three of us woke up, alarms sounding off and the smell of smoke hovered the cockpit.

"Daniel, send out the distress call!"

"Already on it, Marco!"

"Samarra, how are you holding up?"

"I am trying, this is not going to be easy to do under the circumstances but I am trying!"

"Marco, distress call received, they are tracking our position now!"

"Good job, Daniel! Everyone, steady!"

"Fuck, Marco, we are coming in too damn fast, I don't know if I can guide us in! If we have any more damage I won't be able to control it anymore!"

The ship was creaking and banging and we were all terrified. Samarra was fighting as hard as she could to keep control of the ship. I could see real fear for the first time on her face.

"Daniel, how much time do we have before we arrive?"

"A little less than five minutes, sir! And just to let you know, we are headed straight for the Pacific Ocean!"

"Fuck! Any way, Samarra, of getting us to land?"

"Not a chance, Marco, sorry, I am barely hanging on!"

"Shit, we are going to have to use the escape pod! Set our course, Samarra, and everyone get to the escape pod now!"

Samarra set the course but the ride was so violent it was off track in seconds. All of us climbed into the escape pod and quickly strapped ourselves in.

"Daniel, how long do we have before we abort the ship?"

"Thirty seconds, sir, and I hope we have it!"

It was the longest thirty seconds of our lives. Daniel send us off! He hit the button, the thrust of our departure away from the ship was so rough we all blacked out. I awoke to the sound of mechanical noises, my body felt like someone took a club and beat me with it for a week straight. I heard moaning in the background.

"Daniel, Samarra, wake up!"

"Where are we, Marco?"

"I do not know, Daniel, but do you hear that? Something is outside."

Then the escape pod hit something very hard. The top of the pod opened and I could see light and faces staring down at us.

"Welcome home, strangers, is everyone okay?"

"Just get us the hell out of here, please!"

"Hey, Ellis, is it okay if I stay with you tonight?"

"Yes, please do, Eve, it will give us time to talk and I need someone. I am very scared right now and honestly very upset about everything."

"I understand that, Ellis. I will have Radan guard us tonight at your house, my other men will stay and help the people out until we can get some source of normalcy around here."

Later that evening I cooked a wonderful meal. Eve and I sat down at the table.

"Eve, what is Radan going to eat?"

"You know, I am not really sure, pretty rude of me, I guess. I will fix him a plate and give it to him."

"I am sure he would love that, Ellis, thank you for being so nice and thoughtful."

I fixed a plate for Radan and brought it to him, he was hanging out on my front porch.

"Hey, Radan, I am Ellis. I thought you may be hungry, so I brought you a plate to eat. I know you have to be hungry, it has been a long day."

"Thank you, Ellis, that means a lot, I am starving. You and Eve have good talks and do not worry, me and my men are watching everything."

"Thank you, Radan, I know you guys are, if you want more just let me know, there is plenty here."

"I certainly will, thanks again."

"So how was Radan?"

"He was very appreciative for the food, I know that."

We both began to laugh.

"Ellis, now that Tinzo is gone what do you think about running the compound?"

"Never thought about it really, Eve, why?"

"You are very smart, Ellis, and a good person, people would trust you and you would have their best interests at heart. I can see your potential."

"Maybe, Eve, but I am not worthy of such an honor and responsibility."

"Why do you feel this way, is it because you are a woman?"

"No, not at all, I have not always been a good person, Eve."

"Well, none of us were, look at me, I tried to have Marco and his friends killed since they arrived."

"Maybe so but nothing compares to what I have done, believe me."

We heard a big boom and the dark sky lit up like the sun just came out again.

Welcome Home, Children

We were pulled out of the pod and loaded up on stretchers. As we were carted off I could see everyone around us applauding and smiling. It was great to be back home but there was a lot of work to do and they had no clue what was about to happen. Every time I tried to talk they kept telling me to hush. I had been giving meds that were making me loopy. I kept going in and out of sleep. My God, I did need the sleep. I had a dream where I was sitting on a rock in the middle of nowhere. I felt a tap on my shoulder and I looked up. It was Ada. She was all in white again, blinding me by her light. She looked at me with that innocent smile.

"You have done well, Marco, but you know it is not over, you must keep going, time is very short."

"I know, Ada, help me, please!"

"I already have, Marco, just listen to my words. You must go on no matter what happens, you will be given a difficult choice but you will know what must be done to fix it. In your choice, Marco, do not follow your heart, just follow the facts, it will be a choice, either way you will have to bear for the rest of your days."

I woke up crying.

Ellis and I came running out to the porch.

"What the hell was that, Radan?"

Two balls of light came down behind the compound not too far away.

"Shit, Eve, he is back, it is the Giver and I am sure he has brought some friends with him."

"Radan, run to the compound and spread the word, be prepared, we are going to be under attack, go!"

The soldiers got into their battle positions with weapons in hand. Radan addressed the troops.

"Men, the Giver is back, he just landed close to the compound with at least two ships that I could see. We do not know how many of them there are but there is not many of us. Go inside, warn the citizens, tell them to pick up any weapons they can find, we all have to fight together! Have the women and children hide for safety! Get going, they could be here any minute!"

"Eve, what do we do?"

"Here, take one of my knives, you may need it. Ellis, do you have any secret hiding places in your home by chance?"

"I do!"

Ellis picked up a rug and revealed a trap door that went underground.

"Where does it go to, Ellis?"

"It leads to the outside of the compound, it is about two miles long."

"Let's get going then."

"Okay, but we need some light first, Eve, it will be too dark to see down there."

Ellis grabbed an old oil lamp and brought it to the door.

"Okay, Eve, we are ready."

"Great, Ellis, let's get the hell out of here, I need to get back and warn our compound and get more help!"

Eve and I climbed down the stairs and reached the ground floor. It was very dark cold and the air was very musky.

"It has been a long while since I had been down here, I almost forgot the tunnel was here until you jarred my memory."

In my thoughts I kept thinking to myself, Please, Marco, find me in your dawn of time. Both of us were shivering from the cold but we kept moving at a steady pace. All of us soldiers locked the doors and hunkered down, waiting for an attack we knew was going to happen, it was just a matter of time. I was ready for a fight, I had been trained under Eve's tutors since I was eighteen and my life was revolved on being a warrior and dying for my cause. Eve was like my mother that I had when the war took her away from me. I had no one, she took me in and gave me my new name, Radan. She told me then a new name starts a new life. Since then I have worked hard to move through the ranks. I did not know the Giver but what I did know was he was not going to rule over this planet if I had anything to do with it!

"Ellis, how much longer do you think we have until we get to the end?"

"Maybe half a mile to a mile, not really sure, but it should not be much longer."

"Why was this tunnel made from your house to the outside?"

"I do not know, it was already here when I was assigned the house. I did not even notice it until two years after I moved in. Why do you ask?"

"Just curious, it just seems odd, it's like an escape path or something. Do you know of any other tunnels on the compound?"

"Not that I am aware of, but who really knows."

All of us were ready and hunkered down for a fight, all was quiet and I did not like quiet, it usually meant the bad shit was on its way. I peeped out of the window and saw shadows of people slowly moving into the compound. I could not really make out what they looked like but I knew this was not going to be a friendly visit at all. I winked at one of the guards to warn them that someone was here. Several of them left to warn the others, if it was a fight they wanted they had come to the right place.

"I think we are getting close. I can see a light up ahead, let's keep moving, no time to waste."

I could not see anything but Ellis was leading the way.

Ellis turned around and grabbed me. "We are here, Eve, we are free!"

I was somewhat relieved but nervous also, it was a long way back to the compound in the dark and not much protection with just two knives. There was a door in front of us.

"Eve, help me kick it open."

We both kicked it several times but nothing happened.

"On the count of three, Ellis, kick it as hard as you can! One, two, three."

Bam, the door flew open and the room was revealed. In our presence was two guards and the Giver!

"Long time, Ellis, where have you been, my dear?"

"Ellis, what is going on, did you just set me up?"

"No, no, I did not know he would be here, I swear to you, Eve!"

"You said the tunnel leads to the outside."

"It does through the next door."

"Enough talking, guard, place Ellis under arrest now! Oh, Ellis, such high hopes for you over the years and now just look at you! You threw it all away for nothing! I will play the Giver now by letting you know I will not kill you as part of our secret pact from years ago. In return, though, you will be sent back to my planet, we will find things for you to do there once you arrive! Guard, take her to the ship and lock her up!"

Ellis fought and screamed and the guard dragged her by her hair out of the room until I could not hear her anymore.

"You, am I correct when I heard your name as Eve!"

"You must be the Giver, and what the hell are you?"

"I am a superior species and that is all you need to know, you're not smart enough to comprehend anything else!"

"What do you want with this planet, Giver?"

"No need for me to lie now, right as you can see I am not here to hold your hands. Me and my people are here to survive and this planet will ensure we continue to do so."

"Are you the leader of your people?"

"No, not me, I am kinda what you would call a go-to guy on this planet. My leader needs things and I go out and get them, it is really fairly simple."

"Why Earth?"

"Why not, if it wasn't Earth it would just be somewhere else, right? Earth is worthless to your kind now, all of you have made it that way, so now I do the cleanup. You should be happy, Eve, I help out your race and you provide other things I need."

"Like what, humans as food-stealing babies making people slaves for you so you can control their minds!"

"I do not like your attitude, Eve, and you do not want to turn me into the Taker, I assure you! Tell me, Eve, who are you?"

"I am a leader of another compound."

"Where is Marco?"

"I do not know, I am the one who sent my Assassins to kill him and you let him live."

"Oh, I see, your assassin was Raz, correct?"

"Yes, he was. How is Raz now?"

"Dead."

"Good, he was not very good at his job anyway. See, Eve, you and I are not so different, we do what we have to for the survival of our people."

"No, Giver, we are very different, I do not lie to my people and I do not harm others for my own personal gain."

"Oh, but you do, Eve, you humans are too easy, I can smell all of your emotions. Your stench is very high in fear and sadness over conflicts you hold deep down inside of you."

"How much are you charging me for this session?"

"That is good, I like that good ole sarcastic humor, it is really refreshing to hear."

"What do you want, Giver!"

"To take back what is mine. You have a choice to make, Eve, my elite forces are waiting for my command to attack. I assure if they attack the casualties will be more than you could bear!"

"Call off your troops and we will let you go to be free and take back what is mine."

"It is your choice, Eve, of whether your people live another day or be slaughtered like pigs at harvest time!"

"When are they going to attack, what the hell are they waiting for!" We all shrugged our shoulders looking at one another.

One of my troops came crawling up to me. "Radan, what is going on?"

"Not sure, I can still see them and there was a lot of them but they were at a standoff like we were."

"Go back and tell the others to just wait it out and be prepared!"

Minutes went by and I saw a light in the compound streets that lit up the whole area. Was this the start of war? Out walked Eve with a creature I had never seen before in my lifetime.

"What the hell is that thing?"

Eve began to speak. "Soldiers of Eve, I need you to come out and lower your weapons to the ground and talk to me."

"No way, this is bullshit!"

A minute or so went by and I did not respond to her.

"Radan, please, I beg you, it is for the good of us all, please listen to me, you are a smart man."

I sat there for another minute or two not knowing what to do but my blood was still boiling for a fight!

"Radan, please listen to me, I beg you."

I yelled out, "I will come alone to talk to you!"

I walked out slowly with my sword in hand and approached the Giver and Eve.

"Yes, Eve, what can I do for you?"

"Very impressive," the Giver said out loud.

"I am not talking to you, bug!"

"Listen to me, Radan, the Giver will let us leave if we drop our weapons and go. Their weapons and armor is way too much, this war would be a bloodbath and I would rather walk away than be responsible for the deaths of so many without a fighting chance."

"But Eve!"

"No buts, Radan, please just do as I say!"

"I do not like your decision but I will obey your command."

I kissed her hand and walked back to the troops.

"I am very impressed, Eve, you have great leadership skills for your kind. I think we could work very well together, don't you?"

"Maybe, Giver, just maybe."

I went back and addressed the troops and informed them of Eve's orders. A lot of them were against surrendering and so was I, but Eve was smart and she must have had a plan in her head. I would follow her orders.

"Listen, everyone, no matter how we feel we must obey Eve and do as we are told, got it?"

"Yes, sir!"

"Alright, let's go, keep your weapons for now until we have been given further instructions."

All of us walked out slowly in the streets and we could see a lot of his troops behind him, they were just as ugly as he was.

"We are all here, Eve, what do you want us to do?"

"Drop your weapons and back away."

My hand was putting a death grip on my sword. I did not want to let it go. I dropped mine first on the ground and ordered the others to do the same. One of my men did not feel the same, he pulled out a knife and ran towards the Giver. One of the Giver's men stuck its arm out and quickly my man hit the ground screaming, within seconds his head exploded.

I yelled out, "Drop your weapons, it is over!"

Everyone dropped everything they had, we knew then this was a fight we could not win, no wonder Eve gave us those orders.

"Well, thank you for coming to terms with the situation that is at hand. I am the Giver and this is my world now, the sooner you get that the better off all of you will be. I have very much enjoyed talking to Eve, she is a great leader, and I would very much love to be able to work with her in the future. However, now is now! You have a choice, my friends, and listen to me very closely, I do not like to have to repeat myself. I am the leader of this planet now! I have the capability to kill everyone that is left on this planet. My rule and law is the only thing that matters. I am the Giver and the Taker of lives, freedoms, and whatever else you can think of is mine! So your choice is and I will be honest because Eve says she is honest with you. You can learn to live under my law or it is simple you will die!"

"That is not what you said, Giver!"

"Mind your tongue, Eve, you are lucky you are still alive!"

"Not much of a choice, is it, Giver?"

"So what is your answer, Radan?"

"Give me death!"

"Then so be it!"

"Stop, Giver, no!"

"Then Eve, talk sense into your so-called warrior, we are wasting time!"

"Please, Radan, listen to me!"

"I am sorry, Eve, this is the first and last time, I cannot, I am sorry, thank you for everything but I will not stand down."

I knew Radan was serious and I felt like a mother who was losing their child. "Okay, Radan, you are to be first." I dropped to my knees, looked the Giver in his lifeless face, and told him, "I hope Marco fixes all of this, he is on his way back home."

He grabbed my sword and pushed it through my skull, everything went numb, and then I saw a bright light, I was home.

Eve dropped to her knees and began to cry uncontrollably.

"Who is next from the great warriors of Eve? I am waiting, or should I just kill all of you?"

A quarter of the troops bowed down to their knees and accepted death with an open smile and the others voted their allegiance to the Giver. My heart was broken on what I had just seen, I could hardly think. What now was to become of the human race? I was scared and for the first time I did not know how to lead my people.

"As you see, Eve, I am in charge again and tomorrow we will go to your compound and set the record straight for all."

"Okay, Giver, whatever you want."

"That is good, Eve, that is what I want to hear."

"Marco, is everything okay?"

"Who are you?"

"I am protecting your room security, my name is Dan."

"Yeah, I am, I need to talk to the president ASAP!"

"I know they are flying you out of here tomorrow to a top-secret location."

"Will he be there?"

"That I do not know, I don't have that top security clearance to answer that. You have another hour before chow time begins."

"Where is Daniel and Samarra?"

"Daniel is next door to you and Samarra is staying overnight with doctors for examination. I will come back in a hour and take you to chow, sir."

"Okay, thanks, Dan."

I did not sleep at all, who really could? My mind was going a million miles an hour about stopping the war and finding Ellis. I was already missing her badly. I kept hoping everyone was okay at the dumping grounds. I hated not knowing what was happening.

The hour went by very quickly and the next thing I knew was that Dan was knocking at the door.

"Captain Marco, time for chow when you are ready, sir."

"Okay, I will be there in a second. Okay, soldier, I am ready to go."

"You know, Marco, I know you cannot tell me anything and I am not asking you to, but I just wanted to say congratulations on your mission."

"Thank you, Dan, but the mission is not over yet, better pray I succeed."

He looked at me very oddly and did not say a word.

"Here you are, Marco, your friends are inside, your air lift leaves here in a hour and a half, and good luck with the rest of your mission, sir."

"Thank you, Dan, be safe."

I opened up the door and immediately saw Daniel and Samarra getting their food. We had the mess hall to ourselves and I ran over and hugged both of them.

"Samarra, how is the baby?"

"Believe it or not, through the rough space travel and all everything is looking good. They did tell me to take it slow for the next few weeks, I have issues with that."

"Daniel, you?"

"Good, did not sleep worth a shit last night but I am glad to be home."

"I know, me either, really kept having crazy dreams."

"So, Marco, who are we meeting with today?"

"Not sure but I hope it is the president. We have a lot to tell them and they need to get to work ASAP. Let's eat, guys, I am starving and seriously missing our normal food choices."

All agreed on that and began stuffing our faces, having good conversation. As we sat there I looked at both of them and realized how lucky I was to be on that mission with them and they would forever be a part of my life. I did not have a family but now I had gotten one and I could not be any more happy.

A sergeant approached our table. "Good morning to all of you, we have ten minutes before we fly you to the mainland and from there you will be flown to a private location for debriefing. Follow me when you are ready."

"Thank you, Sergeant, are you guys ready?"

"Let's go," Samarra shouted out, "we have things to do."

We walked out on the deck and there was a very small transport ship warming up with the ramp pulled down.

"I take it this must be our train?"

"Yes, sir, have a good trip and good luck."

We boarded the transport ship, greeted the pilots, and strapped ourselves in.

"Pilot, how long is it from here to the mainland?"

"We will have you there in an hour, give or take."

"Where are we going?"

"We will land in Tampa, Florida, and from there, sir, I have no knowledge."

"Thank you, Pilot."

Smooth takeoff, which at this time I really appreciated. I looked at Samarra and said, "Hey, maybe you should take lessons from this guy," and as expected I received the finger.

The flight was quick and a very smooth landing, making me appreciate not being in a bigger ship. We landed at an unknown secret base and immediately was taken from the transport ship to a hangar and boarded another ship. Within thirty minutes we were off again with a two-hour flight time to an unknown destination. Good time for a quick nap. Don't know if it was time travel, space travel, or just plain stress, but I was getting tired. I woke up brushing my face with my hand as I opened my eyes, Samarra was in my face with her finger touching the inside of my nostrils. I smacked her hand away.

"Samarra, what the hell is wrong with you, that's nasty."

Daniel could not stop laughing.

"We have arrived, sunshine, wakey wakey, time to sell our story, dick."

I hated to get up, I was sleeping so good. We got out of the ship and were escorted to a room where a general was waiting on us.

"Congrats, troops, I am General Adams. In a few minutes I will escort you three to a meeting room, the president will be there, along with members of the Congress and Senate, along with some of the top brass. Everyone understand?"

"Yes, sir, and thank you, we have a lot to talk about, sir."

"We are looking forward to your reports and samples you have taken."

We all looked at each other. Samples? Who had time for that? We were in survival mode but they would understand in the briefing.

Say It Isn't So

"Are you three ready?"

"Yes, sir, General Adams."

We walked quite a distance. General Adams opened the door and escorted us in. There was a standing applause and a lot of shouting as we entered the room, it kind of made us feel like rock stars, it was odd but we really enjoyed it. I could really tell Samarra did, she thought she was a queen anyway. Everyone sat down, the national anthem began to play, we all rose and the president walked in through the doors. The president sat and so did everyone else.

"Captain Marco, Captain Samarra, and Captain Daniel, it is so wonderful to see you again. I just want to say thank you on behalf of your country and the world, your return is amazing, all of you have exceeded all expectations in our eyes."

The crowd stood up, chanting, "USA! USA! USA!"

I stood up graciously and began to talk firmly. "Sir, we need to talk now, thank you for the praise, we all really appreciate it, but there are very important matters to discuss."

"What is it, Captain Marco?"

"Everything, Mr. President, the planet we visited was not an unknown planet, sir."

"Then what was it?"

"It was Earth, sir!"

The crowded gasped in disbelief.

"It was Earth, that is why your readings were very similar but off from our standards."

"What are you saying, Captain?"

"It is Earth in our near future, Mr. President, and it is not good."

"Go on, Captain Marco, what did you find out?"

"There is a nuclear war that the whole world is involved in, sir! No one wins and in the process an alien life form comes down and uses the rest of humanity to feed on and eventually take over the planet to be ruled by its people."

Some congressmen and senators began to laugh at the notion.

"Where is your proof, Marco, we do not like jokes."

"Ask Daniel and Samarra, sir!"

"Daniel and Samarra, is this true?"

"Yes, sir, it is, we fought for our lives just to get back here. I was raped, Mr. President, and now pregnant, sir, the planet is in trouble!"

The crowd began to uproar.

"Silence to all!" the president screamed. "Where are your samples and experiments, Daniel?"

"There are none, sir, we were captives and we escaped to come back and warn you, this mess could be happening anytime."

General Adams stood up. "Marco, is this true?"

"Yes, sir, it is, and if it is not prevented the whole planet will go to shit, I promise you!"

More uproar from the crowd.

The president looked very confused. "Marco!"

"Yes, sir, Mr. President?"

"Who starts this war?"

"Abbas Tahan. He downloads a virus, sir, into computers, the computers think they are being attacked and it starts off a worldwide attack that cannot be stopped!"

More roars from the crowd.

"They are racist!" roared from the crowd.

"Race has nothing to do with this! This is what I was told!"

"This man's name is a start and go from there and see what you find out! So Captain Marco, what would you suggest we do now?"

"Kill him and kill him now, who knows who or what he has working with him!"

Half the crowd roared and the other half was silent.

The president slammed down the gavel. "Silence, everyone, silence!"

"I am Captain Marco, I am telling you good people in faith and that you love this country and our planet! This is a reality that is going to come to pass! If you choose to ignore it that is on you, but death is coming soon! I love this country and I love this planet, but you need to open your minds, millions upon millions are going to die and the rest who survive will wish they were dead! Leave politics and political correctness out of this and just do your fucking jobs!"

General Adams stood up. "I hear you, I want to know more!"

The president slammed down his gavel and announced we would meet again tomorrow. "Marco, see me in my office soon, I will send someone to get you!"

"Yes, sir!"

I was escorted by Secret Service and was escorted to the president's private office. The president was standing by his desk.

"Marco, would you like a drink?"

"Yes, sir, I would, thank you."

"Scotch okay?"

"Anything is fine right now, sir."

"Your trip has been very stressful on all of you, I see."

"Yes, sir, it really has opened my eyes on how lucky we are all to be standing here in peace and safety."

"Please, Marco, just call me Tim. Look, Marco, what the three of you are telling me sounds crazy, you have to know that?"

"Maybe so, sir, but that is the truth!"

"Are you sure the time travel did not mess with your heads?"

"How could that be, sir, all of us saw the same things. Look, Mr. President, I know you do not want to see it or is it just too politically correct to take out a terrorist? However, I assure you if you do not do something everything you see and all the people in that meeting will be gone! There is no government left, sir, only groups of sick people living together scattered everywhere."

"Marco, let me assure you of one thing. If you are wrong about this all three of you could be held in contempt and could be sentenced into life in prison! So if you are not being honest you better confess now, my son."

"I am not worried about your courts, sir, or anything else; however, I am concerned with losing millions and millions of lives on this planet!"

The president just sat there for a minute with his glass of scotch in hand, silently thinking. "Alright, when we meet in the morning we will vote on an investigation on this so-called terrorist. For your sake, Marco, you better be right!"

"Not for my sake, Mr. President, for the world's sake!"

"Okay, Marco, you are free to go, we will see you three again at eight in the morning."

"Thank you, sir."

"And Marco?"

"Yes, sir?"

"Thank you for all that you have done, Captain."

"Do not thank me yet, sir."

That night I sat around with Daniel and Samarra at dinner, telling them about the conversation I had with the president and what the meeting was going to be about tomorrow.

"I do not understand them, Marco."

"I do not either, Daniel, it just seems they just do not want to believe that it is going to happen."

"It almost appears to me they know the truth but for some reason they are in denial."

"Well, fuckem is what I think, it is all political as usual, none of them has balls to do anything! The government does not even know how to pick their own fucking noses!"

"Nice analogy, Samarra, but I must admit I agree with you. Let's get some sleep, tomorrow will be a busy day."

"Good morning to you, Eve, I hope you slept well?"

No answer.

"I suggest you change your attitude today, you are going to introduce me to your compound. Eat something and we shall leave soon."

The Giver was sitting in a vehicle that rolled like a tank and had a cover over it that protected him from the sun. He brought twenty of his elite troops for the journey to my compound. I was sick to my stomach from fear and I kept thinking of Radan nonstop.

An hour and a half later we arrived at the compound and the main gates were locked.

"Eve, tell your people to open the gates."

I yelled out, "This is Eve, open the gates," but there was no response.

"Tell them again and if they do not I will smash the gates down. Do as I say, Eve, so I do not have to kill anyone today, that is an order!"

A few seconds later the compound doors began to slowly open and the Giver and his elite rolled into the compound streets.

"Nice place you have here, Eve, there is a lot I could do with this place. Now address the people, Eve, that are starting to gather."

People began to flock over in our direction, they were amazed by the Giver's appearance.

"My faithful people and friends, we have been a community of peace and reason together. Today I am no longer in charge of this compound."

The crowd was in disbelief, they began to gasp and chatter amongst themselves.

"Please listen to what I have to say, it is very important for everyone. The Giver is now in control, he promised me that if you do what you are told under his new law none of you will be harmed. He is setting up a new government here and I will be in charge of getting everything organized the way that he wants it."

A man yelled out from the crowd, "Fuck him, he does not rule us, we do not want that thing in charge!"

The Giver looked at me, then nodded to one of the elite members. The elite guard walked up to the man, grabbed him by the cheeks, and squeezed him so hard his eyeballs popped out of his skull and he dropped dead.

"Eve told you I was in charge, rule one listen to my commands or this is what happens. You can live in peace here as long as you obey my laws. Now everyone, go about your day, I have work to do. Oh, and before all of you leave, if you try to escape my guards will pull your bodies apart, have a good happy day. Okay, Eve, do not be shy, give me a tour of the compound."

I woke up early that morning and met Daniel and Samarra for breakfast before the big meeting with the government officials.

"Everyone ready and prepared this morning?"

"I hope so, this baby is kicking my ass and I am tired and sick this morning."

"I bet your baby bump is starting to show more and more these days. Have you thought of a name yet, Samarra?"

"If it is a girl it will be Tanya, as you already could have guessed. If it is a boy probably Daniel Jr."

I liked that Daniel was so happy he was smiling from ear to ear.

General Adams walked through the mess hall. "Alright, soldiers, time to go, everyone is waiting."

"Yes, sir, we are on the way."

We walked through the doors, a lot of smiles and a lot of disbelievers as well. Everyone was standing as the president walked through the doors.

"Thank you all for attending this important meeting, all of you can take your seats. Today we are here to cast a vote on whether to further investigate the situation with a so-called terrorist. Marco is aware of the circumstances, he may have if we conclude his story is false. So if you please, all in favor of an investigation please stand up."

It was tough to tell, it was going to be close.

"All of you who are not in favor of an investigation, please stand up."

It was close, we won by only two votes.

"I will appoint General Adams and a special team to launch this investigation and hopefully very soon we will have answers. As all of you are aware, this is top secret to the highest level, no one is allowed to discuss this with anyone outside of this room! Everyone is dismissed. Marco, Daniel, Samarra, and General Adams, stay with me for a minute, I need to talk to all of you in private. Listen, General Adams, you need to get started on this investigation as soon as tomorrow."

"Better than that, Mr. President, I will start gathering up my team starting today."

"Great, the quicker the better. As for the three of you, well, you can thank me later. I am sending you off on a one-week leave to wherever you want to go. Better yet, I will send you to the beaches in Mexico, all paid for, and at the end of the week we should have our findings and go from there."

Samarra was smiling from ear to ear and I could not blame her. "Thank you, sir, we appreciate it, when do we leave?"

"This evening around five, we will also have someone pick you up and bring you back as well."

"Thank you once again, Mr. President."

"You are all very welcome, go have fun and blow off some steam and we will see you in a week."

"Holy shit, we are going to Mexico!"

I had never seen Samarra so happy and to be honest there were no complaints coming from Daniel or myself.

Changes

"I have to say, Eve, I am impressed with the tour of the compound."

"Thank you, Giver, we all have worked hard to get where we are at."

"I have decided to leave you in control of this compound under my new law and rule. I will leave some of my elite here with you to assure that everything is up to my standards. You will have protection here for your people. My elite have already rounded up all of your weapons, so you're going to have to rely on us for your defense."

"Understood, Giver."

"Tomorrow jobs will be assigned to your people for things I need to have done."

We walked around the corner and there was roughly thirty old people all hovered up in a circle surrounded by a couple of the elite.

"What is going on here, Giver!"

"These individuals are either sick or over the age limit or a combo of both. They are worthless to your race and now they will become food for mine."

"You cannot do that, Giver, they are people!"

"Not anymore, their meat is now a necessity for survival and they are now frail and no use to this compound."

"You cannot do this, it is inhumane."

"Really, inhumane, your species has been inhumane since your very existence. Do not worry, Eve, they will not feel a thing. We will butcher them here and ship them out, you must get used to it, these are the new way of things."

"I do not think I could ever get used to that!"

"You have no choice, Eve, this is my world now."

As we walked my throat closed up and I could not hold back the tears. I kept thinking, Please, Marco, I hope you are getting closer to figuring this all out and even worse, what if they did not make it back, is this our new destiny?

Daniel and Samarra were jumping around in the water at the beach and I was laid out in my chair on the shore, feet in the water, enjoying a cold beer. All of us deserved this time, we definitely earned it, but I was feeling guilty. I kept wondering what was going on back there and worried about Ellis, Tinzo, and Eve. Seeing Daniel and Samarra living it up and loving each other made me sad. Not in a bad way, don't get me wrong, I was very happy for them both but it just made me miss Ellis even more. I knew for the first time in my life I was truly in love and it really hurt in a good way, but I would keep my promise and find her again and make things right.

"Hey, Marco, get in the water, it's amazing!"

"I can't."

"Why not?"

"I am on a new mission."

"What are you talking about?"

"Save the whales project, in case you wash up on shore I'm in charge."

"Clever, dick face!"

Life was good but I was ready to get to the investigation, but not much I could do at this point until we returned in a week.

"Yes, Giver, you called for me?"

"I did, Sabot, the mud people had a huge part of the attack."

"What do you ask of me, my lord?"

"I want their leader brought to me alive!"

"Who is their leader?"

"I am not sure, but they say he is much different looking from the rest and considerably bigger. According to witnesses, he killed an Ag-Waz with his tongue. I want him brought to me so I can personally cut out his tongue."

"As you wish, my lord."

Sabot waited until dark and at lightning speed ran through the bushes and tall grass, cutting through the thickness of the forest. In the forest Sabot ran upon two men.

"Who are you!"

"I am Sabot."

"What kinda dipshit name is that?"

Sabot pulled back his head gear and reveled his face. The two men were in shock and disbelief.

"It is the name that will end your lives."

Sabot opened up his hands and sharp razors began popping out from his fingers. Before the men could think to run, he was already on them both. Sabot shoved each of his hands and stabbed the two men in their groin, lifted them both up on each side of his face. His chest plate popped open and out came two silver balls the size of golf balls. They rolled up his arm and made their way inside the body of the two men through their groin. Sabot dropped the men to the ground and walked away. Five seconds later their bodies exploded into flames.

Sabot continued until he found a waterway. He kneeled down by the water and pulled out a small vial from his leg area and poured it into the water. Seconds later the water began to boil and instantly the mud people began to surface. Their heads began to surface and Sabot started to speak.

"You tell your leader that the Giver wants to talk with him face to face. If he does not we will swim down and kill all of you. I have warned you, we are not to be taken lightly."

Several mud people came up to attack and Sabot quickly struck them dead.

"Let this be a lesson, you have been warned."

The mud people descended and Sabot left in the quiet of the night.

"My lord, I have left the message with the mud people that you had instructed me to. A few tried to test my patience but they were eliminated."

"Good, thank you, Sabot, I know I can always trust you."

"Yes, my lord."

"Eve, Eve, wake up, my lady."

"Who are you?"

"I am Ada."

"I do not know you."

I jumped out of bed and she was gone. I must have been dreaming but I was up and not in a good mood. Everything was crazy and out of whack. The Giver was gone and now I had the reality of answering questions to all of the citizens of the compound. My day was very hectic, one after another, question after question, where do I go from here? I felt worthless at one point, I could help now, I couldn't do shit, were we doomed? I did not really know but death and sadness surrounded us.

"Sabot, when are they to arrive and greet me?"

"Not sure, my lord, but soon. If they do not I will personally eliminate each one of them slowly and painfully."

"Very good, I eagerly wait to see this so-called leader of the water. Keep up the course, my friend, soon will be the widespread takeover of the planet, we are almost ready."

"I understand, Lord."

It was time to leave beautiful Mexico. I was ready to get back to find out what General Adams had discovered. On the other hand, Daniel and Samarra looked sad.

"Cheer up, guys, with our contracts you will be able to afford to live there if you want."

"You know, Marco, sometimes you make sense, when do you think we will get our money?"

"Not sure, you know how damn slow the government is but we will get it. A lot is riding on this investigation, as you know. We have an hour, guys, before we catch our flight, so get ready, I will see you at the limo."

We crammed into the limo, which I might add had a bar in the back.

"Sorry, Samarra, whales can only drink water but Daniel and I will have a few for you."

"Great, thanks!"

We arrived at a base just inside of Texas and climbed aboard a transport ship. The captain opened up the cockpit doors.

"Welcome, your flight will be two and a half hours, please enjoy your flight."

All of us reclined and took a nap. I was a very light sleeper and the small bump of the landing woke me up.

"Daniel, Samarra, we are here, wake up."

"What time is it?"

"It's time to get your asses moving, let's go."

The walkway of the transport ship opened and we walked off. Another vehicle was there to pick us up and drive us to the base.

"I hope all of you had a wonderful trip and an easy flight?"

"We did, it was great, thanks for asking. Where are we going, Soldier?"

"I have been instructed to take you to a certain location and that is all I know."

We were dropped off in front of some hangar doors and he drove off.

"Great, where is our welcome?"

About a minute later General Adams came walking outside. "It is good to see all of you again, I hope your vacation was pleasant?"

"It was, thank you for asking, sir."

"We have a lot to talk about and questions for the three of you, so I hate to be short but the president is waiting. Grab some lunch, he will be here in an hour."

"Yes sir, General, we are ready to talk."

"Yes, and so am I."

"What do you think is going on, Marco?"

"Not sure, Samarra, but I hope they found something to help our case."

"Hey, enough talk for now, I am hungry."

"What's wrong, Daniel, having sympathy hunger pains for your woman?"

"Maybe, but it is a good excuse, right?"

"Agree, let's eat."

"Josh, where have you been?"

"I have been trying to comfort and help the people on your compound, Eve. I thought you had escaped."

"No, just laying low, helping others and trying to avoid the freaks."

"What are we going to do, Eve, people are worried?"

"I do not know, Josh, I am open for suggestions, I am at a loss at the moment."

"I take it the Giver is gone?"

"Yes, but as you can see a lot of his men are still here keeping an eye on things. We cannot fight them, Josh, we just can't, they are too advanced and way too powerful, if we try it would be a bloodbath."

"My people, Eve, are going to wonder what has happened to me. They will come looking for me thinking you tricked us and the whole alien story was a lie. When that happens they will be enslaved as well. If the Giver discovers another colony, he will take it over also."

"I know, Josh, I really do, I am very sorry but it's not our compounds, he plans on doing this to the whole planet."

"The only hope we have, Eve, is that Marco figures it out because if he doesn't it is all over with."

Eve began to cry and Josh held her tight and consoled her.

"Either way, Eve, life will go on and we will have to make the best of it."

"You're right, Josh, I just can't believe this is happening, I feel so stupid."

"Well, don't. None of us knew this was going to happen."

"Yes, Sabot?"

"The leader of the mud people is here to see you, my lord."

"Very well, send him in."

The doors opened and the Giver stood up very quickly. "Who are you?"

"Me Wom-Pal? Who be you?"

"I am the Giver. Wom-Pal, you are accused of starting a war and killing many of my people while helping a criminal by the name of Marco escape!"

"Me not start war, you be start war on Wom-Pal people."

"Not a very smart answer, Wom-Pal, you did along with Marco and others, and now you will have to pay for what you have done!"

"Wom-Pal do not pay, Wom-Pal only like to eat and he hungry."

"See there, Sabot, they are too stupid to survive and exactly the reason we are here, it actually helps them."

Wom-Pal began laughing very loudly.

"Why are you laughing!"

He kept laughing louder and more out of control.

"Answer me now, what is so funny, or should I just have Sabot kill you now!"

"Okay, okay, Wom-Pal will answer, me not really stupid, Giver."

"Why do you say that?"

He began laughing again. "Wom-Pal so sorry, reason why me laugh so hard is because me not Wom-Pal, me not even know me name."

The Giver was pissed! "Who are you then!"

"Me told you me not know, but there are thousands of us stupid Wom-Pals coming through your gates right now."

The Giver and Sabot looked at each other in disbelief. Wom-Pal laughed so hard he fell to the ground. The Giver and Sabot ran outside to see what was happening. Sure enough he was right, thousands of mud people were flooding the compound and the chaos began. The Giver's elite were killing mud people one by one very quickly, but the numbers were too high. People on the compound were lighting up the walls and homes on fire in retaliation. It was a full-on scale war like no other. The Giver's elite one by one began to slowly fall due to the bites of the mud people and the battle was starting to even up. Sabot was running amok through the streets, killing everything and anything he came in contact with. The Giver disappeared into the darkness as the battle continued to ensue.

Eve and I were looking at the stars, admiring the beauty of it all.

"Eve, what is that?"

"What, Josh, I don't see anything."

"Over there, look."

I could see it now, it looked like lights or fire.

"Shit, Eve, it looks like the compound!"

Ten minutes later the Giver's elite busted through the gates and left the compound.

"Shit, Josh, what is happening?"

"Something serious, it looks like. We can escape now, Eve!"

"You can leave if you must, but I cannot go. I can't leave my people, Josh."

"I understand, I will send some of my people to inform them that before, you are okay with it?"

"I would like that, thank you."

"Great, then it is settled."

Sabot was still in killing mode, he was relentless and brutal and had the knack for killing, he loved it, no wonder he was the chief commander of the elite; however, the numbers were starting to pile up on both sides. The Giver got on to one of his ships and started punching the controls and setting the flight programs. When he was done he closed all exit ways to the ship and prepared for takeoff.

"Where be you go?"

"Who are you and where are you?"

"Me is Wom-Pal, who be you?"

The three of us walked into the meeting. General Adams addressed us all.

"I need you all to sit down, there are things we need to discuss. Well, Marco, I have investigated the terrorist by the name of Abbas Tahan and there are several in which I have found no link to terrorist groups in any of the regions. However, two days ago we do have surveillance tapes of him meeting with a very suspicious character in Yemen. Your terrorist guy has moved a lot in the last ten years but no suspicious activity at all until this."

"What is it, General?"

"He took a trip to Afghanistan, where we have him meeting someone unusually tall. This person was around seven feet tall, give or take. The strange thing is he hands him an envelope. Then he goes in a cave and we never see him again. The man in question was draped in a black hooded coat so we could not see any of his body at all. Not only was he unusually tall, he was also unusually big!"

"So what does this all mean?"

"Relax, Mr. President, I will explain."

"So this big man disappears without a trace. We combed the cave, do any of you know what Sabot means?"

The three of us looked at each other. "No, sir, we have never heard that before."

"Okay, so let me continue. So your terrorist guy has been writing to a junior in college at UCLA who is becoming a teacher. As I said, this junior in college has ties to your terrorist friend, they have communicated only twice by phone but they have been writing letters back and forth. He just mailed off another letter that will arrive to her in two more days. We do know she is a radical against the United States Government and does not like the direction our country is going."

"Who is she, General?"

"Marco, her name is Ellis Hall."

"No, no, that can't be right."

"No, Marco, don't listen, that has to be a coincidence."

"Maybe, Samarra, but I doubt it, she did not want to come, I can feel it, Samarra, it has to be her. Think about it, she was in California, a teacher, same first name, and she could not come!"

"I am sorry, Marco, I hope it is not true."

"Me too, Samarra, we will see. So what are we going to do, General?"

"A raid! I must be allowed to go."

The president interrupted. "No, you can't."

"Bullshit, I will be there, I can handle all of this!"

"No, you can't, Marco! You have done well, but we need to handle this."

"I will be there, Mr. President, whether you like it or not, you owe me that! I will complete my mission, sir!"

"Fine, don't you screw this up, Marco!"

"Me told you I am the Wom-Pal, and me not like you!"

Wom-Pal moved from the shadows from behind the cockpit and knocked the Giver forward, smashing him into the control panels. The ship started to spiral out of control, losing altitude and zigzagging across the sky. Wom-Pal's bites did not have much effect on the Giver, due to his outside protective bio mechanical suit.

"Wom-Pal will kill you now and eat good!"

Wom-Pal shot his tongue out from his mouth as the ship shifted and missed hitting the control panel and it began to spark. The Giver quickly slammed his right hand down with his blades and cut off Wom-Pal's tongue. Wom-Pal fell backwards, shaking his face violently. The Giver stood up, showing his blades to Wom-Pal.

"Now, stupid, it is time for you to die!"

As the Giver started approaching Wom-Pal, the ship quickly dropped and the Giver was thrown backwards into the piloting widow and was pinned. The speed of the ship got faster, you could hear the crackles of tree limbs snapping off and then the explosion.

"Josh, look, did you see that, the Giver's ship went down!"

"Yes, I did, let's grab some horses and head THAT WAY."

Eve and I rode as fast as our horses could go for about twenty minutes.

"Not far, Josh, I can see the smoke from here."

"Yeah, me too, keep going!"

We arrived at the crash scene. We did not see any movement, we were hoping he was finally dead.

"Eve, what do you see?"

"There is a very large mud person here, unusually big, I must say."

"Is it dead?"

I picked up a very large and long stick and poked it. "Yeah, it is definitely dead."

"Do you see the Giver?"

"Not yet, come help me move some of this debris, please."

"Hold on, I am coming."

We began pulling up some debris and then I could see some of his body. I poked him with a stick and no movement.

"Good, it looks like he is dead."

Then a slight quiet voice began to speak. "I need help."

"I am going to help you, Giver, the same way you help others!"

"Eve, Eve!" His voice began to crack and he was having trouble breathing. "You better help me or I—"

"You will do what, Giver, enslave me, use me as food, tell me something I do not already know!"

"I have already sent out a distress signal to my people, they will be here soon."

"Well, that's great, but when they return you will already be dead, Giver!"

"Eve, do you want me to finish him off?"

Eve looked around a little and paused. "Actually, no, I do not, Josh, his ship is on fire and continues to burn. Let him go down with his ships the way humans used to do, maybe he will think about it while he dies."

"Hey, I am all good with that, let the bug burn!"

Eve turned around and spit on him. "See ya in hell, Giver, that is where you're going! Josh, let's get back to the compound and in the morning at sunrise we will go see what happened at the other compound."

"You know, Eve, I cannot believe I am going to say this but you are very hot when you're pissed off."

"You should see how angry I get in the bedroom."

"Eve, I will race you back then."

They both smiled at each other and the race began.

The moon was full and very bright, the sky was clear and the stars sparkled with all their beauty. In the distance you could hear the sounds of limbs and shrubs and grass popping like a stampede was taking place. The trees parted and out walked Sabot.

"My lord, are you in there? My lord, am I too late, it is Sabot?"

Sabot started frantically ripping and slinging parts of the ship off of the Giver. Sabot kneeled down and turned the Giver over.

"My lord, you are burnt very badly, can you hear me?"

There was no answer, just the subtilties of the night.

Sabot leaned down beside the Giver. Out of his finger a sharp large syringe appeared and he stuck it into the Giver's neck. The Giver began to shake but could not speak. "You're still alive, hold on a little longer, help will arrive soon to take us away. If you can hear me, Lord, I promise you when you are healed we will return with a massive full invasion army and fully occupy this planet!"

Another ship arrived from the sky and Sabot and others carried the Giver aboard and quickly shot out into the heavens.

Truth Is Deadly

"Okay, General Adams, the president is not here now, we need to talk! When is this mission taking place?"

"We are leaving at eight A.M., Marco. We have called the postal service, they are on strict orders not to deliver the letter until exactly one P.M. and it is a federal order. That is when she checks her mail. I told them a second earlier and we would file charges. We will fly out at eight, it is only an hour flight from here. When she gets her mail we will surround her and escort her to her apartment."

"Marco?"

"Yeah, Samarra?"

"I have to go with you, I have to be there."

"No, you don't, stay with Daniel, you're pregnant, it's not safe."

"Not safe, what the hell do you think we just went through!"

"I understand that, Samarra, but we did not have a choice but now we do."

"No, you're wrong, you need me!"

"Daniel, please talk some sense into her."

"Sorry, Marco, I agree with her, you need her there."

"Damn all of you! General, stop them, please!"

"Marco, honestly the more the better, a lot is at stake here, she may be valuable."

Samarra grinned.

"Fine, I will see you all on the ship then! Everyone, listen to me, get your rest tonight, no distractions, we will wake you up at six A.M. and start getting ready."

"Yes, sir, got it."

"Good morning, Josh, how are you feeling?"

"Great, Eve, tired as hell, you sure were angry last night."

We both began to laugh.

"Yes, I sure was, I have sent someone for us to receive breakfast in bed and then we will go to the other compound and see what we can do to help."

"Sounds great, but before they bring us breakfast you still seemed a little pissed?"

"Yeah, I still do feel a little pissed."

That was the best breakfast I had ever had and now we were heading out to the compound to see what the hell went down last night. Both of us were happy that the Giver was dead but we knew at some point that they would return. We took about twenty fighters with us but we were low on weapons. We had some cutting knives and some sharpened sticks but we did not know what the Giver did with all our other weapons.

An hour later we arrived, most of the buildings had been burnt to the ground, some of them still smoking. There were way too many bodies to count in the streets. These poor people, they had gone through so much in a short period of time, their lives had been turned upside down. Josh and I stood in the streets and I began to talk.

"People, please listen to me, if you do not know me I am Eve and this is Josh. We offer all of you help. I have a compound that is safe and so does Josh. We want to inform you that the Giver is dead when his ship crashed last night and he was burnt to death. But before he died he said he signaled for help, so others will be coming back. We do not feel you are safe staying here. However, I can't and will not make you leave, it is your choices to make. You are all free, people, but you do have the option to come with us and be strong together."

Some people were thanking us and others were still in disbelief and shock, but this was the new world we had created, good, bad, or indifferent, it was what it was.

"Okay, Eve, I have a lot of people and so do you. I will take them to my place and you escort yours to your compound. I will give my people instructions on what to do and I will come back to you the next day."

"Don't keep me waiting too long, Josh, you know how angry I can get."

"Oh, believe me, I do, but I love your anger."

We both smiled and went our separate ways. I arrived at my lovely tree compound, nothing like being at home. I had a lot of people helping out, making our new friends feel at home. I finally got back to my house and had a few drinks of my special blend that Marco really enjoyed. It felt great going down. I finally began to relax and was thinking very warm thoughts about Eve and the next thing I knew it was morning. It was time. I got up and ate breakfast, hopped on my horse, and at full speed headed out to see Eve. It was funny, when I arrived she was already at the front gate waiting on me. I jumped off my horse and we hugged and kissed. This was one thing I never would have ever had happen in a million years, but I was falling in love. We spent the day together talking to the people, reassuring them things would be okay and getting everyone settled and relocated. There was no time for lunch or any breaks, so much work to be done. Finally we had some alone time and decided to have dinner together. We had a great meal and wonderful conversation opening up more and more to each other.

"What would you like to do now, princess?"

"I would love just to go outside on the roof, lay down, look at the stars, talk, and just relax, been a crazy day."

"Sounds good to me, Eve, and guess what?"

"I cannot imagine what?"

"I brought my special fun drink that everyone loves so much."

"Interesting, I have never had it before."

"Well, good, hopefully it will make you very angry later."

We both laughed.

"Yes, I would love some."

We climbed to the highest point on the compound. The moon was full, the stars were abundant, and the sky was very clear.

"Eve, you know what?"

Silence.

"Eve, you know what?"

She began to laugh. "What, Josh, I was messing with you."

"I am falling madly in love with you."

"You, Josh, really, I do not see it."

"No, I am serious, I cannot believe it either, I really do love you."

"I know you do, Josh, I feel the—"

Loud, ear-piercing booms and lights filled the air.

"Josh, what the hell is that!"

"I do not know!"

"Shit, Josh, it's the massive invasion, it is starting, we're all going to die!"

"Let's go, Eve, we have to run, no one can defend against this!"

"Maybe so, but we have to warn everyone and take our chances and run!"

"Take my hand, Eve, no time to waste, let's go!"

Face to Face

"Get up, everyone, time to move, shit, shower, and shave time for breakfast, we have a plane to catch."

Six A.M., that was the longest night of my life. All I did was think about confronting Ellis, she would not remember me but it terrified me to the core. What would become of her once we captured her scared me as well. I did not know the answers to any of it, but we had to stop her and hopefully this was just one big mistake.

I met Daniel and Samarra in the chow hall.

"Marco, how did you sleep?"

"Not well, Samarra, I am really worried."

"I know you are, I am sorry, that is why I wanted to be there for you. I wasn't trying to bust your balls."

"I know you do, Samarra, thank you."

"Good morning, troops, hope all is well?"

"We are, thank you, sir."

"So I wanted to give all of you a very interesting and productive feedback. By the way, when this is all done the three of you are going to receive the highest medal ever awarded in military history!"

"That is great, sir, we are very honored, but you have our full attention, what is it?"

"Special forces captured your terrorist Tahan in a second trip to Afghanistan. I ordered him to be interrogated. He was not compliant with our kindness, so I had to turn up the heat on him."

"You captured him?"

"We certainly did, it was not very hard either."

"I thought the president did not want him touched without any proof of wrongdoing?"

"Well, you are right, but however he gave me complete control of the investigation and I feel we needed his information. You see, I do not go by political correctness, I am not a politician, I am a general and my mission is to stop a war or finish it. We sleep deprived him and filled him with the newest and best truth serum. Boy, did he talk."

"What did he say?"

"He was originally greeted by a member of a new terrorist organization named WERG."

"What does that stand for, General, I have never heard of them before?"

"Me either, Marco, none of us has, not even the Homeland Defense Department."

"It stands for Western European Repent and Giver."

All three of us just looked at each other in disbelief.

"Do not be surprised just yet, guys, there is more. Tahan was very scared, he did not want anything to do with it. He had no choice, no one to turn to, and was afraid if he did not cooperate his family would be in harm's way."

"So they used him because he was completely innocent so he would not be on the radar."

"You got it, Marco. He met with someone in a cave named Sabot, as I told you someone put his name on the wall inside the cave. Sabot was always covered up from head to toe in a long black cape with a hoody. Tahan never saw what he really looked like. Tahan could only say he was very tall much taller than any human he had ever seen. Sabot told him to mail this letter to a certain address, that it was filled with critical information and if he did not he would have to die. The address that he was given is Ellis' address. Sabot told Tahan that Ellis would do the rest and that he would be free and Sabot gave Tahan several million dollars in his currency for his work."

"Talk about wrong place and wrong time."

"You are right, Marco, we are still holding him until our mission is done. We will eventually let him go, he really is not guilty of knowing what is happening, he was scared and bullied by this Sabot."

"The Giver has been staging everything since the beginning, guys."

"It appears that way, Marco."

"So none of you know of Sabot?"

"No, General, we never saw or heard of him while we were there, but the Giver we all know too well."

"Finish up, troops, it's time to go to California. It is time to save the Earth, there is no second guessing things anymore, we know what we have to do!"

"Yes, sir, we will be ready, sir!"

Samarra and I loaded up with the rest of the team on a military transport. Daniel stayed behind but was waving at us goodbye as the doors began to shut. The transport took off, it was going to be a very short flight, only an hour, and I was already starting to sweat.

"Relax, Marco, everything is going to be okay."

Samarra grabbed my hand and squeezed tight. As much as she and I had fought in the past she was there for me, and I couldn't appreciate it any more.

The flight was over and we slowly started to land on the runway. The transport landed and the doors opened.

General Adams addressed the team. "Briefing is in ten minutes, follow me and do not waste time."

"Yes, sir!" we all shouted.

"My God, Eve, hold on tight to my hand! Let's go, let's go, we got to leave!"

"Where, Josh, where?"

"I don't know but we have to warn everyone."

"Josh, I am scared, very scared!"

"Me too, come on, please."

We climbed down to the bottom of the compound. We began to yell, "Leave, leave now, danger is coming, everyone get out of here!"

Panic started to ensue, the sky was on fire with the lights of all the ships descending from the atmosphere. This was my compound, I ran it with peace and structure. I saw women with children in arms running in fear. I watched the chaos unfold, I used to be able to protect my people, now I had failed all of them. What did I do that was so wrong? None of us deserved this, not now, not ever. Time slowed down and I lost myself.

"Eve, Eve, what are you doing?"

"Sorry, Josh, I am so sorry."

"Stop it now, we have to go, time is wasting."

I was terrified and sad. I felt like I had let everyone down and was helpless.

The lights from the ships were so bright, it looked like daytime except it was a pale green color. Josh and I ran through the streets, the compound was falling apart, chaos ensued, people were trying to escape. Fights broke out, the people turned on each other, stealing supplies from one another out of fear. Tears rolled down my face. I was ready to die. I did not want to see any more.

Josh and I got outside the gates and headed for the woods. It was dark and dangerous and we had no weapons on us. We stopped and fell against some trees, we were so tired we could hardly move. The massive ships hovered and then they started releasing smaller ships that descended to the ground. We watched them land and many elite forces of the Giver's came running out and seized the compound.

"Josh, my people are all going to die!"

He pulled me to him and put his hand over my mouth and held me tight.

"Please, Eve, be quiet, I know, I am sorry but we have to survive for all humanity."

One of the big ships slowly descended to the ground outside of the compound walls. Around a hundred elite forces came to greet the ship. The doors of the great ship opened up and a tall dark figure walked out onto the ground. All of the elite got on their knees and started screaming, "Sabot, Sabot, Sabot!" I tried to scream but Josh had my mouth secured and was holding me tightly.

Sabot walked out and motioned for his elite to arise and began to address them. "My special elite, thank each one of you today. It is another great day in our civilization's history, another planet conquered! The Giver will be so pleased with each and every one of you! He has been badly injured but he will be okay, he is very strong, as you all know. In his absence I will take over command, he has taught me well over the years. The humans that resist will be killed and used right away for food. The others we will control, produce more human babies for future food, and harvest the others as they serve no more breeding purposes. This is the law of the Giver!"

I was screaming so hard on the inside, nothing would come out. I watched them load person after person aboard the ship.

"Josh, what do we do?"

"We leave, Eve, go back with me to my people, they do not know about us yet."

"But they will, Josh, they will!"

"We have no other choice, we have to go."

I knew he was right. I cried the whole way.

"Please, God, I thought you were a myth or a story, but please help us all!"

The whole way back to Josh's people, I kept seeing the girl in white that was trying to wake me up but I did not know her. I thought she said her name was Ada. As we ran she kept whispering in my ear that all would be better, that life would become whole again.

"I think I am losing my mind, I cannot take much more."

As we approached Josh's compound she smiled and started to slowly fade away.

I screamed out, "You are a liar, leave me alone!"

Josh grabbed me. "What the hell is wrong with you?"

"Nothing, Josh, I am sorry, just scared!"

"Get a hold of yourself, we need to live."

"What is living, Josh, answer me that? Do you know, Josh, or is it just for sex?"

"Shut your mouth, Eve, you know I love you! Why are you doing this now? I love you, dammit, you need to understand that!"

I did but it was my instinct to go farther and question everything. We looked into each other's eyes and I knew he got me.

"I will die with you, Josh."

"And I will die with you, Eve, I swear."

We began to kiss and the Earth started to shake like no other. We held each other tight and could feel and hear the ships landing one after another.

Josh addressed his people. "Please listen, everyone, we need to all go inside, blow out your candles and fires, we do not need any light to be seen.

The enemy is here, we have to hide, we cannot fight them, hide so they do not find us."

Everyone scattered off to hide. I took Eve's hand and we climbed up into my home.

"Wow, Josh, I am impressed, it really is comfortable up here, especially for being a man's place."

"It will do, my other wife decorated it for me."

"What! What did you say!"

"Relax, it is a little end-of-the-world humor, can't stop being funny now, right?"

"Ahh, you're such an ass, Josh, but you had me going."

"Eve, guess what, I have some of my secret juice left, ha-ha."

"Sorry, Josh, I am not really in the mood at the moment."

"Not for sex, my dear, damn, do you think I am a rooster all the time? I am talking about just to relax."

"Sure, fill my glass, big man."

Both of us were on our third shot and starting to calm down some.

"Josh, what do you think is going to happen now?"

"I am not sure, but I do know this is the beginning of the worldwide invasion! I think they have been preparing for a while and here it is."

"You know, Josh, I am really ashamed of myself now."

"Why is that?"

"Well, after the war I was very young, a lot had happened. I managed to work my way up through the ranks and became in charge of the compound. My ideology was hatred to technology, I blamed technology on everything that happened. Maybe I was not completely right in my way of thinking. I still believe technology is bad but yet I wonder if technology could defend us now, or could it have stopped this invasion from ever happening?"

"I do not know the answers to your question, Eve, but I do know one thing."

"What is that?"

"You cannot blame yourself for what has happened. You did not start this, it was other people's choices that created all of this, you and I and everyone else unfortunately are the ones who have to deal with their poor choices. You know me, Eve, my people wanted technology back, maybe there is a good middle ground that would have been nice, you know?"

"Maybe you are right, Josh, I just do not know too much to think about now. Hey, Josh?"

"Yes?"

"You are slowing down on the drinks, speed it up, man, no time to waste. So tell me, Josh, what was your other life before the great wars?"

"Well, I was eighteen the day it happened. I lived out West. My parents owned a bunch of property. I grew up hunting, fishing, and learned how to farm, unusual for those days' standards. Farm life, that was to be my career, while all of my friends were going off to college. It was a beautiful day, eighty-some degrees, low humidity, not a cloud in the sky, sun was shining and I was working the fields. My mother came running out, told me to come into the house, she was in panic mode like I had never seen her. We all gathered around the TV and heard words of the first blast on TV and my parents and I went down into the basement to hide. Two days later the TV and radio were dead, we had a lot of food stored in the basement. We stayed in the basement for six months or so until we all became stir crazy. My father had enough and all of us were ready to get out and move around, anywhere but the basement. My mother and father had pistols with them, and we opened up the basement door and entered the outside. It was very strange, it was daytime but foggy looking and cold as hell. Out of the fog came something of a person deformed by radiation, grabbed my mother, bit her neck, and started dragging her off. She dropped her gun and was screaming, my father started running after her and he was knocked down by another one that he did not see coming. I froze for a minute, I was scared to death. My mother's screams were gone but this man was on top of my father, biting and eating his face. I picked up my mother's gun and shot the man that was on top of my father. I went looking for my mother, I did find her, there was a man on top of her eating her and I blew his fucking head off. After that I lost it for a bit, Eve. I cut both the heads off. I took shoulder pads from my football gear and put spikes on each shoulder. I put both heads on them! I went from place to place, looting and killing anyone who got into my way! And now I am here, Eve, better but still lost for words."

"I am so sorry, Josh, I should not have asked you that."

"No, I am glad that you did, you are the first person I have told that to."

"I am special then."

"More than you know, Eve."

"Hey, Josh, one more drink and let's lay down, I want you to cuddle me, please, I need you."

"Sounds good, here you go."

"Last briefing, is everyone ready?"

"Yes, sir!"

"As all of you know, I am General Adams. If you do not know, then get the fuck out! Relax, men and women, I have always wanted to do that. Listen up, this is the most serious mission you will ever go on in your entire life. And if not it will be the last mission any of us ever do! Pay attention to the screen, this is our target, her name is Ellis. She is twenty-one years old, a junior in college, and is an anti-American protester! She will receive her mail at two o'clock this afternoon and it has been arranged. We need that envelope and we need her alive no matter what! If that is not possible, then you are free to kill! Understood!"

"Yes, sir!"

"I cannot give you all the details, but this mission is top priority, if we fail millions upon millions are at great risk for death! Do you understand me!"

"Yes, sir!"

"Good, we will be separated into teams and will be staked out around her apartment building so there is no way to escape. We will be watching every move that is made, and listen to your leaders and stay focused on the mission. There can be no fuck-ups on this one shot only, do or die!"

"Yes, sir!"

"You have one hour, get yourselves mentally prepared. In one hour, ladies and gents, operation take back the planet begins!"

It was early in the morning. I was thirsty and the sun had not peeked above the horizon just yet. I rolled over, looked at Eve, her back was facing me. She was so beautiful, sleeping like a baby. I kissed her back and rubbed my hands all over her. She flipped over, began to smile with her eyes closed, and asked me what I was doing.

"Nothing, just admiring such a beautiful and smart woman, is there anything wrong with that?"

"Not at all, hold me, I am a little cold."

We held each other tight and quickly fell back to sleep. We both woke up to the sounds of screams coming from everywhere.

"Josh, what is going on?"

"I don't know, hold on." I jumped out of the bed with no clothes on and peeped outside to see what was happening. "You're fucking kidding me!"

"What is it, Josh?"

"Shit, they're here! There are hundreds of them outside!"

"What are we going to do?"

"I don't know!"

Then a knock at the door.

"Who is it?"

"Josh, it's Anna."

"Are you alone?"

"Yes."

"Do not lie to me, Anna, are you alone?"

"Josh, I swear I am!"

Eve nodded.

"Okay, come on in. Anna, what is going on?"

She began to cry. "I am sorry, Josh, they know you are the leader and they want you to come outside. They say if you do not they will burn down all of our homes and make us slaves. You have five minutes to come outside before they start killing people."

"You okay, Anna?"

"No, Josh, I am very scared."

"I know you are, I am sorry, tell them I will be out soon, okay?"

"I will, thank you."

"Josh, what the hell are you going to do?"

"I do not know but I have to do something. Those are my people, either way we are screwed."

"I do but I cannot lose you now, Josh, I can't."

"Listen, I will strike a deal, okay, trust me, I will do my best, okay?"

"I love you, Josh."

"I love you too, stay strong for me, okay?"

"I will."

Josh got dressed and quickly climbed down from his home and was greeted by a lot of elite troops. A big, tall, dark figure pushed his way through the crowd and knocked Josh to the ground.

"Get up and meet your new ruler!"

Josh slowly got up. "Who are you?"

"My name is Sabot, and what was once yours is mine now!"

"Well, it is nice to meet you, I guess, but what makes you so sure my stuff is yours now?"

Sabot slapped him down to the ground once again. "It is the new way of things now!"

"What do you want with us, Sabot, we are a peaceful people who keep to ourselves."

"Not anymore, my lord now runs this planet, his name is the Giver!"

"I know of your Giver and he is a liar!"

Sabot knocked him down again. "You have only one choice, Josh, you are under my rule or all of you will die!"

"Not much of a choice, Sabot, is it? Can you and I talk one on one about it, Sabot, I am sure it will be in your favor."

"Where?"

"In my home. Anna, please clean up the mess in my room so Sabot can have the best experience we have to offer."

"I will, Josh."

Anna quickly climbed up into Josh's place and grabbed Eve.

"We have to go now, Eve!"

"Why?"

"Josh is bringing Sabot up here. Come with me, Eve, we will go underground."

"Sabot, are you ready?"

"I have been, time is wasting."

Sabot and I climbed up into my home. I was nervous but did not have much of a choice, my people's lives were at stake.

"Since you are the new leader, Sabot, I would like to officially welcome you and offer a token of friendship."

"What is that!"

"I am the maker of the best drink in all the planet, not many get the opportunity to have it but you are special, so I would like to toast the beginning of having a good working relationship."

I went to the counter and poured two drinks, came back down, and sat in front of him.

"Here you go, Sabot, drink up."

"No!"

"What, are you rejecting my hospitality?"

"You drink from both first!"

"Not a problem, the more for me is better." I began to chuckle. I took a shot from both glasses. "Wow, that is a good batch indeed, what's wrong, you think I am going to poison you?"

Sabot took the drink. His mouth morphed around the rim of the cup and down it went all at once. "Strange taste, but it makes you feel better, interesting."

"Yes, that is what us humans use to help us relax when we are stressed or just to have a good time."

"I want some more."

"You can have as much as you like, it is your compound now. Help yourself, the jug is right over there."

He kept drinking and drinking. I was impressed, my newest batch was almost gone. I had never seen anyone that could drink that much. His alien anatomy must have been catching up to him, he began to become confused and started falling and stumbling into the walls, at one point he fell over my kitchen table. I guess aliens can't hold their liquor either, not much different than humans.

He fell to the floor once again and started to laugh, it was creepy, I did not know they could even do that.

"You fooled me, human, you did!"

"No, Sabot, you fooled yourself with your arrogance, thinking you're the only race capable of living free!"

"Do not make me kill you, Josh," and he began to laugh.

"Good luck trying, Sabot, while you're at it care for another drink?"

"Yes, I am the ruler, give me another!" he yelled out loud.

"Sure, here you go, my master!"

"The Giver will really like you, Josh, he really will!"

Another two shots and Sabot was barely breathing. He must have drunk enough to kill ten humans. I was looking for his weakness but was having trouble finding one. I pressed a couple of areas on his face and his face plate popped off. I did not know what I did but it was open.

I walked into the bathroom and found an old toilet plunger we had as a decoration we had found. I pulled the plunger part off and stabbed the stick through his head, it wasn't easy but it went down to his brain. What would be effective now, and the old me came out! I cut Sabot's head off and cleaned out the insides. I put his head over mine and walked outside. The crowd gasped in shock!

"I am the new ruler, you must obey me, I am the new Sabot, he gave up his life because he knew we had the new weapons to kill all of you! This is your last chance, leave now or all of you will die!"

All of them fled, scared and confused of just what had happened. I was even more scared on the inside but it seemed to be working. Anna and Eve came running out to join me.

Josh addressed the crowd. "Today, my people, is the start of a new beginning and new world order, where us humans rule our planet together! They may come back when the shock is over, but we will never back down from them again, this is our planet!"

The crowd roared with excitement.

"Find weapons and start making them, we will be prepared and show them if we must what the human race is capable of if we all work together for one cause, are you with me!"

The crowd roared again and excitement and hope filled the air.

Eve was happy, she had tears going down her face, she patted Josh on the arm and said, "Great job, I will get our people in position."

We had landed and all of us were separated into separate undercover vehicles. Samarra and I and General Adams were in one vehicle together.

The general grabbed the radio. "Listen up, people, lock and load, keep the chatter quiet. Let's fall into positions around the apartment complex."

We drove for about twenty minutes until we reached ground zero. The name of the complex was called New Horizons. Ironic, I thought, yes indeed, the horizons were going to be new for sure. I was already starting to panic about seeing Ellis and what was going to happen at the raid.

Samarra must have seen it on my face, she grabbed my hand and looked at me in the eyes. "Marco, it will be okay, I am here for you."

"I know you are, thank you."

Everyone pulled into position.

General Adams got on the radio. "Listen, in ten minutes the mail will arrive, we wait until we see the suspect get the mail and then we follow her up."

It was a good plan, the building had two separate stairwells of steps on each side. We had separate teams that would be occupying them. Inside were two elevators that were going to be covered, nowhere to escape. We waited and exactly on time the mailed arrived. Now it was a waiting game.

A few minutes later a young woman went to the mailbox. "General, that is not Ellis, sir."

"Well, no matter who it is we must move if she gets the mail."

The young woman picked up the mail, flipped through it a few times, and walked into the apartments front main lobby.

"Okay, men, when she gets on the elevator we move! Okay, she is on, go, go, go!"

Doors opened up all around the complex and the investigation team poured out of the vehicles as bystanders looked on in shock. Very well-trained soldiers sealing down the area and advancing with a purpose. A lot of us reached our destination, both sides of the corridor were sealed with soldiers. Guns up and with stealth, we approached the apartment door. General Adams knocked on the door.

A soft voice replied, "Who is it?"

"Pizza guy."

"We did not order pizza."

"Yes, ma'am, we have two larges for this address."

"Sorry, dude, no order from here."

General Adams pointed at one of the soldiers to kick down the door. One swift kick and the door went down. We flooded in the door with guns raised. The young woman had her hands up screaming and fell backwards to the floor. One of the soldiers put a gun to her head and she began crying.

"Who are you!"

"Who are you!"

"Tonya, please don't hurt me!"

"Where is Ellis!"

No answer.

"Where the fuck is Ellis, lady, don't make me pull this trigger!"

She nodded to the back bedroom.

Samarra stopped General Adams. "Please, General, let me try and get her out."

"Okay, Samarra, be careful."

Tonya was taken off in handcuffs for questioning.

"Listen, Ellis, you do not know me, my name is Samarra, but you did know me in the future, we were friends. I know that may be hard to understand."

No answer.

"Look, Ellis, the virus you were given you think is only to destroy the U.S. computer system but you were lied to."

Silence.

"What it actually did was start a nuclear war all over the planet, millions upon millions will die! In return the one who gave you the virus is an alien who takes over the Earth and enslaves the people that are left and uses them for food. Are you listening to me?"

"You are a liar, Samarra, just like this country's government, no wonder you work for them!"

"It is not a lie, Ellis, please come out and talk to me!"

"Never not going to happen. I am almost done with the download now!"

"No, stop. No!" Samarra kicked down the door.

Ellis jumped up, pulled the trigger, and down went Samarra.

I grabbed my gun, screaming, "Nooo!" Pulled the trigger and shot Ellis in the head, she dropped to the ground dead.

The rest of the team rushed in. Ellis still had the virus in her hand and did not execute its deployment. Everything went into slow motion for me. I kept seeing Ellis' face in a pool of blood. Seeing Samarra with medics all around her trying to rush her out of the building. I dropped my gun and dropped to my knees. I heard others trying to talk to me but I just blacked out. I kept having strange dreams, one after the other. One minute I saw Ellis' face and loving kisses. In others her head lying in a pool of blood, looking up at me, crying, "Why did you do this to me?" In others I saw Daniel and Samarra with a beautiful family raising children and she would give me the finger. My parents in front of me telling me I was a huge failure, just ripping me apart. Visions of Jappel and I sharing food and good conversations. I thought I was dreaming, but was it real?

Then the Giver showed up, pointing his long crooked finger at me, threatening to kill everyone. Then all of a sudden the room became white and felt at peace. A white hooded figure appeared and destroyed the Giver from my sight. It kneeled down in front of me and I realized it was Ada. A sense of warmth and compassion entered my body.

"Relax, Marco, it is only me, you are safe. I have been with you for a while now."

"What has happened, Ada?"

"What was destined to happen, Marco."

"What does that mean?"

"You have to figure that out for yourself, you will understand in time. Oh, Marco, by the way, someone needs to talk to you. Thank you, Marco, you won't be forgotten," and she kissed my forehead and disappeared.

Then I saw Ellis just as she was when I saw her at the compound.

"Hi, Marco, now do you understand why I could not go?"

"No, you should have told me, Ellis, we could have fixed it together."

"Not true, Marco, what I did was very wrong, that is why I did not deserve someone like you."

"You do, Ellis, you still do, you were fooled by the Giver, everyone deserves a second chance."

"That part is over now, Marco, you gave me more love in that short period of time than some people get in a lifetime, and I thank you for that. I am paying for what I have done, and part of that punishment is not being with you right now. Do not be sad or angry about me, please, we will see each other again, it just won't be right now. I love you, Marco, but your work is not done, when the time is right we will be together soon. Live and love life, Marco, you have a wonderful future ahead of you."

The bright light faded and I woke up screaming in a hospital bed.

"Calm down, Marco, it's okay, it's me, Daniel, you're okay."

"Who, what, where is Samarra!"

"Relax, everything is okay and Samarra is fine."

My breathing started to slow down but I was pouring sweat. "Where is Ada and Ellis?"

"Marco, I am sorry but you know they are gone."

I paused for a bit and reality hit me hard.

"Go to sleep, Marco, Samarra will see you in the morning."

I woke up, the sun was shining on my face and when I opened my eyes Samarra and Daniel were there.

"Hey, Captain, how are you feeling?"

"Like I am dead."

Samarra laughed. "You look and smell like it as well."

"Samarra, how bad was the shot?"

"Lucky for me I was only grazed by my shoulder, sore but I am fine. It's over, Marco, it is done, we did it, we saved the planet!"

"How do you know for sure?"

"The virus never got deployed. Guess what?"

"What?"

"After the virus was never deployed my pregnancy never happened, life has been altered, no one on the other planet will ever have to live their lives that way."

I just turned over and wrapped the sheets around me. "Sorry, guys, I just need some rest."

Both of them patted me on the back and left the room.

Full Circle

Two weeks later we received medal after medal. It was great but I still felt lost. The money came through, all of us were retired and could live the rock star life if we wanted to with no financial worries at all. I had to find myself again, no family, no spouse, I just needed to go out and see the world that I put my life on the line to protect. The thought of what Eve told me before still puzzled me. Musician going to Seattle to make it big, I am pretty sure the girl on the plane said her name was Trina. I had all the money in the world and for shits and giggles decided to go hang out in Seattle and catch up on the music scene.

    A few weeks later I saw that girl performing in a very popular nightclub. They did introduce her as Trina and surprisingly she was pretty talented, I thought. The show was over and I caught her walking off the stage.

"That was a great show."

"Thanks."

"Can I buy you a beer?"

"Yeah, if you want, old man, but no sex!"

I started to laugh. "No sex, just five minutes of your time."

"Sure, fuck it, next party is in an hour."

"Do you remember me? On the plane I fell asleep and you just left me there?"

"No, not really, what do you want, creeper?"

"Nothing, just glad to see you, Eve, you are doing what you always wanted to."

"Hey, jackass, my name is not Eve, it's Trina, damn, do you have Alzheimer's?"

"Sorry, you're right, my mistake."

"You are a weirdo, my friend, but I do like the name Eve. Eve, the beginning of a new rock era and dominance. Hey, man, thanks for the beer and new idea! Hey, old man, maybe I will see you in the future?"

"You have, Eve, enjoy your new life."

"Seriously, dude, lay off the drugs, later."

"Good luck, Eve, kick ass!"

Samarra and Daniel were both really doing well. They got married and had their first kid together and of course named her Tanya. All of us stayed very close. We were a family, and believe it or not I found time to eventually have a relationship. I met and fell in love with a woman named Allison. Wonderful, beautiful woman, very smart, and we had a lot in common. We were the same age and neither one of us had children. We had a great life, we did as we pleased, life was fun and exciting, we lived it to the fullest. I never got over Ellis completely, but in time it was easier and I knew we had done the right thing.

Allison and I one night went to bed after a wonderful dinner of steak and wine, it was perfect. My secret government phone for emergencies only went off at four-fifteen in the morning.

Allison woke up. "Marco, what is that?"

"Oh, shit, it's the secured line."

"Answer it, Marco. What do you think they want, you're retired?"

"Hopefully they called the wrong person. Hello?"

"Marco?"

"Yes, it is."

"This is the president, we need to talk ASAP!"

"What is wrong?"

"The planet is back!"